Carson Swift may look exactly like his twin brother Cody, but they're as different as tie dye and camouflage. Reliable, responsible, and usually the designated driver, Carson is also over being his brother's keeper, but suddenly his plans to break free are complicated by the woman they fish out of Hidden Creek . . .

Lily Price is not your typical damsel in distress. Infidelity, infertility, and downsizing provide a triple threat to her ego, but falling into the swollen river nearly ends her life. If not for the handsome stranger—make that two handsome strangers—she might not have had a chance at having a baby by any means necessary . . .

As Carson helps Lily overcome her fear of the river, she helps him save his rafting business from going under. She also saves him from abandoning all that is important to him in order to get a taste of freedom. Together they find that love is the ultimate adventure.

Books by Kristina Mathews

More Than A Game Series
Better Than Perfect
Worth the Trade
Making A Comeback
Earning A Ring

Swift River Romance series
Swept Away

Published by Kensington Publishing Corporation

Swept Away

A Swift River Romance

Kristina Mathews

LYRICAL PRESS
Kensington Publishing Corp.
www.kensingtonbooks.com

First Electronic Edition: July 2016
eISBN-13: 978-1-60183-922-0
eISBN-10: 1-60183-922-7

First Print Edition: July 2016
ISBN-13: 978-1-60183-925-1
ISBN-10: 1-60183-925-1

Printed in the United States of America

To my husband and brother-in-law who went fishing one day, rescued a tourist, and inspired this story.

Author's Foreword

Many years ago I met a guy who spent his summers on the river. He had strong arms, an adventurous spirit, and funny tan lines on his feet. Our first trip together was a long weekend rafting on the Tuolumne River. It rained the whole time, and he was so manly, he didn't need a tent. We ended up sleeping under an upturned raft. But I was hooked. On the guy, and the sport. He bought me a lifejacket long before he bought me any jewelry. A very romantic gift—he wanted to protect me and make sure I was able to join him in something that was a big part of his life.

Marriage, kids, and careers pulled us away from the river for a number of years. But a used bucket boat (as opposed to the modern self-bailers) and kids old enough to paddle have brought us back to the river. So what if the first time I'd been tossed overboard and hit my tailbone on a rock was ten days before my first Romance Writers of America national conference? It just provides more inspiration for future books.

And yes, Carson and Lily's story was inspired by real life adventures. My husband and his brother went fishing one day and came back with a story of how they rescued a tourist from a swift moving river. I changed the brothers to twins and made the tourist a woman and the rest just burst forth like a natural spring. I hope you enjoy this story of love- the ultimate adventure.

Chapter 1

"Man this water's really pumping." Carson Swift hiked a few steps ahead of his twin brother, Cody. His feet landed firmly on the familiar trail to Hidden Creek, but his thoughts were a million miles away. Make that eight hundred miles, give or take, depending on whether he took Highway 50 or Interstate 80 through Nevada. "With the water this high, I don't think we'll catch a lot of fish."

"Good thing we have steaks in the fridge." You'd think he was nine, not twenty-nine, by the way Cody trotted along excitedly, skittering small bits of gravel along the well-worn path. He was too damn happy with his life. "We're not pulling anything out of the river today."

"At least it's finally warming up." What a coward. Carson had dragged his brother out here to have a serious conversation. Instead, he was discussing water conditions. The weather.

"I thought winter would never end." Cody would probably still catch a fish or two. He had that kind of luck. Women and trout landed at his feet without much effort. "But summer's coming and it's going to be a hot one."

Another summer stretched out in front of them. Long, hot days on the river. Longer, hotter nights at the Argo—throwing back a few beers, shooting pool, picking up pretty strangers. Who wouldn't want the easy life of a whitewater guide?

"June bookings look pretty solid." Carson tried to look at the sunny side of the creek. Business was good. That wasn't why he wanted out.

"We should get quite a few bachelorette parties." Cody had suggested advertising in the regional bridal magazines. His idea was to offer Girls' Weekend trips, complete with a selection of local wines and discounted cabin rentals. It was one of the few times he'd taken an interest in the business itself.

Most of the time Cody was all about the fun. Hot babes and cold beer on a warm summer night were the only things he seemed to care about. Except in winter, when he'd head up to the mountains to ski. Leaving Carson to take care of repairs and maintenance.

"Plenty of family trips too." All those intact families. Smiling. Laughing. Bonding. Being there for each other. Reminding Carson of what he didn't have.

"Don't forget bachelor parties." Cody was always up for a good time. The man lived his life as though it was one big party. A lot of guys would give up their flat screen TVs to walk in his sandals. "Man, we've got the best job in the world."

"Sure. A day's work for us is a vacation for most people." Carson still loved the heart-stopping rapids and Zen-like calm stretches on the river. He still loved helping people connect with nature and discover a little something about themselves along the way. And he still loved the constant, yet ever-changing force of the river.

It was the change that called to him now. He might as well be guiding the jungle boats at Disneyland. He was seeing the same sights, telling the same jokes over and over again until he felt like one of the automated characters. He needed a change of pace. A change of scenery. A change of company.

"Yeah, we've got it made." Cody trotted along like a kid on the first day of summer vacation. He had no idea his brother didn't share his enthusiasm for the status quo. Carson was afraid of becoming stagnant. A breeding ground for bad blood.

It wasn't that Cody was a bad guy. He was just there. Always. They lived together. Worked together. Ate together. The only thing they didn't do was sleep together. Although there had been women who would have been willing to take on them both. Cody probably could have been talked into it, but it was bad enough sharing breakfast and small talk with his brother's dates. Carson wasn't about to share anything more.

He should just get it over with. Say the words. *I'm leaving.* But the lump in his throat rose like the spring runoff, drowning out his voice. If he could think of another way to get Cody to grow up already, he'd take it. But the only way to get him to change would be to force it on him. He had to toss his brother overboard and hope he'd come up swimming.

"What the hell?" Cody skidded to halt. "Is that woman actually swimming? In this high water?"

* * * *

Damn. This water is cold.

Lily came up for air, sputtering and spitting out a mouthful of river water. She grasped for something—anything she could hold onto. But the current was too fast, too strong for her to grab hold of anything. She tried to find her footing, but the force of the river kept her from getting her legs underneath her. Quickly she realized that it was probably for the best. If anything, she could end up breaking a leg if she slammed against a rock. Or worse, her foot could become entrapped and it wouldn't be long before the river pulled her under, drowning her.

She wondered how long it would take to find her body. Would some fisherman stumble upon her days, weeks, or even months from now? Or would the current eventually pull her downstream, where she'd wash up lifeless on the shore?

For the first time in her adult life, Lily was thankful she was childless. There was no baby to leave motherless. Left to be raised by her rat-bastard ex-husband.

Water shot up her nose, and Lily coughed. She tried once again to regain control of her body, but she was caught in a force too powerful to fight.

The movies were all wrong. Her life didn't flash before her eyes. Nothing but water and sky and regret rushed past her as she was carried downstream.

Lily didn't want her last conscious thought to be about her ex. About her failures.

As a wife. A daughter. An employee.

A woman who hadn't been able to conceive.

She tried to think of something positive. Relaxing her body, she willed her last thoughts to be about something beautiful. Like Hidden Creek. She'd always loved it here. The smell of the pines and the whisper of the wind through the trees. How the night sky was so clear and the stars shone so brightly she felt as if she could reach up and touch them. Blackberries that would be ripe in another month. She could bake a pie in the cozy kitchen of her cabin.

Her cabin. The one thing she'd fought for in the divorce. The place where she'd hoped to raise a family.

But now it would go back to Brian.

Over my dead body.

With a new sense of urgency, Lily fought back against the current, flailing about as if her life depended on it.

* * * *

Carson turned his attention to the river. He expected to see the slow, graceful movements of a woman out for an afternoon swim. He expected smooth, easy strokes and efficient flutter kicks as she propelled herself through the water. He expected to pass her by without another thought. Instead, he felt his muscles tighten, his heart rate accelerate, and his vision narrow as the realization that she was in trouble hit him like a flash flood.

Instinct kicked in. He dropped his rod, pulled his keys and phone from his pocket, and raced into the raging river. He dove into the waist-deep water, swimming aggressively toward her. The current was strong. He had to be stronger.

"Just relax. I've got you." He kept his voice steady, projecting strength, confidence, and competence. He couldn't let her panic. *He* knew he was trying to save her, but there was no way of knowing what was going through her mind.

She struggled briefly, mumbling something, as he wrapped his arm around her waist and pulled her against his chest. The buzz of adrenaline flooded his system, blocking out the cold, the current, and everything but the need to keep her head above water and bring her to shore. He kicked hard to propel them away from the strongest part of the current. Working with the flow of the river and not against it was crucial in getting them both out alive.

The river slowed as they approached the eddy. Carson adjusted his grip and his hand slid up over the smooth curve of her breast. He corrected his hold on her, but not before his thumb grazed her nipple.

Focus.

Get her out of the water.

All the hours of training drained from his head. This wasn't the first time he'd rescued someone from the river. It certainly wasn't the first time he'd touched a woman's breast. He should be able to get his mind back on track. Once they made it back to dry land, then he could think about her perfect breasts. When she was safe, he could let his mind wander in the direction his fingers had wanted to go. Not to mention his mouth.

"I've got you." He tried to sound calm, in control. Like someone who knew what he was doing. Her life was still in his hands. "Trust me."

Her body relaxed against his as she wrapped her arms around his neck. Relief flooded him as he realized she wasn't going to panic and try to fight him. He still had to get her out of the water. Then get her somewhere warm. The image of his bed flashed through his mind and he brushed it away like a pesky mosquito.

Cody stood downstream, holding his rod case over the water. A rope would be better, but they'd left the hoopi in the truck. The tubular nylon webbing, often used by climbers, was one of their most valuable pieces of river gear. Almost as versatile as duct tape, and Carson wished he had some with him. He did have his brother. Cody might not remember to pay his cell phone bill on time, but get him on the river and he was one of the most reliable men around.

"Hold tight." Carson reached for the case, and grabbed hold as Cody pulled them toward the shore, reeling them in like a couple of steelhead. Carson got his feet under him and helped the woman stand.

"You're okay. You're going to be just fine." His legs felt like wet beef jerky now that the adrenaline drained from his system. His heart rate should be returning to normal, but he'd just felt her up in the middle of the river and he didn't even know what color her eyes were. Let alone her name.

"Thank you." She shivered.

Hidden Creek would be a very different river in another month. Once the runoff slowed, it would be marked with gentle riffles, calm pools, and some of the best trout fishing in Northern California. Today, it was a surging flow carrying a winter's worth of snowmelt as it merged into the South Fork of the American River. Not as cold as it had been a few weeks ago, but still cold enough that twenty more minutes might have led to a different ending.

Carson tore off his wet shirt and pulled the woman against his bare skin. "I've got to get your core temperature up." He massaged her arms and torso briskly, hoping she wouldn't think he was some kind of perv. But, damn, she felt good pressed against him, soft in all the right places and naked except for her bikini bottoms. The idea was to warm her up, but he was the one on fire.

"Cody. Give me your shirt." His words came out harsh and demanding. His brother obeyed, pulling the dry T-shirt off and tossing it to him in one swift motion. Carson slipped it over her head, breaking the contact but not the impact of her bare skin against his.

"What's your name?" Carson asked.

"Lily Johnson." She held her hand out, but quickly retreated. "Sorry. It's Price. Lily Price."

She shook her head before extending her hand again. Her grip was firm and surprisingly warm. Had she recently changed her name or was her confusion because of injury? He glanced down at her left hand. Bare. But that didn't mean a thing. The river was a thief. She'd been known to take jewelry, sunglasses, and bathing suits. Even lives.

"I'm Carson Swift." Carson dropped her hand, but he still felt the charge as if he'd been struck by lightning, and the water only intensified the conductivity. "This is my brother, Cody."

"Oh, so there are two of you." She let out a sigh of relief. "I thought I was seeing double."

"We're twins." Cody reached out to shake hands. "Identical."

"Nice to meet you both." Lily glanced from one brother to the other. The glazed look in her honey-gold eyes told Carson she'd have to work at telling them apart. They were too much alike. On the outside.

"It's our pleasure." Cody emphasized the last word, letting her know that he was interested. Then again, Cody rarely met a good-looking woman he wasn't interested in.

"Well, thank you both for…" Lily held her breath just long enough for Carson to suspect she was not as calm as she pretended to be. "Saving my life." She flashed them a fake smile to let them know she was fine, thank-you-very-much.

"Hey, no problem." Carson wanted her to believe it was no big deal. All in a day's work.

Except it was a problem. A big problem. He couldn't just walk away from her now.

Physically, she'd recover. She'd be sore for a few days, but the color had already returned to her cheeks. She stretched her arms overhead and rolled her head from side to side. He almost expected her to throw a few jabs in the air just to prove she was a fighter. But she kept casting glances at the river as if it might reach up and swallow her. Carson worried more about her emotional state. Fear could creep in like an unwanted vine and if left unchecked, it would take over, choking the life out of her.

"Let's get you someplace warm." Carson took her arm to lead her back up the path. "My truck is just down the creek."

"Oh, that's okay." Lily eyed the water again with mistrust. "My cabin is right on the river."

"Cedar shingles? Green trim?" Cody asked. They had fished this stretch of the river enough times to know the place she was talking about.

"That's the one." Lily's face lit up with pride. There were only a few residences along the way and hers was by far the most welcoming.

"Trust me," Carson said. "My truck is much closer."

She shrugged and then bent down to pick up his keys and phone.

"You might need these then." She handed the keys to him and their fingers brushed, sending a shiver down his spine.

"Is there someone we should call?" Carson asked as he took the phone.

"No." Lily shook her head. Sadness flickered across her face, disappearing almost instantly. "I'm enjoying the solitude of Hidden Creek."

"So you're all alone out here?" Cody's voice dripped with invitation. Could he be any more obvious? The woman had just been plucked from the river and Cody was trying to get her into bed.

"I'm taking a much-needed vacation." Lily's voice held a hint of defiance. "The first since my honeymoon seven years ago."

"So will your husband be joining you?" Carson's voice cracked like a thirteen-year-old boy. He half-hoped she was still married. Then he could just forget about her.

Yeah. Right.

"My *ex*-husband can go to hell." Lily's voice shook a little. As if she wasn't used to using such strong language. Or maybe she wasn't used to standing up for herself. "Did I say that out loud?"

"You did." She made him laugh, in spite of everything.

"I am so embarrassed." Lily blushed, a deep, dark pink. "I'm not really the bitter ex. I swear."

"What, did the guy cheat on you?" Cody asked. Leave it to his brother to use a woman's divorce as an opener to hit on her.

"Yeah. Among other things." Lily looked down at the trail, as if it was the most interesting thing in the world. Obviously she didn't want to talk about it. She marched forward, but stumbled on an exposed root.

Carson grabbed her arm. Just to steady her. The sooner he got her back to her cabin, the better.

"Let's get you home. Get you warmed up, and we'll be on our way." Carson would sleep better knowing she had no lasting effects of her ordeal. Besides, he already felt responsible for her.

He needed someone else to worry about like he needed another Swift River Adventures T-shirt.

Maybe he could use another shirt. His was dripping wet and covered in dirt. Lily was the only one of them wearing a shirt, dry or otherwise. And damn, if she didn't look really good in it. Her hips swayed ever so slightly as she walked. She wasn't very tall, but her legs stretched long and lean beneath the faded blue shirt. Her damp hair fell just below her shoulders. Carson couldn't tell if it was light brown or dark blonde, but either way it would look great spread across his pillow.

He didn't need to peek at Cody to know he was thinking the same thing. They were way past the age of acting like horny teenagers. Or they should be. Besides, Carson wasn't going to stick around; he had no business lusting after her.

She was just something else he would leave behind.

* * * *

"So, Lily, what were you doing swimming in such high water?" one of the brothers asked. The one who'd pulled them both from the river. He'd also given her the shirt off his back. Literally.

"I wasn't swimming." Lily didn't like the defensive tone in her voice. "I… I fell in."

"Well, it's a good thing we came along when we did," the other brother said. He tried to keep his tone light, but Lily sensed an undercurrent of worry. They all knew what might have happened if the brothers hadn't been there.

Some Mother's Day this turned out to be. Not that she was fortunate enough to be a mother. And instead of being a good daughter, spending an uncomfortable day not talking about her divorce with her mom, she'd decided to relax in the sun, finally diving into that novel she bought for herself last Christmas. With everything that happened to her in the last few months, Lily hadn't had time for small pleasures. Now she had all the time in the world. The next few months, at least. She planned on taking the summer off before looking for another bookkeeping job, or even landing clients of her own.

Lily had felt a little reckless sunbathing on that rock like a teenager. She'd even switched to SPF 15 instead of her usual 50. UV rays had turned out to be the least of her worries. She should have waited for the paperback or gotten an eBook. With the bulk and weight of a hardcover edition, the book had slipped out of her hands and as she reached for it, she'd tumbled head first into Hidden Creek.

She was a strong swimmer, an experienced swimmer, but the swift current had taken her by surprise. She'd tried swimming back toward the rock, but there was no way she could fight the force of all that water. Disoriented and a little ticked off at the twenty-seven dollars she'd spent on that book she'd never get to finish, she'd started flailing about, reaching for something, anything to grab onto so she could get her feet back under her.

She'd been in the water ten minutes, maybe longer, when she'd heard a deep male voice, felt strong arms around her, and realized she wasn't alone in the water.

The rest happened so fast. She was in the water. Then out. Somewhere along the way, she'd lost her bathing suit top and this man was holding her close. There was a second man, identical to the first. He gave up his shirt and flirted with her. The first guy seemed worried about her. But she was fine. Really. They were making too much of a fuss over her. "Sorry to interrupt your fishing trip." Lily tried to steady her voice, to sound like a woman who could take care of herself.

"Hey, it's okay," one of the guys said. "The water's a little high for good fishing, anyway."

"We caught something much better." His brother smiled and spoke with a light-hearted tone. He was definitely flirting with her. She remembered flirting. It's what her ex had done with every woman but her.

"Tell me again who's who." They'd reached the end of the trail. Lily was trying to keep them straight, knowing it must be hard to be constantly mistaken for your twin.

"I'm Cody, the good-looking one." The first brother flashed his dimples and smoothed back his blond hair in an over-the-top, I-know-I'm-good-looking way.

"Yeah? When was the last time you got a haircut, you hippie?" His brother gave him a friendly shove. Lily's gaze strayed to his wet shorts. He'd been the one to jump in the water after her. He'd been the one to really save her life. She shivered at the thought. And at the way the damp fabric clung to his muscular thighs.

"At least I don't look like an escapee from boot camp, like Carson here." Cody snapped to attention and offered a salute.

"I like it short." Carson sounded a little offended. "Besides, my hair's so thick if I go more than four or five weeks without a trim, I have to put stuff in it."

"And it would just run out into the river, poisoning the fish." Cody recited the words like scolded schoolboy. "Lighten up, man."

"So I care about what gets washed into the river." Carson shook his head and chuckled. "You only care about what you pull out."

"Hey, at least I catch something once in a while."

"I'm not talking about the fish."

They teased each other, but there was genuine affection in their banter. Lily envied their closeness. As an only child, she'd envisioned a large family of her own someday. Three, maybe four kids running through the house. Walking down to Fairy Tale Town or the Sacramento Zoo. Baking cookies and hanging their artwork on the refrigerator door. The only thing hanging on her refrigerator now was an appointment card for Foothills Fertility Clinic.

She followed the twins to a white double-cab Toyota truck. Carson clicked open the locks and held the front passenger door for her. He offered his arm to help her climb up into the cab. A jolt, almost as startling as the icy-cold water, shot straight through her.

How long had it been since she'd been touched, really touched, by a man? For the last few years, sex had been entirely clinical. An act of procreation—and desperation—that had nothing to do with intimacy.

But he hadn't really touched her. Not like that. He was only trying to help. Like he'd been trying to help when he pulled her against him. And he was only trying to help when he'd touched her breast. Lily wasn't going to read anything into it. She didn't need a man. She definitely didn't need two of them.

Carson went around to the driver's side and Cody slid into the backseat. Lily clicked her seatbelt in place. If only she could restrain her nerves so easily.

"So tell me." She turned so she could converse with both of them. "What do you two do when you're not rescuing topless women?"

Masculine laughter filled the cab. The deep, rich sound warmed Lily from the inside out. Carson started the ignition and turned the heater on full blast, to warm her on the outside.

"We run Swift River Adventures, a rafting company out of Prospector Springs." Carson's smile showed a man who took pride in his work.

"It's not far from where gold was first discovered in California." Cody leaned forward, inching closer, making her aware that there was entirely too much testosterone in this tiny space. They were big men. Strong men. Very good-looking men.

It took twice as long to drive to the cabin as it had for her to float downstream. At last, she was home. *Home.* Even if it was only temporary.

"Nice place." Carson shut off the engine and turned toward her. His eyes were as warm, and as blue, as a summer's day. "Are you renting for the summer?"

"Nope. It's mine." She was still getting used to the idea. "All mine."

"Is it a vacation cabin?" Cody asked from the backseat.

"Not exactly." Lily turned to find Cody's eyes were just as startling and blue as his brother's. "My house in Sacramento sold a lot quicker than I anticipated. So this is home. Until I figure out where I want to end up."

"Well, I'm glad you're here now." Carson's voice was slightly lower than Cody's, without the teasing note. She just hoped she'd be able to find other ways to tell the two of them apart. They both wore faded khaki shorts, complicated athletic sandals, and nothing else. Carson had tossed his wet shirt in the back of his truck and she was still wearing Cody's.

"So, Lily." Cody didn't seem to want his brother to get the last word in. "What do you do when you're not charming the shirts off a couple of fishermen?"

"I'm an accountant." Or she had been.

"No way." Cody leaned forward again. "You're much too interesting to be an accountant."

"I think that was supposed to be a compliment." Carson shot his brother a disapproving look. "What kind of accounting?

"I don't have my CPA license." Lily was making excuses again. Focusing on what she lacked, not what she could do. "I do general bookkeeping, payroll, just about anything except income taxes. But my company decided to outsource my duties, so here I am."

She exited the truck and approached the front porch steps. Both men followed her across the wraparound deck and through the front door of the two-story cabin. The place had been built in the 1940s, when things were made to last. The floors were well-worn oak planks, the fireplace had been built with rocks gathered from the area, and a large picture window overlooked the river below. Three bedrooms, plus a loft, would provide plenty of space for the large family Lily still hoped to bring back here someday.

They entered the bright, spacious kitchen, with its knotty-pine cabinets, butcher-block counters, and a large cast iron sink big enough to bathe small children in. Lily had so many dreams for this place. None of them involved being divorced, jobless, and alone.

"Do you have any tea?" Carson eyed the kettle on the back burner of the gas stove. "Or hot chocolate? Something to warm you up?"

"How about some whiskey?" Cody suggested. His grin made her somehow think of those old cartoons with the big St. Bernard lumbering through the snow with a barrel of whiskey on his collar.

"Um, yeah. Tea bags are in the cabinet over the stove. There's beer in the fridge." Lily pointed to the old-fashioned Frigidaire. Not the most energy efficient appliance, but it reminded her of a simpler time. Back then, fresh fruits and vegetables replaced microwave popcorn as a snack. Cupcakes were made at home, not ordered online and delivered to your door. And families were created when a man and a woman loved each other very much and wanted to share that love with a child. It didn't take a credit check or a series of lab tests. "Make yourselves at home while I go change."

"You should take a long, hot shower," Carson suggested. His voice warmed her and made her shiver at the same time.

"Are you offering to wash my back?" The words just slipped out. She wasn't the kind of woman who traded suggestive comments with a man she'd just met. She'd never even made that kind of statement to her ex-husband.

"He doesn't have the skills." Cody stepped closer, invading her space. "But I'm very skilled." He lowered his gaze to her chest and licked his lips subconsciously. Or maybe it was on purpose. He seemed like the kind of man who knew exactly what he was doing when it came to women.

"Sometimes it takes more than skill." Carson shot his brother a disapproving look. Oh dear, they were fighting over her. Not fighting really, just competing for her attention. She should warn them that she'd vowed to go the rest of her life without ever having sex again. She'd spent the last few years with pillows propped under her hips every Tuesday and Friday from 10:15 to approximately 10:27. All for nothing.

Water under the bridge. Over the dam. Spilled out into the ocean by now.

She closed the bathroom door and slipped the oversized T-shirt over her head, catching a glimpse of herself in the mirror. A large bruise bloomed along her left side, stopping just below her breast. More bruises appeared along her hip and back. Tears stung her eyes as she realized just how lucky she was that Carson and Cody had decided to go fishing that day.

"I'm going to fix you a cup of tea," one of the twins said through the door. "Do you need any help in there?"

"No, I got it." Lily tried to make her voice as strong as possible. She didn't want whoever it was to think she was weak.

"Just checking." His voice was strong, steady, and very sexy. "Let me know if you need anything. Despite what Cody says, I'm very good at washing backs."

It was Carson. Her heart fluttered as she remembered the feel of his arms around her. His hand on her breast. The way he'd pressed against her, trying to warm her up. He was so solid, rock hard arms, chest, and well, if that was shrinkage…

She turned on the shower. It would take a few minutes to warm up. The water, that is. She was already warm in all the wrong places. Maybe she should take a cold shower instead. Like that would help get her mind off the two hunks in her house. Either one of them was twice the man Brian was. And put together? She shuddered as she stepped under the hot water.

The warm spray did wonders to release the tension in her body. It wasn't just the day's events, but the last eight months of stress that she needed to wash down the drain. She had turned thirty wondering why it was such a big deal. She had a good job, a nice house in a desirable neighborhood, and a smart, successful husband to share her life with. The only thing missing was a baby. They had been working on that.

But then she'd lost her job. No big deal. They didn't need the money. She was going to quit when she got pregnant anyway. But they had been trying for three years. Two years longer than most people waited to get tested. The results were more than disappointing. It had been the final straw that had broken the overstrained backbone of their marriage.

Damn. She must have gotten shampoo in her eyes. The stinging sensation couldn't possibly be tears. She had nothing to cry about. She was alive. That had to count for something. She still had plenty of time to have a baby. She had options. Maybe even right there in her living room.

Stop. Don't go there.

She wasn't desperate. Gone were the days when only a married couple was given a chance at having children. She could probably even adopt, if it turned out that Brian wasn't the only one with fertility problems.

With a little effort, Lily managed to dress after her shower. A bra was out of the question, considering the bruises on her side. The guys had already seen her girls in all their glory, so she slipped on a dark green T-shirt, hoping she wasn't asking for trouble. She'd just have to go out there and be herself. If only she knew who that was.

That's what she'd come up here for. To live life on her own terms. And that meant taking one step at a time, starting with marching into the kitchen where her rescuers were waiting.

"Oh, good. You're both still here." Lily put on a brave smile. "I'm not sure how to thank you. For everything."

"Don't worry about it." Carson handed her a cup of tea. "We're just glad we could help."

"I could make you dinner. Or something." Lily tried to think if she had enough food for three.

"No. That's okay," Carson was quick to decline. "You should get some rest."

"We could light your fire," Cody offered, and his brother gave him a quick elbow to the ribs. "In the fireplace. To make sure you stay warm."

"Oh, that's not necessary." She wasn't sure if Cody was trying to be funny, but the way Carson glared at him made her suspect that Cody's over-the-top flirtation was a sore subject between them.

"Is there anything else you need?" Carson's concern was a little overwhelming. She needed to get a grip on her emotions. Her hormones. All she had to do was finish her tea and thank them for saving her life. She wasn't looking to create a new life with either of them.

Chapter 2

Carson leaned against the counter and watched Lily sip her tea nervously. She was obviously still rattled. "Are you all right?" It really wasn't any of his business. He shouldn't get involved. Yet, here he was, involved. Wanting to help. Caring about her.

"Sure, I'm fine." Lily opened the door of the old refrigerator. "You sure you guys don't want something to drink?"

"That would be great." Cody would accept her offer. "Can I use your bathroom?"

"Be my guest." She swept her arm in the direction she'd just come from, fresh from the shower. Carson wondered if it was still steamy.

"This is a sweet old fridge." Carson tried to shake off the image of her in the shower. Naked. "Classic."

"Thanks." Lily pulled out a couple bottles of beer and shoved the door closed with her hip. "I'm sure it's horribly inefficient, but it reminds me of the good old days."

"Our Granny had one just like it." Warm memories flooded him. She'd always kept it stocked with gallons of milk for two growing boys. Plenty of fresh fruit they could help themselves to. And a bottle of sticky, red grenadine for those special occasions when Granny made them Shirley Temples while she enjoyed a glass of wine with Granddad. They had taken the boys home from the hospital and had done everything they could to give them the life their daughter couldn't have.

Lily handed him a beer and reached around him for a bottle opener. Her right breast grazed his arm.

"Sorry." He pulled his arm away. She must really think he was some kind of jerk.

"It's okay." Lily laughed—a crystal-clear sound, like the deepest pool on the river. "It's not like it was the first time."

"No. Sorry about that too." Carson felt his cheeks warm. He'd really hoped she hadn't noticed.

"Hey, no big deal." Lily struggled with the bottle opener, a blush creeping across her cheeks.

Carson took the bottle and the opener from her, setting both on the counter. "You don't have to entertain us."

"I don't mind. Really. Entertaining is one of the things I'm good at." There it was again. Her vulnerability tugged at his heart, making it impossible for him to just walk away.

"Oh hey, Sierra Nevada." Cody returned from the bathroom, making himself at home by prying the caps off both the bottles. "One of my favorites."

"Sit down." Lily indicated the heavy oak chairs at her kitchen table. "If you won't stay for dinner, let me at least put out some snacks. I think I have some chips and salsa."

"That won't be necessary." Carson was on edge.

"Great." Cody sat back and took a nice long pull on his beer. He seemed to have no intention of going anywhere anytime soon. Not unless Carson dragged him out of there by his ankles.

What had gotten into him? He'd just met Lily, and he was ready to club his own brother for just looking at her. He'd never reacted to a woman like this before.

Sure, he'd been with his fair share of women. He enjoyed their company. Liked to be able to please them. Give them what they needed. Some women just needed someone to talk to. He was a damn good listener. Others needed someone to hold them, a warm body to keep them from feeling the chill of loneliness. Then there were the women who needed to be touched. To have him stroke both body and ego, letting them know just how incredible and powerful and sexy they were.

But with Lily? He didn't have a clue. He didn't know what she needed or what he wanted from her. It was like heading down an unfamiliar stream in the dark, without a map, or even a paddle.

* * * *

"So tell me more about your rafting company." Lily put a dish of salsa and a basket of tortilla chips on the table.

"We run several one- or two-day trips a week from April to October." Carson spoke with enthusiasm. "We take kids as young as eight and as old as eighty. We take families, scout troops—"

"Singles groups and honeymooners." Cody chimed in. "And we have a campground that's open year-round."

"We got a late start this year, though." Carson's tone took on a more serious note. "The late storms, while great for the water reserves, put a damper our business. But things are picking up. Come Memorial Day we'll be booked pretty solid."

"Isn't all that rain good for business? In the long run?" Lily was curious about their way of life. So different than the life she'd led. So much more relaxed. So much more real.

"The American River is dam controlled." Carson leaned forward with a sparkle in his eye as he talked about the river he called home. "The first few weeks the river is higher from the runoff, but mostly it's pretty consistent."

"Except for drought years," Cody added. "Some years there's barely enough water to release. But every season is slightly different—the rapids change with higher or lower water, the river changes course, and we're always meeting new people."

"The tributaries, like Hidden Creek, are much more affected by the heavy snowpack," Carson informed her.

"Tell me about it." Lily had learned that the hard way. She'd come here, hoping to start over, to stand on her own two feet, to be the strong woman she knew she could be. If it wasn't for these two, she wouldn't be standing at all. "I'll be sure to steer clear of the river from now on."

"That would be a shame." Carson glanced over at her, trapping her in his gaze. The sensation of being pulled under was stronger than it had been in the river.

"Yeah," Cody added. "The river is life."

They talked for a while, the guys becoming more and more animated as they discussed their lives on the water. Their passion for their jobs and the outdoors was clear. They had been shaped by the river. Not just their bodies—those sculpted arms, shoulders, and abs certainly didn't come from a gym—but who they were on the inside was a result of the years spent guiding.

"You should come rafting with us," Cody suggested.

"No, that's okay." Lily shivered at the thought of being on the river. "I think I'll stay away from the water for some time."

"Don't give in to the fear." There was something in Carson's voice that reeled her in. "I'd hate for you to miss out on one of life's great pleasures."

"You're that good?" Lily finished off her tea, wishing she could forget the feel of Carson pressed against her. His hand on her breast. His strength completely enveloping her.

"Honey, we're the best," Cody joined in, lightening the mood. His flirting, she could deal with. He made her feel feminine and attractive, but she knew he didn't mean anything serious.

"I'll think about it." They were right, of course. But still, she was afraid. Of the river, sure, but she was more afraid of spending too much time with the Swift brothers.

* * * *

They had a problem. Carson gripped the steering wheel of his truck as he backed down the long driveway. Lily was safe and warm in her cabin. She'd showered, dressed, and finished her tea. After playing hostess, offering them drinks and snacks, she no longer seemed dazed or confused as she'd been when Carson had first pulled her out of the river.

But he was confused. Not about why he and Cody both found her attractive. That was perfectly understandable. No. What he couldn't figure out was why he felt such a strong need to protect her. He was looking for less responsibility, not more. Yet some instinct rose inside him. It was almost primal.

And it made him want to spar with the other male competing for her attention.

"You went a little overboard with the come-ons in there." Carson wasn't sure if he was more jealous or embarrassed by Cody's blatant flirtation. "I mean, 'We can light your fire?' Who says that?"

"I was just trying to be helpful." Cody had that innocent, "Who me?" tone in his voice.

"It was too much, even for you."

"What's that supposed to mean?" As if he didn't know.

"Helpful would be maybe waiting until she dried off before trying to get her into bed."

"You're the one who felt her up on the side of the river." Cody sounded a little defensive.

"I was trying to keep her warm. Hypothermia can be a real danger, especially this time of year when the water is still barely above freezing."

"Listen to Mr. Boy Scout." Cody chuckled. "You want her and you know it."

Carson didn't respond. There was no use arguing, so he concentrated on the road. On putting distance between him and Lily.

"So if I said I saw her first..." Cody wouldn't drop it.

"I went in after her," Carson reminded him.

"I like her. I really like her."

"You like every attractive woman you meet." They'd had this conversation too many times. "Until you get them into bed."

"Lily's different." Cody almost sounded sincere.

"Leave Lily alone"

"I don't think so. I'm not going to step aside just so you can have her."

"She's not a prize to be won." Carson couldn't help himself. He was protective of her. A little possessive, even.

"Afraid of losing?"

"No." Carson had learned a long time ago that it was easier to let Cody win. But not this time. "It's just that I'd hate to see her added to the tailings of your pathetic love life."

"The tailings of my love life?" Cody choked out a laugh. Maybe Carson's words hit a little close to home.

"Yeah, all those women you just tossed aside. After you dropped your shaft, you couldn't care less about the destruction you left behind."

"Hey, my shaft is bigger than yours." Wow. A penis metaphor. There was something new.

"You don't get it, do you?" Carson gripped the steering wheel tighter. "You can't treat women that way."

"Hey, I let them know up front what they're getting into."

This wasn't just about Lily. It was a conversation they should have had years ago. They weren't twenty-two anymore.

"Yeah, and you think they actually believe you." Carson couldn't believe his brother didn't know the difference.

"What's that supposed to mean?"

"Sure, they agree—no strings, no worries," Carson said the words through a clenched jaw. "But most of them tend to think that maybe, just maybe, they're special. That they might be the one woman who can tame the raging beast inside you."

"Lily could be that woman. Give me a little credit, will you?" Cody cranked the volume on the radio, tuning his brother out.

They were traveling in uncharted territory. Amazing that they hadn't ever both been interested in the same woman before. Or maybe Carson had stopped being interested in the kind of women Cody lured into his bed and sent out the back door the next morning because he didn't care enough to walk them to their car.

Maybe Carson was ready for something more. Something that didn't involve Cody.

"So not everyone stays friends with the women he sleeps with," Cody said after several minutes of silence between them.

"What's that supposed to mean?" Carson kept his eyes on the road ahead. They were almost to the highway.

"I mean, you manage to stay on speaking terms with every woman you bring home." Cody's voice held a note of contempt, and maybe a little bit of wonder. "Hell, some of them even invited you to their weddings. What's up with that?"

"I didn't sleep with all of them," Carson admitted. But he wasn't sure if he was proud of the fact or not. "Some were just friends. That's why they stayed friends."

"So you're saying you never slept with any of those women?" Cody's voice rose an octave.

"No. I'm just saying I haven't slept with every woman I've brought home."

"What's wrong with you?" Cody wondered aloud.

"Nothing's wrong with me." Carson shook his head, still not looking at his brother. "I just don't have to prove anything to anyone by sleeping with every woman I meet."

"You know they have pills for that now," Cody teased. As always. It was starting to wear on him. No. It had grown old years ago. It was just now he had a way out. A plan to make a life of his own.

Carson fiddled with the radio, switching from music to sports talk radio. The Giants had lost their game earlier and the callers were demanding drastic measures. A trade. Bringing up that prospect. Dumping the guy who'd been the big hero last year.

Was that what Carson really wanted? A major shake-up?

"I know I've always been kind of a catch and release guy." Cody wouldn't let it go.

"You're bummed we didn't get a chance to fish." Carson couldn't help but get in one more jab. "I kind of thought it was worth it."

"That's what I'm trying to say, asshole." Cody raised his voice, acting like a spoiled child. "I never hung on to a woman because I never met a woman worth hanging on to."

"Until Lily." Carson sighed.

"Lily's not like any woman I ever met." Cody sounded like he actually meant it. "She's like coming home. Just not any home we ever knew."

"What are you, Tom Hanks?" Carson quipped. "No, that's right, you've never sat through a chick flick for a woman."

"What are you talking about?" Cody sounded beyond irritated.

"So you really feel something for her?" Carson said, all teasing gone from his voice.

"Yeah." Cody leaned back into the seat. "I just wish the hell I knew what to do about it. I mean if it's just sex, that's easy. But maybe I want something more."

"Really?" Carson was skeptical. He knew Cody all too well. "Since when?"

"Since I realized it's time for us to grow up," Cody grumbled. "I can't take another summer doing the same old thing."

"The same old thing, as in a different woman every weekend?" Carson wasn't going to make this easy on him. "You're ready to try something different? The same woman every night?"

"If Lily's that woman, you bet."

"Nah, I don't like to take bets with you. You tend to get stupid lucky."

"So that's it, you're just going to step aside?" Cody sounded skeptical. "I don't think so. I think we both take our best shots. Let Lily decide who she wants."

"What if she doesn't pick either of us?" That would be the best thing. For everyone.

Chapter 3

Lily slept in until seven-thirty—late for her. As tempting as it was to stay in bed all day, her mind was racing. Yesterday's events replayed in her mind and her dreams. The river. The river guides. The sensation of being swept away both by the water and the emotions of being caught up in their world. Surely it was the added excitement of being rescued that made them seem much more attractive than they really were.

After a cup of coffee and another dose of Advil, Lily booted up her laptop, thankful to have internet in such an out-of-the-way place. She quickly found the website to Swift River Adventure Company and Resort. The home page showed a picture of the twins, smiling at her as if they knew what she looked like naked. So maybe they did. Mostly. But they also appeared as if pulling half-naked women out of the raging river was something they did every day.

She browsed the website, paying special attention to safety information. Impressive. All of their guides were experienced and well trained. Most had been trained in CPR, first aid, and several of them—including the twins—were certified in swift water rescue techniques.

Lily had nothing to worry about. It would be as safe as driving down the highway. Or hiking one of the nearby trails. If she'd wanted to stay holed up in her house with bars on the windows, she could have kept her house in Sacramento. If she was going to live here, she couldn't be afraid to walk out her front door. Especially since the river was right there, just a few steps away.

No, she would brave the river with the Swift brothers as her guides, and then she'd get on with her life. It wasn't like meeting them was a life-altering experience. Life saving, maybe, but not life changing. She knew better than to fall for that kind of fantasy.

She printed the list of items she would need for a day trip down the river. In a boat this time. They would provide the raft, a life jacket, and their expertise in guiding her down ten miles of rapids. She hoped their store would supply her with the few items she'd need to bring with her—a bathing suit chief among them.

Lily grabbed her purse, keys, and a spare pair of sunglasses. Now was as good a time as any to face the river. And the two men who'd pulled her from its chilling grasp.

Lily turned off the main road into quite possibly the most beautiful setting she'd ever seen. The morning sun filtered through numerous pine, oak, and cottonwood trees. Blackberry brambles tangled around a rock building that looked like it had been there since the gold rush.

"Welcome to Swift River." A cheerful young man stepped out of the information booth. Part surfer, part mountain man, he had longish sun-bleached hair and a scruffy looking copper-colored beard. "What's your pleasure? Are you here to get wet or get dirty?"

"Pardon me?" Was he flirting with her? She'd gone years without being noticed by the male population, least of all her ex-husband. Now she seemed to have a neon sign above her head advertising her newly single status. And the last thing she needed was another man distracting her.

"Are you here for rafting or camping?" he asked with a twinkle in his eye that made Lily think those weren't her only options.

"Actually I'd like to just look around, if that's okay?" Now that she was here, Lily wasn't sure if she could go through with it.

"You can do anything you want." His tone was suggestive. Somewhat flattering, even. "If you decide to stay, come on back and I'll fix you up."

"I bet you will." Lily laughed, feeling about ten years younger. She took the map he offered and drove slowly into the compound. She peered through the trees at the small cabins and tent sites cleverly tucked away so that each spot was its own oasis. Even the RV sites were hidden from each other, offering privacy and a feeling of being someplace special.

Picnic tables dotted the edges of a large meadow, the perfect spot for lunching on a lazy afternoon. Horseshoe pits and a volleyball court provided recreation for those seeking a more active distraction. Log benches surrounded a fire pit and a granite slab looked like it could serve as a stage. Or an altar for small, intimate outdoor weddings. Not that she was ever going to walk down that aisle again. She'd learned her lesson—happily-ever-after didn't exist.

She parked behind the large log building that housed the main office. A wide porch lined with benches overlooking the river looked like the perfect spot to sip a cold drink and chat with friends old and new. Guests could mingle on the porch or duck into the store for last minute supplies.

Lily stepped inside, bells tinkling overhead as she opened the door. Coolers along the back wall displayed soda, sports drinks, beer, and wine. One whole section contained locally produced juice and fresh fruit. There were packages of deli meats and a variety of cheeses for picnics. They also sold four different kinds of trail mix, including a nut and gluten free mix for those with allergies.

She found displays of T-shirts, bathing suits, sunglasses, and hats. Not to mention sunglass straps and those funky sandals the twins wore. Sunscreen, first aid supplies, and... Oh my, condoms were also available for purchase.

Thumbing through the racks of bathing suits, Lily looked for a replacement for the one she'd lost. Could she be bold enough to try on a brightly colored string bikini? What the hell? New life. New rules. No more boring black. No more subdued colors to blend into the background. She grabbed a siren red, skimpy little number. The kind that would surely turn heads. The question was, whose head was she hoping to turn?

"Lily? I thought that was you." The voice ran down her spine like warm honey. "It's me, Carson."

"Yes. Of course." She turned and saw that he was just as big and strong as she'd remembered. She hadn't built him up in her imagination. "I thought I'd check your place out."

"You still up for rafting?" His smile both reassured her and made her even more nervous about coming here.

"If the offer still stands." Lily hoped the slight tremor in her voice wasn't too obvious. "If you're busy or something..."

"Never too busy to help out a friend." Carson said the word like it was something exotic and dangerous. Like friendship was the last thing on his mind.

"Well then, I'm here for my first time down the river." Lily tried to keep her voice steady, pretending she wasn't afraid at all. "In a raft."

"You've come to the right place. I'll text Cody and see if he still wants to go."

"And if he doesn't?" Part of her hoped he had other plans. But then she'd be alone with Carson. In a boat. On the river. *Just the two of them.* She wasn't sure what scared her more.

"We can go down without him." The look in his eyes said he hoped Cody was unavailable. "Or we could do it another time."

He pulled his phone from his pocket. His thumbs flew over the screen and Lily couldn't help but wonder what else he could do with those skilled fingers.

"He's on his way."

"Do I have time to change?" Lily held up the bikini, and she noticed his eyes widen in appreciation. "If it fits, I'll pay for it before we go."

"Yeah, sure. Meet us in the boat barn around back."

Lily nodded.

"Oh, and make sure you have on plenty of sunscreen."

As if that was going to keep her from getting burned.

* * * *

Carson was pleased to see Lily ready to brave the river again so soon. He was pleased to see her, period. So he'd had a bit of a squabble with Cody about her last night. They were mature, responsible adults. They'd be able to move past their petty jealousy and show her a good time on the river. Couldn't they?

"Lily will be down in a minute." His brother was busy pulling out gear for their impromptu trip. "She had to pick up a few things from the store."

Like a red hot bikini. Was she trying to torture them? And why didn't they stock one-pieces? Something modest, like the wool suits they wore in the 1920s. It wouldn't matter because he already knew what she looked like underneath. He already knew what she felt like, and he had a hard time pushing the memory out of his mind.

Cody just grunted as he continued to gather the necessary supplies and equipment. So, he was still ticked off at him. Good. About time he learned the lesson that he couldn't always get everything he wanted, when he wanted it.

The two men quickly fell into the routine of getting ready to put-in on the river. They must have done this a thousand times. He and Cody knew each other so well, they didn't need to talk to communicate. A good thing since he didn't feel like talking to his brother right now. He'd noticed the way Cody looked at Lily. Like he was dying of thirst and she was a fresh mountain spring. Jealousy bubbled up to the surface and Carson fought to keep it under control.

Normally he'd just step aside. Let Cody have his way. But he couldn't let Cody have Lily.

Carson helped Cody pull out the boat and load it into the back of the truck. They gathered throw ropes, hoopi, and a hand pump. Carson grabbed his guide's paddle and threw three others into the back of his truck. Having an extra paddle on the trip was a good idea. Having an extra guy along? Not so much.

A first aid kit, water bottles, and bailing bucket—all this equipment for just a couple of hours. They finished loading the gear, and Cody tied down the load, making sure everything was secure. Carson threw extra hoopi in the back of the truck. He didn't want to be caught without one again.

Lily appeared in front of the boat barn wearing her new bikini and a tentative smile.

"Let's get you fitted for your life jacket." Cody handed Lily an orange life jacket and she wriggled into it. Carson nearly knocked Cody over as he moved in to check the straps. Cody shot him a look that made it clear he didn't appreciate Carson stepping in, but he didn't care. He needed to make sure Lily was safe. Even if it meant keeping her away from Cody.

Carson pulled up on her shoulder straps, but it was too loose. When he tugged on the chest strap, Lily let out a sharp gasp.

"Sorry." He'd forgotten about her injuries. "Are you sore from yesterday?"

"A little." She held her breath while he tightened the lower strap. "But I'm sure you know what you're doing."

"Proper fit is important," Carson assured her. "If it's too loose, you might as well be wearing nothing at all."

"Been there. Done that." Lily managed a smile, but her face was a shade paler than it had been.

"You can take this off until we get on the river." Carson unhooked the buckles and slid the life jacket down her arms. It was only then that he noticed the bruises on her side. His concern deepened. So did his admiration. Getting back on the river so soon took courage. Plenty of it.

"Let's roll." Cody slammed the tailgate of his truck and glared at him before shooting Lily his most charming grin. "Lily, you can sit up front. Next to me."

"Sure." She stepped toward the red truck and then stopped in her tracks. "I thought the truck was white."

"That's Carson's boring truck." Undertones of resentment seeped to the surface. "I like a little more excitement. I really like red."

Cody fingered the string of Lily's new bathing suit top, grazing her neck with his thumb and sending a noticeable shiver down her back. This could be a very long trip. Carson would have to keep an eye on Cody. Make sure he didn't get too close to Lily. The river was too shallow to hide his body for long.

As he drove, Cody filled Lily in on what to expect on the river. When it came to doing his job, the man was a true professional. He delivered his standard safety speech flawlessly, injecting enough humor and personality to guarantee that guests felt like they were in good hands.

Trust was their most important equipment. More important than the boat, life jackets, or safety ropes. On the river, Cody was more than trustworthy. He not only made his passengers feel safe, he also made each and every one of them feel like the trip had been designed just for them.

If only Carson could trust his brother on dry land.

"Let's get the boat inflated." Cody parked at the put-in spot and jumped out of the truck. He started pulling the raft out of the back of the truck all by himself. Showing off, probably hoping Lily would notice his muscles flexing with the weight of the raft.

"Let me help you with that." Carson was at his side in an instant. "You know better than to try to lift one of those things by yourself."

"That's right. You're in charge here." Cody nearly dropped the boat on his foot.

"No. You're head guide for this trip." Carson had decided to let Cody be the guide. If he was focused on the river, he'd have less time to make a move on Lily. "I'm just your grunt."

He pulled the rest of the gear out of the truck while Cody inflated the boat with the electric pump plugged into the outlet provided for commercial and private rafters' use. Carson double checked the first aid kit, and made sure there was plenty of water.

"Is there anything I can do to help?" He hoped Lily hadn't overheard the way they snipped at each other. Not a good way to instill confidence if she was worried about them taking a paddle to each other's heads.

"No, you're our guest." Cody turned on the charm. It was as if he'd never even thought a harsh word in his life. "Just relax and get ready to enjoy the ride."

"Should I put on my life jacket?" There was a hint of anxiety in her voice, but Lily was doing her best to control it.

"Sure, but you don't need to buckle it until we get down to the water." Carson wanted her to be comfortable. He needed to start by making amends with Cody. They were a team. It was time they started acting like one.

"If you want to put any personal belongings in this ammo can, it will keep everything dry." Carson opened the metal box.

"Okay, sure." She tossed her keys and her T-shirt into the can. "Is this an actual ammunition case?"

"We get them from the military supply store," Carson told her. "They come in several sizes, for everything from first aid kits to groovers. And they're completely watertight."

"Groovers?" Lily looked skeptical.

"Porta-potties. For overnight trips." Carson hadn't been on many lately. Cody preferred to take the two-days. "They're actually quite convenient. They take up a lot less space than commercial models. Watertight, odorless, and surprisingly comfortable."

"Probably more than I needed to know," Lily said.

Carson shrugged and threw his own wallet and cell phone into the can. "Cody, what do you want in the dry box?"

Cody drew his wallet out of his pocket. The unmistakable ring of a condom marked the well-worn leather.

"You know you really shouldn't keep those in your wallet." Carson whispered to his brother.

"Hey, I don't carry a purse." Cody kept his voice low so Lily wouldn't overhear. "Besides, I use them up long before they have a chance to deteriorate."

"Good to know you play it safe." Carson dug his nails into his palms. Sometimes he marveled at the fact that he wasn't an uncle.

* * * *

Lily didn't want to be nervous. But the closer they got to actually getting on the river, the harder it was to remain calm. It didn't help that there was unmistakable tension between the brothers that hadn't been there the day before. She hoped it wasn't her fault. Maybe they didn't really want to take her down the river. Maybe they were just being nice. Or maybe they thought she was wasting their time.

Since they'd come this far, and they'd gone to this much trouble, she figured she'd have to go through with it. She just hoped she wasn't getting in too far over her head. Even with the snug fitting life jacket, she worried about falling in.

She watched as they slipped the raft into the water. It was a calm spot, but she knew it wouldn't be like that the whole way down.

"Now remember, if you fall in"—Carson's voice was calm, assuring— "just lean back and put your feet downstream, like you're relaxing in a lawn chair. We'll come to you."

"I'm sure you will." Lily offered a quick smile.

Carson would keep her safe. She had to keep telling herself that. It was the only way she could put one foot in front of the other. It was the only way she could step into the boat.

"Ready?" Cody asked. "You hop in first. Take your paddle with you."

"Oh, I thought you guys would do all the rowing." Lily was now more than a little nervous. What if she couldn't paddle hard enough? What if she dropped the paddle in the river? What if she fell in?

"I'm just your humble guide." Cody smiled at her, flashing his dimples. She was sure if he wasn't wearing sunglasses, he would have winked at her. "You and Carson take the front and follow my commands."

"Oh, so we're going with age before beauty?" Carson quipped. "He thinks he's so cool because he's older than me."

"Just better looking." Cody ran his hands through his hair, shaking his head like a model.

"Are you two going to bicker, or are you going to show me a good time?" Lily crossed her arms over her life jacket and stood there, daring them, hoping their banter was more friendly than serious rivalry. Anything to keep her mind off the thought of being tossed into the river, unable to get her feet under her. Unable to breathe.

"You'll do just fine." Carson leaned over and whispered in her ear, "Paddling will keep you engaged. You won't have time for fear to creep in."

Sure, except for the fact that the man seemed to read her mind.

Carson held her arm as she stepped into the boat. She tried to concentrate on keeping her balance, not on the feel of his hand on her skin. He let her take the right side and showed her how to keep her weight centered and use her paddle to keep herself balanced. After practicing paddling and a few simple commands, they were underway.

It didn't take long for Lily to feel like she'd been doing this all her life. It didn't hurt that the twins worked so well together. They were in such perfect sync that she couldn't help but think they had some secret communication ability only identical twins had.

"Wow. This is great," she said. "I wasn't sure if I could actually do this, but it's so relaxing. And exciting at the same time."

"Yeah," Cody added. "But we haven't even gotten to the good parts yet."

"It can't possibly get better than this." Lily lifted her face to the sun, soaking up its rays. Soaking in the experience. Here, on the river, the rest of the world drifted away. There was no such thing as stress or heartache. All the pain of the last year, all the disappointments from her marriage— from the obvious like the cheating and the inability to get pregnant, to the little things, the way Brian had always managed to make her feel inferior—were swept into the river, carried away like fallen leaves.

The river took her professional setback and put it into a new perspective. It wasn't the end of the world, just a new course for her to take. And she was armed. She could paddle her way to the right future for herself. She could steer around the obstacles that cropped up. She wasn't just a passenger, but an active participant in her own life.

"Whoo-hoo!" Lily shouted as they dropped over an exciting rapid. "This is living."

"The next one is a swimming rapid," Cody told her. "You up for it?"

"A swimming rapid?" Her voice squeaked.

"It's one with a deep channel, few rocks, and big waves," Carson explained. "It's kind of like nature's waterslide."

"Sure, why not?" Lily tried to sound like she was up for anything. Here in the safety of the boat, she felt perfectly safe. Out there? She wasn't so sure.

"You don't have to do this if you don't want to." Carson meant to be reassuring, but instead she took it as a challenge. She was through being treated like a delicate flower.

Cody steered the raft to the side of river. He wedged his paddle under the tube behind Lily. He stood and grabbed the straps of her life jacket, picked her up and tossed her overboard.

"Keep your feet downstream!" he shouted. "Relax and have fun."

After spitting water from her mouth and shaking her head, Lily leaned back to enjoy the ride. It was such a rush to be carried over the waves with just her body. "This is awesome!" she cried out with her arms outstretched. Much better than her last trip downstream. This time, she was in control. She was wearing a life jacket. And this time, she knew the Swift brothers would be there to keep her safe.

The raft came alongside her as the current slowed. Carson leaned over and grabbed the shoulder straps of her life jacket.

"Just kick as I pull you up," he instructed. "Kick hard."

She kicked with all her might as he lifted her into the boat. She must have kicked a little too hard because they fell together to the bottom of the boat. She lay on top of him, breathless, both from her swim and from the feel of his hard body beneath her.

Their eyes locked and Lily felt a connection that made her heart stop. For a moment, it was just the two of them, floating in a world all their own.

Carson groaned.

"Damn it, Cody, you could have avoided that rock." His voice was as sharp as the pain she remembered from hitting a rock or two yesterday. "Don't tell me you didn't see it."

Lily picked herself up and returned to the front of the raft.

"Oh, if you think you could do better…" Cody stood up. "Come get the big paddle."

"Fine." Carson switched places with Cody for the rest of the trip. There were several more rapids, some calm stretches, and an overwhelming sense of peace as they made their way down the rest of the river.

"That was amazing!" Lily exclaimed once they brought the boat to shore. The trip ended at their campground, so there were plenty of guides around to help with the equipment. "Thank you. Thank you so much."

"Anytime." Cody helped her out of the raft. She was trembling all over. From the excitement, from working her muscles, from the cold water temperature.

"It's our pleasure." Carson helped remove her life jacket. His hands brushed her skin and it burned. Like a sunburn, only deeper. And no amount of SPF could protect her from his touch.

He tossed the jacket on the ground and went to gather the rest of the gear from the raft. Lily followed to grab the water bottles and spare paddle.

"I'm hooked," she said with a big smile on her face. "You may never get rid of me."

"Glad to hear it," Carson said. She could hear the pleasure in his voice. "I knew you'd conquer your fear."

"Of the river? Sure." Lily was still a little afraid of the feelings that had been growing since she met him. He was like the river. Rugged, wild, yet never completely out of control. He could be exciting and reassuring at the same time. And she suspected he had depth, hidden parts that she wanted to explore.

Cody promised a shallow adventure. What you see, is what you get. He'd be pure fun—nothing more. She'd felt his gaze on her as they'd floated down the river. When he caught her eye, he made sure to smile, showing off a world-class set of dimples. He said all the right things, the kind of lines she'd only wished had been thrown at her when she was younger. And as flattering as his attention was, she didn't quite react to him the same way. He may look just like Carson, but he didn't make her feel that bone-deep longing that his brother did.

The question was, what was she going to do about it?

Chapter 4

Lily followed the guys to the equipment shed. The barnlike building housed the rolled-up boats, spare paddles, life jackets, and various equipment she was sure had names and purposes, but none she could think of. She hung her damp life jacket on one of the drying racks and tried to make herself useful, but even with the neatly labeled shelves, she had no idea what most of that stuff was.

Cody dropped hints about going someplace called the Argo—a restaurant or bar of some sort. He'd talked it up like it was the place to be after a day on the river. But spending more time with the two of them probably wasn't such a good idea. As much as they made her feel welcome, she wasn't really a part of their world. She was really more of an indoor girl. She belonged in an office.

Today had been a nice escape. But it wasn't reality. She could tell herself she'd hang out all summer, soaking in the sun, forcing herself to relax. But she wasn't in her twenties anymore. She'd need to find something to keep herself busy. To give herself a purpose in life.

She fantasized about opening her own business. Working from home. Bookkeeping services were always in demand. She could provide small businesses with help on financial tasks, payroll and such. And many businesses believed that outsourcing was more cost effective than having someone on staff. Hadn't she learned that from experience?

If she got organized enough, she could establish a client base before she had the baby. And by working from home, she wouldn't have to leave her baby in the care of someone else for ten hours a day. Maybe she'd hire a part-time nanny while she met with clients. She could get a lot done while the baby napped, or played quietly nearby while she input data into a computer.

Who knew that floating down the river could be so empowering? She wished there was some way she could repay them for the afternoon's adventure. She felt like a new woman, like she could do just about anything. Getting on the river so soon had been a good thing. A really good thing.

And there was something about this place that drew her. That made her not want to leave. So maybe she hadn't been camping since the sixth grade. Maybe she hadn't stepped foot into a natural body of water since college. At least until yesterday. And maybe she'd never look as at home in the great outdoors as the female guide who was just getting off the river and heading over to talk to Carson and Cody.

Tall, tan, and very fit, the woman had biceps most guys would envy. She reminded Lily of a cougar, but not in the older women dating young men sense of the word. She moved with the strength and grace of a mountain lion. Slender and agile, and possibly territorial, as she glanced at Lily with a serious look on her face, like she was taking inventory. She must have passed inspection because the woman broke into a wide grin and introduced herself.

"Hey, I'm Fisher." She offered a firm handshake.

"Pleased to meet you." Lily smiled, despite feeling somewhat intimidated by her. "I'm Lily."

"The chick these guys rescued. Cool." Fisher gave a slight nod before following the twins back to the boat barn. "So, I know I'm the last person anyone would expect to have any gossip, but did you hear about Heather?"

"No. What about her?" Cody tossed the throw ropes into a bin. He shook out Lily's now-dry life jacket and hung it up in a bundle with five or six others.

"Heather's our bookkeeper," Carson explained to Lily. He double checked the contents of the first aid kit before putting it on the shelf.

"Not anymore," Fisher informed them. She tossed her long braid over her shoulder. "She totally ran off with some dude she met online."

"I thought she was married." Cody seemed only remotely interested in the news.

"What about her kids?" Carson sounded more concerned about the situation.

"Left the husband, left the kids." Fisher shook her head, tsking softly to herself. "Those poor girls."

"When you say she left," Carson said. "Do you mean she left town?"

"Oh yeah. Back east somewhere." Fisher grabbed the paddle Lily had used and leaned against it. "Aubrey ran into her husband at the market. He was stocking up on mac n cheese and frozen pizzas."

"He's a nice guy, too." Carson shook his head. "Too bad he hasn't had much construction work lately."

"I know, it totally sucks." Fisher shrugged. She replaced the paddle in the bin with all the others. "Well, I thought you guys should know. So you don't worry when she doesn't show up for work tomorrow."

"Hey, wait." Carson's voice was tight. Tense. "You don't mind picking up a few extra trips for me?"

"Sure." Fisher flashed another smile. "No problem. I guess you'll have stay behind to do the payroll and stuff."

"I could help." Lily had been listening with only mild interest about the love life of someone she'd never met, but when she heard the word "payroll" her heart rate ticked up a notch. "I don't have my résumé with me, but I could e-mail it to you when I get home. I worked for Crawford & Associates for almost eight years. I'm sure they'd be more than happy to provide a reference for me. My being let go was purely a financial decision."

"That's right, you're an accountant." Cody had been avoiding the conversation so far, but he was more than interested now. "So you can do payroll and all that financial stuff?"

"Sure, payroll, accounts payable, bank recs." Lily's voice sped up with her enthusiasm. "I can even handle phones, reservations, whatever you need."

"Whatever I need?" Cody moved in. He dropped his gaze, assessing her in a way that should have made her feel exposed. But she was still riding high from the rafting trip. Let him look.

"I can start work right away. I was planning on taking some time off, sort of a vacation, but I'd hate to see you guys fall behind." Lily was excited at the prospect of working for them. She knew she didn't want to go back to a corporate job. Once she became a single parent, the logistics of long hours and a lengthy commute would be difficult to manage. She could open her own bookkeeping business, but she was new to the area and worried about being seen as an outsider. Working for an established, local business was just the opportunity she'd hoped for to give her experience with the needs of a small, family-run company.

"Maybe we should discuss it over dinner?" Cody suggested. He leaned in, giving her a smile that hinted at very little actual conversation.

"There's nothing to discuss," Carson cut him off. "Lily starts tomorrow."

"I'll e-mail my résumé as soon as I get home."

"Just bring it with you." Carson sounded a little weary. Not exactly enthusiastic about the idea. She wondered if he'd made the offer more to shut Cody up than anything else. "We'll hammer out the details in the morning. I'm sure everything will work out just fine."

"Great, I'll see you in the morning." Lily wondered if she'd overstepped her bounds. Maybe he didn't want to hire someone to replace the last girl. Maybe he needed to downsize and this would have been a good opportunity to do so. But Lily had just jumped right in, offering her services. It was so unlike her. She was normally the type to research and contemplate. She was a planner. Before she even applied for the job at Crawford, she'd looked into their company profile in the online business journal, could project their next four quarter profits, and had the company's mission statement memorized.

She said she would help, so she would. If anything, she could at least get the next payroll out on time and make sure the bills weren't late. Then if they decided it wouldn't work out, there would be no hard feelings on her part. She would just be testing the waters, so to speak. It's not like they were going to set up a partnership.

* * * *

Carson finished putting away the rest of the gear, jotting notes on the equipment where needed. It took him awhile to fully absorb the news that his bookkeeper had skipped town. Having Lily jump in could be a good thing. Tomorrow, he would check her references and contact her former employer. But he trusted her. The way she had trusted him when they were in the river together.

Hopefully, she'd catch on quickly and they'd be able to make a smooth transition. Then he could go through with his plans to take off for Utah. He'd promised his buddy, Eric Sims, he'd fill in for him on the Yampa River. The secluded canyon would be the perfect place for him to carve out a new identity. He wanted a chance to be someone else. He needed a chance to just *be*. To go along for the ride instead of always having to be in the driver's seat.

The river was only runnable for six weeks in the summer. Just enough time to give him a taste of something different. But not so long that he couldn't return if he had to. It would be a trial separation. If it turned out that Cody couldn't handle things on his own, then Carson would return. If he decided to stay out there, he could look into expanding the business. The American wasn't the only river in the Western United States. It just happened to be the one in which he'd first dipped his paddle.

He just hoped he could handle having Lily in such close proximity every day. He was already troubled by how strongly he reacted to her. Part of it was the physical contact. Too much, too soon. He'd have to be careful not to cross that line, because the instant he did, it would be like fireworks. And in this part of the state, they were a fire hazard. Not to mention illegal.

But mostly, he was shaken by the way she made him feel. Like there was something he'd been missing his whole life, and she was it.

Carson did one last sweep to make sure they hadn't left anything behind when they got off the water. He breathed in the faint smell of the river, damp, fresh, and full of life. It soothed him, almost like a drug, as he felt the tension drift away with the current. He would miss that most of all. He didn't know the names of all the plants that grew here, but he knew their smell. Familiar. Comforting. Smelled like home.

He'd still be living on the river. He'd never trade the lulling sounds of moving water for city streets. But it would be a different river. The sounds would be different, the water gliding over sandstone instead of granite. The wind whispering through rock cliffs instead of pine and oak. The smells would be different, too. Different plants, different trees. Even the air would be different. Drier, quieter, and at around five thousand feet, thinner.

Cody wouldn't be there. Wasn't that the whole point? To see who he was as his own person, not as one of *the twins.* They had never been separated since the second week of kindergarten, when it had become painfully obvious Cody couldn't handle school without his brother right by his side.

Maybe he was taking a big risk, leaving Cody to fend for himself. He'd always done more than was necessary to help him out. Probably even more than was healthy. But he had been the reason their mother died. He'd been the reason their father left. So he felt like he had to keep an eye on Cody. He had to make it up to him.

The problem was that Cody had become too dependent on him. He seemed reluctant to be alone, even for the eight hours or so he spent sleeping. Carson had started to wonder if going back to bunk beds was the only way to get Cody to stop using women to keep from getting lonely at night. At some point, his good looks and fun-loving manner weren't going to be enough. Someday Cody might want to actually get a life.

"So that's one way to make sure we get to see more of Lily." Cody waited until she was on her way home to start talking about her. "Maybe this way she can take her time figuring out which one of us she wants."

"If she's working here, she's off limits." Carson hoped he could follow his own command. "We don't mix business and pleasure."

"Sure we don't." Cody laughed. It wasn't that funny. "We never meet women on our trips. We never spend time with them once we get off the river. And two guides never hookup by the end of the summer."

"That's different," Carson reminded him. "If Lily is our employee, she's not someone either one of us can just hookup with. There's a little something called sexual harassment."

"Look, I know where the line is, and I won't cross it," Cody said. "Lighten up. You know me, I'd never do anything with a woman that's not one hundred percent consensual."

"Still, you're technically her boss," Carson warned. "So you need to be even more careful."

"And what about you? Are you going to be careful? Are you going to keep from thinking about how hot she is? Are you going to be able to work next to her, day after day without thinking about kissing her? Touching her? Wanting her?"

"Yes," Carson lied. He'd have to. Either that, or he'd have to leave a whole lot sooner than he'd planned.

"Sure." Cody shook his head, chuckling mostly to himself. "This I gotta see. I might just have to stop by the office more often. Just to make sure you're not crossing a line."

Carson glared at him. He wondered, not for the first time, what it would be like to be an only child.

"I saw the way you were watching her." Cody wasn't finished. "I saw the way she was watching you. You can talk the talk, but you're going to have a hard time walking the walk, bro. You're going to have a hard time just walking."

"Shut up."

"Look, if it's too much temptation for you," Cody kept at it. "I can take her off your hands."

"No one's going to take her anywhere."

"Lighten up, bro. I'm just kidding."

"There's something new."

"Yeah, you want to see how serious I can get?" Cody squared up, ready for a challenge. "I can get just as serious as the next guy. I can get just as serious as you."

Sure. Why didn't they just trade places? Cody could take over making sure the bills were paid, the employees got their checks, and the septic tank wasn't backed up. And Carson would be the one to make Lily laugh. He'd be the one to show her the local sights. He'd be the one to capture her heart.

Chapter 5

"If I'd known you'd be here so early, I would have brought you a cup of coffee." Carson held the door for her, and she had to tell her heart to settle down. This was a job, not a date. She'd been awake since before dawn. First day jitters and the prospect of spending time with the twins—specifically one of them—had her insides churning like the biggest rapids they'd run yesterday.

"That's okay, I had two cups already. More than that and I get a little jumpy." Lily steadied her breathing and followed him into the small office. Maybe she was making a huge mistake by going to work for a man she was clearly attracted to. And then there was Cody. Even though he was over the top, she couldn't help but like him. Cody was good for her ego. He made her feel pretty and flirtatious and fun.

"I know the feeling." He was trying to make her feel at ease, but it would work better if he didn't talk. His voice sent her heart racing like twelve double-shots of espresso.

"This will be your desk." He indicated the one closest to the door. The other desk was pushed up against it, so they were facing each other. "Technically, Cody and I share the other one, but he rarely comes in here."

"Great." She was here to do a job. One she was good at. It felt good to be useful again. While it was nice to feel wanted, it was quite another thing to be needed.

Lily looked around the office. Along one wall, the copier/printer/scanner sat on top of a small metal cabinet. A bookcase and two tall filing cabinets stood on the far side. High windows let in plenty of light, but she'd have to stand on a chair to look outside. She had enough distractions already, she didn't need a view.

"I'll be in and out, depending on my trip schedule." Carson held the chair for her and she plopped down in the seat that was a little low for her comfort.

"Sorry." Carson pressed the lever to raise the seat. "I have to lower it all the way, otherwise my legs don't fit."

Lily's eyes were drawn to his long, lean, and powerful legs. He had to be at least six-three. Maybe six-four. And solid. His legs were tan and muscular and covered in silky golden hair. She already knew his strength. She owed her life to it.

"I usually like to check in first thing in the morning, even on days I'm not on the river. So the best time to catch me, if you have questions or something, would be before eight-thirty." He sounded like he was making apologies for not being around all day long. "If I'm not on the river, I stop in throughout the day. But if I'm on a trip you'll pretty much be on your own."

"I can come in around seven-thirty." That would give her at least an hour with him. In case she had questions. Or something.

They spent a few minutes firming up her schedule, agreeing on a salary and discussing expectations for the job. Her main duties would be payroll and bookkeeping. Most of the trips were booked through the website, but there were always a few people who didn't trust technology and would want to talk to a real live person. He showed her how the online calendar worked and the basics of scheduling.

"This is the program we use for all our bookkeeping." Carson indicated the familiar icon on the desktop screen.

"I've used this software for years." What a relief to be able to just jump right in without having to work with an unfamiliar program. "So what do you want me to start on first?"

"Here's the in-basket." He pointed to an overflowing tray. "It looks like Heather was spending a little too much time with her online boyfriend, and not so much time on work."

"I'll dig right in." Lily mentally rubbed her hands together in anticipation of the challenge. "I can get these invoices input and processed, streamline the filing system, and run reports to make sure everything is where it should be."

"Don't worry about the reports just yet." Carson frowned, as if the thought of something being amiss just hit him. "The guides are expecting their checks tomorrow, that's our number one priority. Then the outgoing bills."

"You probably should check your accounts." Lily didn't like the idea that someone had been messing with them, but when a bookkeeper skipped town unexpectedly, it could be trouble. "I'd feel better if I had an up-to-date balance to reconcile. And you might want to change your passwords."

"Good point." Carson sat down at the computer opposite her. He logged on to his bank's website and printed out a current balance. "What's your birthday?"

"October 17th, why?" Lily didn't think he was the horoscope kind of guy.

"The new password is your name and birthdate." He tossed her a quick smile. "If Heather wanted to access the accounts, she'd never guess that."

"No, I suppose she wouldn't." Lily felt a little embarrassed that he'd used something so personal to her. But then again, it would be hard to hack. "So does the balance look about right?"

"Yeah. The main account looks good." His shoulders relaxed a bit. "And the payroll account has enough to cover this pay period."

"Good. I'll be on the lookout for anything even remotely suspicious," Lily assured him. "But let's get these paychecks out first."

She clicked on the screen for Employees and Payroll. Scanning the list of employees, she could see she had her work cut out.

"Do you really have that many people working for you?" Lily indicated the seventy plus names. Many were obvious duplicates, but it looked as if every single person who'd ever worked for them was still on the active roster.

"No, some of those guys have been long gone." Carson leaned over her shoulder; the heat from his body threatened to overload her entire system. "And look, Fisher is in there three times. She does work three times as hard as most people, but…"

"I can get this cleaned up, no problem." Lily tried not to inhale too deeply, but the scent of soap, sunscreen, and pure male made it hard to breathe. "I'll print out a list of employees who haven't been paid yet this year, and you can tell me who will likely be back this summer."

"Sure, that's a great idea." He backed away. Relief, mixed with disappointment, washed over her. She concentrated on processing a quick report using the parameters she'd described. She hit the print key and watched Carson retrieve the paper and sit down at the other desk. Lily wondered if it would have been better to have Cody get her started. But she got the impression that Carson knew a lot more about the ins and outs of running this place than his brother did. Cody seemed to be more of a hands-on guy when it came to the physical part of their job.

The paperwork required a different approach. Lily was glad she could help them both out.

"These three guys should be back in the next couple of weeks." Carson handed her the list with three names circled. "Everyone else is long gone."

"Good." Lily made quick work of making the former employees inactive. "Now tell me how the hours are reported each pay period?"

"Time cards are due today by noon, but we could move the deadline up since you're coming in early." Carson brought over a stack of papers already turned in. Fisher's was on top. "Cody and I are on salary. Guides are paid by the trip, since the river doesn't keep a time clock. Anyone working at the store or campground is paid at their standard hourly rate."

"Sounds simple enough." Lily thumbed through the timecards. It looked like only someone named Tyler's was still missing. "What should I do with Heather's final paycheck?"

"I suppose I could drop it by her house." Carson's voice took on an edge. "If her husband decides to deposit it in their joint account and use the money to feed their kids, that's their business."

"That sounds like a good plan." Lily's heart lurched at the way he thought of Heather's kids instead of wanting to withhold her final check. This way he'd be covered, and hopefully her kids would benefit.

Carson returned to the other desk. He looked up at her and smiled. "And Lily…thanks. You're a lifesaver."

"I'm the one who should be thanking you." Lily tried not to let him know how excited she was. "It feels really good to be useful again."

"I'm glad we could help each other out." Carson turned his attention to his own work and Lily dug into the overflowing inbox. She started by sorting bills from bank statements, deposit slips from junk mail.

Every once in a while, Lily got the feeling that Carson was watching her. The tension between them hummed as loud as the twin computers. It had nothing to do with the fact that he was entrusting her with his company's finances. He was attracted to her, but he fought it. Was it because she was working there? Or was there something else going on?

She was just about to bring it up when Cody sauntered in.

* * * *

"Well good morning, Lily." Cody leaned against her desk as if he owned the place. He did own the place, but still, Carson didn't like the way he treated Lily so familiarly. "You sure do brighten up the place."

"Thank you." Lily looked over at Carson and flashed an embarrassed smile. He thought they'd already discussed the fact that Lily was an employee. She was off limits. For both of them. "I've certainly got my work cut out."

"Well, if there's anything you need," Cody drew out his words, letting her know that he was offering more than just a certain type of pen or an ergonomic keyboard. "You just let me know. I'll take care of you."

"I'm good," she said in a clipped tone. "I just need to concentrate right now."

Carson bit back a grin. She'd put him in his place. A rare occurrence. Cody was the kind of guy who could make a university president blush like a schoolgirl with just a smile.

Cody picked up the stapler, turning it over in his hands. Clearly the man didn't know what to do with himself. He was so used to having women melt with nothing more than a glance and a grin. Lily's dismissal must really rub him raw. Carson found it entertaining as hell, though, and that bothered him almost as much as the fact that he hadn't been able to get a lick of work done with Lily so close.

It was going to be a long month if today was any indication. He wanted her. He wanted her more than he'd ever wanted any other woman. And he couldn't do a damn thing about it. She was at least able to concentrate, biting her lower lip as she input information into the computer. When she chewed on the end of a pen, Carson thought he was going to explode.

Cody had walked in just in time.

"Hey, Cody, could you check and see if the printer has plenty of paper?" Carson suggested. He couldn't stand having Cody just sitting there, doing nothing but making all of them aware that this was far from business as usual. "Lily mentioned some reports she needs to run, and I'd hate for her to run out in the middle of the job."

"Yeah sure." Cody strolled over to the printer, staring at it like it was a foreign object.

"The extra paper is in the cabinet below." He really shouldn't take such pleasure from his brother's cluelessness. "If there isn't enough, there should be two or three cases out in the barn."

"I knew that." Cody shot him a deadly glare. "I was just thinking I should check the toner as well."

"Good idea." Carson glanced over at Lily, who was trying to hide a smile as she worked. Her fingers clicked and clacked over the keyboard, and she had managed to make quite a dent in the in basket.

Cody rummaged through the cabinet, loaded the printer with paper, and stood there looking like a man who'd just performed open-heart surgery using a pocket knife. Lily didn't seem to notice.

Carson could just sit there watching his brother looking like a lost little kid or he could jump in and save his ass. He threw him a line. "I think we need to update our website. Maybe you could give me a hand with the copy? I'm sure you could think of some way to make it more interesting."

"Sure. I can write up some tips to make the first time more enjoyable." Cody seemed relieved to have something to do besides stand there and look pretty. "Lily could help."

And that's what he'd really come in for—an excuse to get close to Lily. Carson had just flung the door open and Cody waltzed right on through.

"Sure. I'd be happy to help." Lily looked up from her screen. "But I need to get my work done first."

"Maybe we could discuss it over dinner?" Cody was smooth. Too smooth.

"I started at seven-thirty. I'm sure you don't want to pay overtime," Lily said. Carson realized he'd been holding his breath, fearing she'd take the bait.

"Guess not." The disappointment in Cody's voice was priceless. He'd taken a big blow to his ego and Carson loved Lily for it.

Wait a minute. *Love* was a little strong. He liked Lily. Admired her, even. He was most definitely attracted to her. But love? That was the last thing on his agenda. As soon as he got her settled in the job, and informed Cody of his plans, he was gone.

He'd planned on driving out around Memorial Day. Take a little vacation, do some exploring along the way. Now he'd have to put it off until he was sure the business would stay afloat. Which reminded him, some of the rafts were getting old and should be replaced sooner rather than later.

"While you're at it..." Carson realized he'd been staring at Lily. "Why don't you run an inventory on the boats? Anything with more than three patches should be replaced."

"Why don't you run an inventory on the boats?" Cody came around to his side of the desk and sat down on the edge. "I need to use the computer to update the website."

Shit. He should have thought of that. This office was feeling a little too crowded. Since Cody wasn't budging, he figured he'd have to be the one to step aside. Leaving his brother alone with Lily. Giving him a chance to do his magic.

"Here's my cell." Carson jotted the numbers on a yellow sticky note. "Text me if you need anything."

He wanted to add, "If you need me to rescue you from Cody," but he kept that thought to himself. Maybe she wouldn't want rescuing.

"I'll be sure to take good care of her." Cody was dialing up the charm. She'd resisted so far, but eventually she'd succumb. It was like trying to control the river—sure, it could be contained for a while, but eventually nature would take its course. In the natural order of things, Cody would get the girl. He always did.

"I can take care of myself, thanks." Lily gave Carson an encouraging smile as she grabbed the next stack of papers and started thumbing through them. "At least on dry land."

Carson's heart swelled uncomfortably in his chest. He needed to take inventory of the boat house. He needed to take inventory of his feelings. The boat house was nice and organized. His emotions were a jumbled mess.

After a good hour of inspecting the boats, Carson found that there were two, actually, three rafts that should be replaced. There just never seemed to be any of that extra money lying around. Sure, they had enough to cover their expenses. Even paying himself and Cody a small salary. But there was never quite the surplus that could be put into really upgrading the place the way he'd like it. Sure they had solar, and the cabins were well maintained. But if he wanted new boats, he'd have to use credit. He'd pay the loan back with the salary he wouldn't draw once he left.

* * * *

"So, Lily." Cody moved over to her side of the desk after about fifteen minutes of fiddling on his computer. The way he'd moved the mouse, she almost thought he'd been playing a couple of hands of solitaire. He leaned on the edge, crossing his arms over his chest. "I know you aren't interested in a dinner date, but how about a bike ride after work?"

"I don't have a bike." Lily didn't even look up from her screen. A lesser man would've quit by now. But she had a feeling Cody wouldn't give up so easily.

"You could rent one at Paddles and Pedals." He picked up one of her pens. Well, she supposed they were technically his pens, but still. She knew he was just trying to play it cool. "It's right on the river. They rent bikes and kayaks. There's a trail that follows almost all the way to the lake. It gives you a whole different perspective of the river."

"I don't know. I'm not much of an outdoor girl." Lily scooted her chair back slightly and turned to face him.

"You could be." Cody lowered his voice, trying to tempt her into going along with him. "If you spend a lot of time around here, you'll be an outdoor adventurer in no time. You've already conquered the river."

"I took one rafting trip." Lily sighed. She wasn't going to get rid of him easily. "That hardly counts as 'conquering.'"

"I'll see if Carson wants to come with us." Cody pushed off from the edge of her desk. "We can pack a picnic. Just a casual sort of thing."

"Well, I guess I should get to know the area," Lily relented. "The trail isn't too difficult, is it?"

"Nah, you'll do just fine." Cody grinned. "We could meet at the bike shop."

He wrote down the address on a sticky note. After jotting his phone number, he slid it across the desk just as the young man she'd met when she first arrived at the resort rushed through the door.

"I didn't forget my timecard." This must be Tyler. His face lit up when he saw Lily. "I see you did more than just look around a bit. I guess you liked what you saw."

"Sure." Lily's cheeks flushed with warmth. "I'm making sure those of you who help people get wet or dirty get paid."

"Nice." Tyler stuck out his hand and Lily shook it. "Welcome. I'm sure you'll love being part of the team here. Every day is definitely an adventure. Hey, boss, we got a group coming in fifteen." The way Tyler used the nickname it almost sounded like he couldn't tell the twins apart. "You want me to meet them and get 'em started?"

"No, I'll be right down." Cody ran his hand through his hair. "Lily, I've got a bachelorette party and there's no way I'm leaving this up to Junior, here. It's kind of our signature trip. But I'll see you this evening. Say six? I mean, we'll see you this evening."

"Oh right." Lily barely looked up from her computer. "I almost forgot. I'll meet you there."

Chapter 6

Payroll completed, checks signed, and most of the filing complete, Lily left the office feeling satisfied with a job well done. She decided to celebrate her success with a shopping trip to Prospector Springs. She currently owned one pair of shorts and she had a feeling she would have no need for grey suits or black skirts. And two-inch heels? She'd make do with the river sport sandals she'd bought along with her new bathing suit. Comfortable and waterproof. What more could a girl want?

She bought three pairs of cropped pants, two pairs of khaki shorts, and five cotton blouses. She picked out a couple of sundresses and a pair of flats that would go with pretty much everything, and she suspected her life would change along with her wardrobe. With the exception of the river, life here moved at a much slower pace. Lily could get used to the idea of stopping for lunch when she was hungry. And instead of going to a trendy restaurant, she could eat under a hundred-year-old oak tree.

She was going to like living here.

Lily arrived at the bike shop before the guys, so she decided to go ahead and rent a bike. The clerk was helpful and friendly, and she wondered if everyone in Prospector Springs was just as welcoming as the twins. Or maybe she was no longer so worried about making the right impression, so she was the one who was friendlier. Either way, she liked her new community. She felt at home for the first time in her life.

She was all set with the bike and helmet and was making practice runs around the store when Cody pulled up. Alone. Would Carson drive over in his own truck? Or was this a set-up?

"Hey, Lily, it looks like you're all set here." Cody shouldered a backpack and lifted his bike out of the bed of his pickup truck. "You ready for the ride of your life?"

"Is Carson meeting us here?" Lily ignored his innuendo. She wondered if he really thought he was clever, or if it was just a bad habit he'd fallen into. "Or is it just the two of us?"

"He got hung up at the camp. Had a lot of work to do." A flash of guilt crossed his face, but then he dialed up the charm. "But he said to tell you not to worry. You'll be in very good hands with me."

"Oh really?" Since she'd already paid the bike rental, she figured she might as well go through with it. Maybe she could set him straight. "I have to warn you, I haven't been on a bike in years. I don't think spin class counts."

"I'm sure you'll remember what to do." Cody moved in on her, getting a little too close for her comfort. "And I'll be here to catch you if you fall."

No need to worry about that. He wasn't her type.

Lily strapped on her helmet and mounted her bike. It didn't take long to get a nice rhythm going. It really was a skill that came back, even after years of not riding.

"Wow, this is a really beautiful trail." Lily paused to take a sip from her water bottle. She was in pretty good shape for someone who didn't spend a lot of time outdoors. She had her workout tapes, but she'd left the treadmill behind. She'd left a lot of her old life behind. "It's hard to believe this is the same river that runs through downtown Sacramento."

"Yeah, normally I'd rather be on the river than next to it." Cody took a long drink of water and glanced over at her, drinking her in. "But it's worth it just being next to you."

"I'll bet you say that to all the girls." Lily might as well play along. She'd decided it was just his habit. Flirting was his native language.

"I've never brought a date here." She had a feeling Cody was trying to impress her. "You're the first."

"Where do you usually take your dates?" Lily asked with a playful grin. "Straight to your bed?"

"Well...yeah." Cody took his sunglasses off and a slow, sensual smile spread across his face. "Most of them are tourists, just up for the weekend, so there's not a lot of time to get to know each other."

"So what, do you just snap your fingers?" Lily could see how women would be attracted to him, but wondered how so many of them just jumped into bed with him so quickly. "And these women just agree to meaningless sex?"

"It's not meaningless." He sounded defensive. Maybe even a little hurt.

Lily shrugged and hopped back on her bike. She started to say something about how she wasn't the kind of girl who could engage in meaningless sex, but then she realized she'd been doing it for years. Sex couldn't get more meaningless than her futile attempts at conceiving a baby. She and Brian had long ago stopped pretending it meant anything else. Foregoing the wine, the music, the sexy lingerie, they'd made no attempts at foreplay. They'd made no attempts at connection.

"Hey, slow down." Cody pedaled alongside her. "Are you okay?"

"Yeah, sure." She stopped. Straddling her bike, she took a slow, deep breath. "Sorry. Who am I to judge what you do with your personal life?"

"I'd like for you to be a part of my personal life." For the first time since she'd met him, Cody sounded sincere. "What do you say we stop for a picnic?"

"Sure." Lily dismounted her bike and flashed him an apologetic smile. He wasn't a bad guy. At least he was honest. Besides, there was a good chance that Carson wasn't all that different. He probably had his share of casual relationships, too.

She parked her bike on the side of the trail and followed him to a soft grassy area surrounded by thick tangles of nearly ripe blackberries. The river flowed over small stones and gravel, making a soft, almost musical sound. It was the perfect spot for a picnic. It would even be romantic, with the right guy.

Cody pulled a thin blanket from his backpack and spread it on the ground. He brought out a loaf of bread, a container of sliced cheese, a bunch of red grapes, and a bottle of wine. He pulled two plastic wineglasses out of his pack and undid the cork with his pocketknife.

"Can I help you with anything?" She was starting to feel a little nervous. He'd gone to a lot of trouble putting this together and would most likely expect her to fall for it. To fall for him.

"No. I got it. You just sit there looking gorgeous." He poured them each a glass of wine and set to work on the bread and cheese.

"Oh please, I have horrible helmet hair." Lily caught herself trying to smooth it down. She didn't want to draw any more attention to her appearance.

"I like helmet hair. Almost as much as bedhead." Cody drew the words out, slow and seductive. It was almost comical. But Lily knew he was serious. He really thought he could win her over this way.

"Okay, you win." Lily took off her sunglasses and inspected him closely. "You've got the right build. Broad shoulders, narrow hips. Tall, probably six-three at least. Lean and strong. Any major diseases run in your family?"

"What?" He seemed thrown off balance by her sudden change in attitude.

"You want to have sex with me." She plucked a grape from the bunch and popped it into her mouth, watching him watch her. "And I want something too. I want to have a baby. So…we might as well get down to it."

"A baby?" He couldn't have looked more terrified if a grizzly bear, a mountain lion, and a rattlesnake had snuck up behind her.

Lily laughed out loud. "You should see your face. I take it you're not interested in becoming a father any time soon."

"No. Definitely not." Cody let out a relieved breath. "I'd make the world's second worst father."

"Who would be the first?"

"The bastard who left me and Carson in the hospital when our mother died." The bitterness in his voice was sharp, and certainly justified. "He just walked away and didn't even contact us for three or four years."

"I'm so sorry." Lily couldn't imagine what kind of man could abandon two helpless infants. Especially after they had already lost their mother.

"Hey, it is what it is." Cody shrugged. He reached for his wine. "Besides, I think we turned out okay."

"Yeah, you did." They had managed to run their own business despite being orphaned at birth. "So who raised you?"

"Carson." Cody didn't hesitate a moment. "Our grandparents took us in, but Carson was the one who was always there for me. Especially after our grandparents died and we had to go live with Joe—our biological father. Carson's responsible for making me the man I am today."

"So you two are really close?" It wasn't really a question. Lily already knew the answer. She wondered if she'd get lucky and have twins. They wouldn't have a father, but they would at least have each other.

"We were." Cody sounded a little disconcerted. "Until recently. Until you came along."

"I don't want to come between the two of you." Lily shifted uncomfortably on the picnic blanket. They'd been through too much together. She wasn't worth splitting them up.

"I've never tried to steal a woman from my brother." Cody was in full confession mode. "I've never lied to him about where I was or who I was with. Until today."

Lily tore a small chunk of bread and stared at it as if she couldn't figure out its purpose. "But you lied to me, too. You tricked me into coming on a date. I thought Carson would be here too."

"So you like him better than me?"

"No. I thought we'd all just be friends," Lily lied. Sort of. She did want to be friends. She didn't want to hurt his feelings. She also couldn't explain why she felt something for Carson and nothing for him. So she figured it was best to just change the subject. "I wasn't kidding about wanting to have a baby. But don't worry. I don't need your help. I'm going to use an anonymous donor."

"A sperm bank?" Cody looked surprised. She'd have to get used to that look. He wouldn't be the last person to be shocked by her unconventional parenting strategy. "Seriously?"

"Yes. I am serious." Lily picked at her bread, took a bite of cheese, and washed it down with a sip of wine. "I've wasted too much time already. This is the best way." Maybe even the only way.

"Really?" Cody didn't seem to agree. He looked out over the river. It probably wasn't a subject he'd put much thought into. "How's the wine? It's made just up the hill by a small, family-owned winery."

"It's very good." Lily took another sip, savoring the red wine from a plastic cup. She glanced at the label, *Lost Mine Wine*. It was quite a discovery; she made a mental note to pick up a bottle or two. "You know, if you ever do decide to bring a date here, I'm sure she'll be impressed."

"But you're not?" His voice sounded light, teasing, yet with an undercurrent of disappointment. "I could try to change your mind."

"Can you settle for being friends?" It was all she could give.

"For now." Cody flashed a lopsided grin. His dimples deepened and his eyes sparkled with mischief. "But I won't give up completely."

"No. I suppose you won't." Lily felt a little warm and fuzzy. Maybe it was the wine. Or the perfect late spring evening. Maybe it was the attention from an attractive man who wasn't entirely scared off by her plans to become a single parent. Too bad he was the wrong man.

"Besides, who says you can't have a little fun?" Cody slipped right back into his charmer role. A role he'd come close to perfecting.

"Fun, I can handle." Lily started cleaning up the picnic, gathering the empty cups and cloth napkins. "As long as you keep your hands to yourself."

"You don't know what I can do with my hands."

"I'm not planning on finding out, either."

"You just might change your mind."

Doubtful. But she knew he'd keep trying. That's just the kind of guy he was.

* * * *

Carson had a lot of work to do. He had a little more than three weeks to make all the necessary repairs and improvements on the resort property. Plus, he'd needed to get out of the office, before things got too heated. Having Lily there was going to be a challenge. But she was good. Efficient, professional, and she had no problem letting Cody know she was there to work, not play.

The late rains had been great for the state's water reserves, but it put him behind schedule on routine maintenance. A few cabins had suffered from storm damage. He'd repaired the broken window in cabin number nine right away, but the loose shingles had been waiting for better weather.

If he had more time, Carson would prefer to go ahead and reroof the damaged cabins. But unless he hired someone, he wouldn't be able to complete the job before he left. A patch job would have to do. The rest of the roof was still in good shape, just a few loose spots where winds and fallen tree branches had taken their toll.

He'd managed to replace the shingles on two of the three cabins in need of repair, but he was losing the light. Not to mention the ability to keep his mind off Lily. What worried him most wasn't the sizzling attraction between them. Or even the fact that his brother was hot on her tail. What worried him most was the way she seemed to fit into his life. She'd slid right into his office with such ease. He could picture her slipping into other parts of his life.

He could see Lily as someone he'd want to settle down with. Except for the fact that he was trying to break out on his own. He was trying to be free for the first time in his life. He wanted to be in a place where he only had to look after himself, and the five or six passengers in his boat. He didn't want to be tied down. Even with someone as great as Lily.

If he could keep his feelings in check, focus on the necessary work around here, and spend as little time alone with Lily as possible, then he could get on with his life.

"Hey, boss." Tyler was heading out from the guides' house. Probably to the Argo. He was like a younger version of himself and Cody. At twenty-two, the kid had his whole life ahead of him. "So it looks like our man Cody has finally met his match."

"What do you mean by that?" Carson was tired and a little cranky. He wasn't in the mood for games.

"He's totally into the new bookkeeper, Lily." Tyler shook his head, a look of envy and awe on his face. "Can you believe he's blowing off a group of hot single ladies from that bachelorette party?"

"Doesn't sound like Cody." Carson packed his tools in the back of his truck. He was ready to head home, take a long hot shower, and maybe catch the last few innings of the Giants game tonight.

"Hey, there are plenty of women to go around." Tyler seemed almost giddy. "You want to come down to the Argo and be my wingman? Or I could be yours."

"No thanks. I had a long day." Carson could use a beer, but he wasn't into crowds right now. Hell, he would have given up on the bar scene a long time ago if it wasn't for Cody. "Cody's really skipping out on you, huh?"

"Yeah, he's taking Lily on a picnic," Tyler informed him. "And we both know how that will end."

Yeah, with Carson making her breakfast in the morning. Only instead of sending her off to wherever she came from, he'd be sending her off to their office. Hopefully she would get caught up before Cody broke her heart.

With a sick feeling, he drove across the bridge to the house he shared with Cody on the other side of the river. It was a big place, more than they needed for just the two of them. But they each had their own master suite, on opposite ends of the house, so they had privacy when they wanted it. Right now, they could have rooms on opposite sides of the country and it wouldn't be far enough for Carson.

Cody wasn't home when Carson pulled in the drive. Great. He must still be with Lily. Maybe they'd gone back to her place. So instead of listening to them, he'd have to picture the two of them doing what Cody did second best.

Carson made himself a sandwich, grabbed a beer, and went out on the deck to sulk.

Cody pulled in not too long after dark. He seemed to be alone, but that didn't mean jack.

"Hey." Cody brought a half-empty bottle of wine and a glass out on the deck. "What are you doing out here in the dark?"

"Just sitting." He took a long drink of his beer. He'd returned twice for a refill. It didn't do anything to dull the sick feeling in the pit of his stomach.

"Mind if I join you?" Cody didn't wait for an answer before he pulled up a chair and poured himself a glass of wine.

Carson couldn't think of anything nice to say, so he kept his mouth shut.

"What a night." Cody leaned back, looking up at the stars.

"You can quit with the bullshit." Carson didn't want to sit out here and wait for Cody to gloat. "I already know you were with Lily tonight."

"Okay, so I saw her after work." Cody had the slightest tension in his voice. Like it hadn't gone quite as planned. "We went on a bike ride. No big deal."

"Really?" Carson wasn't sure if he believed him or not.

"Yeah, we rode down by the river. Had a picnic." Cody heaved a long sigh. Frustration? That would be a first.

"So you thought a picnic would be a good way to welcome Lily to our company?"

"Yeah, that's what it was. A company picnic." Cody stretched his legs out, making himself comfortable.

"What about the rest of the staff?" Carson was tired of this conversation. Tired of Cody. "I didn't see a memo."

"What's your problem, man?" Cody drained his glass and then poured the rest of the bottle.

"Nothing." He couldn't wait to get out of here. He couldn't wait to be free. No more entertaining his brother. No more making sure he didn't screw up. No more giving a shit about anyone but himself. It would be like…well, like being Cody.

He gathered up his empty beer bottle and went inside without another glance at his brother. So maybe Cody hadn't gotten very far with Lily. He should be happy. Except that it made it that much harder to stop thinking about her. That much harder to stop wanting her.

Chapter 7

"So, how was your date with Cody yesterday?" Damn, he'd told himself he wasn't going to bring it up, but Lily had been in the office twenty minutes before the curiosity threatened to kill him and any cats within a twelve-mile radius.

"What date?" Lily didn't even look up from her computer, she just clicked away at the keyboard. "Oh, the bike ride. I thought it would be a threesome."

Her cheeks flushed, and she looked up from her computer. "I mean, I thought you were coming, too."

So, Cody had tricked her. It should have made him feel better, but it didn't.

"No, I was working." He wasn't sure if he should mention that he wasn't invited.

"Cody mentioned you had some things to do. But the trail was nice." She smiled. It made him think of sunny days, blue skies, and the kind of freedom he hadn't felt since his first summer on the river. "It's a different perspective than going down the river in a raft."

"Sure it is." Carson realized he'd been holding his breath, waiting for Lily to tell him how great Cody had been. That Cody had only pretended to be frustrated last night. "But even in a raft it's different every time."

"So you don't get bored?"

"Bored?" That wasn't exactly the word for it. But it was something along those lines. Dissatisfied, maybe. Needing something different. Something more. "No, not bored."

Should he tell her his plans? Maybe it would ease the tension between them. If she knew he could never be more than a temporary fling, she would lose interest. She didn't seem like the casual relationship kind of girl. No she was a woman. A woman who deserved more than he or Cody could give.

"What do you do on your days off?" It was a legitimate question.

"I don't take a lot of days off," he admitted. "When I'm not on the river, there's always plenty to do. Paperwork, maintenance, ordering supplies. Doesn't leave a lot of time for much else. Except maybe the occasional fishing trip to Hidden Creek."

"The occasional fishing trip can be life-changing." A moment passed between them, a reminder of the two of them in the water, his hand on her breast. Somehow he knew they were both thinking of that moment. He knew it the way he often knew what Cody was thinking.

He understood his connection with his twin. He didn't understand how he could feel an equal, if not deeper, connection with Lily. He'd only known her a few days and yet…

"Cody doesn't seem to let work get in his way of having a good time." Lily kept talking, keeping his mind from lingering too long on her earlier question. Or on the possibilities.

"Of course not." He wondered if she picked up on the bitterness in his voice. The family ties were getting too tight. He needed to sever them before one of them ended up hanging from the nearest tree. "He knows I'll take care of things around here."

"But you guys are partners. Doesn't Cody share in the workload?"

"Sure." Cody was his equal partner on paper. He took an equal share of the profits, but not an equal share of the work. "Cody spends more time on the river. I keep an eye on everything else. So I guess it evens out."

"If it works for you." Lily smiled politely before turning her attention back to her computer screen.

"That's weird." She looked intently at the screen, their conversation forgotten for the moment. "No, that can't be right."

Carson came around her side of the desk, leaned over her shoulder, and looked at the computer. He wasn't sure what he was looking at. He was used to one of two reports that Heather e-mailed him on a weekly basis. He hadn't looked through the actual data in months, if not a year or more.

"Is something wrong?" His stomach started to churn. Heather had disappeared suddenly. Now his new bookkeeper had found something weird. One plus one could equal trouble.

"I'm not sure." She clicked through a series of screens, her brows furrowed in concentration. "It could be a glitch in the software. Or it could be something else."

"What did you find?" His heart hammered in his chest. Was it from the accounting or simply from being so close to her? He could smell her shampoo, fresh, clean, not-too-sweet, with a hint of citrus.

"Well, there are duplicate entries on some of the transactions." Lily adjusted the screen so she could view two windows at once. "It looks like the withholding was taken from both the payroll account and the main account. But I don't know where.... I'm going to need copies of your bank statements, going back the last year, maybe longer."

"I'll dig them up for you." Carson walked over to the filing cabinets; his feet felt like lead. This could be big trouble. And like always, it would all fall on his shoulders.

"Oh and I need copies of the payroll tax reports, too." Her tone was focused, determined. She didn't take her eyes off the computer screen. "State and Federal. How long did your last bookkeeper work for you?"

"Three years." This was bad. Very bad.

"Bring me three years' worth of records then." Lily looked up then and must have seen the panic on his face. "It's a good thing you changed the passwords on all your accounts. She can't do any more damage."

"How much?" He raked his hands through his closely cropped hair. He'd started to feel like his feet were about to be swept out from under him. "How much damage has she already done?"

"It could be nothing." Lily sounded like it was no big deal. She dealt with this kind of thing every day. He imagined he'd sounded a lot like that when he told her it was no big deal to pull her out of the river. "Like I said, it could just be a computer glitch. Or a problem with the setup. I won't know until I see the statements. Do you just have the two accounts?"

"Those are the only active accounts." He logged on to the bank's website. He had to navigate through a few screens to bring up the information on the main account and the payroll account. Both seemed to have a healthy balance. But if there had been an error on the withholding, there would be penalties. Not to mention having to deal with State and Federal tax agencies. What a nightmare.

This had happened right under his nose. How could he even think about leaving when he couldn't prevent disaster while sitting a desk away? There was no way Cody could deal with this.

"Hey, we'll figure this out," Lily said. "Don't worry."

Sure. Nothing to worry about. Payroll taxes would just take care of themselves. Or he could let Cody handle it. That would be a catastrophe, unless the auditor turned out to be a lonely female willing to trade tax amnesty for sexual favors.

He was so screwed. They both were.

"Well isn't this cozy?" Cody strolled in while Carson was digging out the old bank statements. He had the current year and the previous years' statements, but he'd have to go into storage to find the rest. "What are you working on, spreadsheets?"

Translation: *Why don't you come spread out on my sheets?* Cody needed to tone it down a bit. Like all the way. Carson didn't have time to deal with his antics right now. Neither did Lily. They could be in for real trouble, and Cody was just in the way.

* * * *

"Nope. Just payroll tax reports." Lily didn't even look up from her monitor. She wasn't in the mood for flirting. Especially not with Cody. "Nothing too exciting."

"Oh, I think you'd make an audit exciting." Cody leaned against her desk, not a care in the world.

"I actually like audits." She looked up from the computer. "An internal audit can give you a clearer picture of your business. They can show the true value of your assets, including property values, equipment, inventory, and accounts receivables. Not to mention your investments in personnel, interest bearing accounts…"

"You remind me of this girl I met from Sao Paulo." Cody leaned closer, a slow grin spread across his face. "I didn't have a clue what she was saying—she spoke Brazilian—but she was sexy as hell."

"Portuguese." Lily resisted the urge to roll her eyes. "A woman from Brazil would speak Portuguese."

"Really?" Cody shrugged off his mistake. "Anyway, all this accounting talk makes as much sense to me as Portuguese. Maybe you could explain it to me."

"Some other time." Lily tucked a stray lock of hair behind her ear. She was trying to keep her annoyance in check. He was her boss, but he was acting more like a child demanding her attention. "Right now I have a lot of work to do."

"Hey, you don't have to work so hard, you know." Cody wasn't taking the hint. "What's that old saying? All work and no play?"

"Are you suggesting I'm a dull girl?" Lily turned her chair, squaring off against him.

"Oh, no, Lily. You're anything but dull." He flashed a lopsided grin. Did he practice in a mirror?

"And I already told you," Lily gave him a stare that told him she meant business. "I don't want to play with you."

Cody shoved off the desk and held his hands out in front of him in a defensive pose.

"Hey, I'm just trying to be friendly." He attempted one last smile. It wasn't his usual cocky smile, hey-let's-get-naked smile. It was more of a so-this-is-what-rejection-feels-like smile.

"I really need to focus right now." Lily dismissed him with a backhanded wave.

"Wow." Carson came over to Lily's desk after his brother slipped out the door. "I have never seen anyone put him in his place like that."

"Sorry." Lily hadn't meant to be rude. She was just in the zone. There was a problem that she wanted to solve. A mystery. And as every girl knew, the way to a man's heart was through forensic accounting. "I guess I forgot my place."

"No, it was great." Carson stepped closer, taking the space Cody had just vacated. A smile teased the corner of his lips. "I think Cody is the one who forgot his place. If he makes you uncomfortable in any way, just let me know. I'll take care of it."

"And what if you make me uncomfortable?" She should not have said that out loud.

"Do I?" Carson's voice deepened, making her feel a little bit nervous, slightly flustered, and a whole lot less than comfortable. "Do I make you uncomfortable?"

"No." Lily held her breath, waiting for the smoke alarm to signal her pants catching fire. "I'm, uh, joking. Yeah, just joking with you."

"Oh. I see Cody's rubbing off on you." His words were teasing; his tone was not.

"He wishes." Lily was surprised by how easily the words slipped off her tongue. "But I'm a professional. I can handle your brother. He's basically harmless."

"Yeah. I guess you're right." Carson crossed his arms over his chest. Lily tried to ignore his bulging biceps, the heat radiating off him as he stood just inches from her, and she tried to ignore the way her heart rate had jumped up a notch once they were alone again.

She needed to focus. Find the anomaly in the accounting that could be a simple error or it could be fraud committed by the former bookkeeper. Numbers were simple. Numbers didn't say one thing and mean something else. Numbers wouldn't break her heart.

He handed her a file folder and her heart skipped a beat. The bank statements. Not a dozen roses, but eighteen months of financial records.

"Thanks." Lily reached for her water bottle. Her mouth felt unusually dry. "I'll go through these carefully and see what we can find."

"I'll head out to storage and dig up the rest." Carson hesitated. He had to be worried. She sure was. "Let me know if there's anything else you need."

"We'll get to the bottom of this." Lily wanted to find the answers, not just to satisfy her accounting nerd curiosity, but because this was personal. She didn't want to let him down. Let them down. Amazing that the minute Cody was out of the room, she forgot all about him. She couldn't say the same for Carson.

Carson was much harder to forget. He was on her mind when she drifted off to sleep at night. He was on her mind when she woke up each morning. And he was on her subconscious mind while she slept. The fact that he was her boss didn't seem to matter. It just made her that much more eager to get to work each morning.

It seemed to bother him, though. He fought the attraction between them. Like a fish caught on a line, he struggled to break free.

* * * *

Carson was in the back storage area of the boat barn, searching through boxes of old bank statements. Cody wandered in, followed by Fisher, one of their most trusted guides. Neither of them seemed to notice Carson was there.

"Hey, the river's that way." Fisher gave Cody a friendly nudge on the shoulder. "Or do you want me to meet with the passengers?"

"No, I'll be right there." Cody sounded a little defeated.

"So why are you so grumpy?"

Cody just grunted.

"Didn't you have a date with Lily yesterday?"

"Yeah. We had a nice ride, but…" Cody parked himself on the rolled up boat. "I don't know. What do women want?"

"It all," Fisher said as if it were obvious. "And the perfect pair of jeans."

"No, I mean it." Cody was actually asking for advice. "What impresses a woman? Besides six-foot-three inches of lean muscle, abs of steel…"

"So you struck out, huh?" Fisher teased him, almost like a sister.

"I just was wondering what I'd do if I wanted to woo a woman."

"How do you woo a woman?" Fisher sat down on the other rolled up boat. "Who are you and what did you do to my friend Cody?"

"Maybe I'm his evil twin." Cody joked.

Fisher took a moment to answer.

"Take it slow. But not too slow. Get to know her, but don't tell her everything about you all at once. Leave a little mystery."

She paused again, as if was searching the inner recesses of her mind for that golden nugget of truth.

"Oh, how the hell do I know?" Fisher shrugged and hopped up. "I've had just as many serious relationships as you."

"Come on." Cody pleaded. "Help a guy out."

"Why don't you ask your brother?" She turned her back on him and mumbled to herself. "It's not like anyone sees me as a real girl."

She stalked off toward the river.

Carson stepped out from behind the stack of boxes. He could barely contain a chuckle. His brother really didn't get women. Not their minds, anyway. He had a pretty thorough knowledge of their bodies. But that wasn't going to help him here.

"I think what Lily wants is to be left alone. So she can do her job."

"You don't seem to be leaving her alone." Cody accused, seemingly unfazed by the fact that Carson had overheard his conversation with Fisher.

"We're working." Carson clutched the thick file folder containing the bank statements. "Don't worry, I won't bore you with the details."

"Of course." Cody's tone was light, like nothing bothered him. "None of my business. I'm just the pretty face on the webpage."

"Oh, so now you're interested in accounting procedures?"

"Sure. Why not?"

"You're just interested in the accountant." Carson shook his head. "Typical. But you need to be careful. She's not here for your personal pleasure."

"Or yours."

"You think I don't know that?" Carson was more than a little irritated. "You think I don't realize that having her in that office means neither one of us can have her anywhere else?"

"Look, I'm not stupid." Cody was frustrated, too. That much was obvious. "I'm not going to hit on her and then drop her just like that. I like her."

"You like her?"

"Yeah. I like her. She's different. Special," Cody said. "She's smart, too."

"Smart enough not to fall for your tired old lines."

"She inspires me."

"Really?"

"Yes. Really. She makes me want to be a different person. A better person."

"Wow. I had no idea she meant that much to you." Carson couldn't tell if Cody was sincere, but he decided to give him the benefit of the doubt. Frankly, he was surprised Lily had held his attention this long. "Still, I think you need to try a different approach."

"Like what?"

"You can't just throw out one-liners. Not if you want more than a one-nighter."

"I figured that." Cody just hadn't ever known any other way to relate to women. Except for Fisher, he'd never really interacted with women outside of his job. And part of his job was to be charming. Whether they were grandmothers or Girl Scouts, he put on the same act of the outgoing outdoorsman.

"Maybe you could show a legitimate interest in the bookkeeping." Yeah, that would happen.

"I wouldn't even know where to start," Cody admitted. "I mean, it's not like that stuff is really interesting."

"It is to her."

"Yeah, but…" His brother had always avoided anything to do with numbers and finances. As long as he had gas in his truck, beer in his fridge, and a roof over his head, money just wasn't something he worried about. Besides, Carson took care of that stuff. He didn't need to bother with it.

"I bet you don't even know what bank we use for our business accounts."

"Prospector Savings?" Cody was just guessing.

"Okay, what about our propane delivery? Who do we use for that?"

"The guys in the big white truck." Of course he didn't pay attention to those details. Propane was propane. As long as the heat came on when he needed it, that's all that mattered to Cody.

"You know it wouldn't kill you to take more of an interest in the business." Especially since it would soon be up to him to run the place.

"I work hard. In fact, I have a group of sixteen that are counting on me right now," Cody huffed. "I gotta go."

And once again, the conversation they needed to have was put off.

Chapter 8

It felt like a millennium since Lily had enjoyed a girls' night out. She'd been too focused on work and the dual problems of duplicate withholdings and her inability to withhold her gaze from settling on Carson as she worked. Damn that man for having the restraint his brother seemed to lack.

Fisher had invited her to Mario's for pizza. Lily suggested they bring the pizza back to her place instead. They'd have a little wine, maybe catch a movie or two. Throw in plenty of discussion about life in general and men in particular, and they'd have themselves a party.

"Would you prefer red or white?" Lily welcomed Fisher into the kitchen with a smile. "Or I have beer."

"I usually just have beer." Fisher set the pizza in the center of the table. "So wine sounds good. What would go better with sausage, fresh mozzarella, and basil pizza?"

"We could open both," Lily suggested. "And do a taste test."

"Now you're talking." Fisher found the plates and glasses while Lily opened the wine.

"This is an interesting combination." Lily handed Fisher a glass of Chardonnay and lifted the lid of the pizza box.

"I kind of discovered it by accident." Fisher took a sip and smiled. "I wanted tomato and basil, Carson wanted sausage and mushroom, but Cody doesn't like mushrooms or roasted tomatoes."

"Does Cody always get what he wants?" Lily had a feeling she already knew the answer.

"Pretty much." Fisher shrugged, dishing up the pizza. "Until you."

So much for keeping a low profile.

"So did Cody say something?" Lily wondered just how much Fisher knew. "Should I be worried about ending up on the front page of the *Prospector Springs Sentinel*?"

"Oh, he's got it bad." Fisher giggled like a seventh grade girl. "He actually asked me for advice."

There was just a hint of disappointment in her voice.

"But since I'm the only other woman who's ever turned him down," Fisher picked a piece of sausage off her pizza and popped it into her mouth. "I guess he figured I'm an expert."

"So, you turned him down." Lily studied Fisher's expression. A look of regret flashed across her face. "And now you're wondering if you missed out?"

"Oh, hell no. We're good friends now." Fisher's tanned skin deepened a shade. "Besides, he hit on me, like, five seconds after we met. He's way out of my league, and I didn't know how to respond. So he moved on to someone else. Several someone elses."

"But you like him." Lily could see her new friend consider denying it. But Fisher seemed uncomfortable coming up with anything less than the truth.

"Like I said, we're just friends." Fisher swirled the wine in her glass, avoiding Lily's gaze. "I won't get in your way."

"What if I told you I'm not interested in Cody?"

"Why wouldn't you be?" Fisher looked up with surprise. "I mean he's good-looking, strong, sexy…" She actually sighed. "And he's determined. I know he can seem kind of laid-back and all, but when he really wants something, he's unstoppable."

"And you think he wants me?"

"I know it." Fisher drained her glass. "Let's see how the red wine tastes with this pizza."

"Sure. But I'm thinking we need to make this a slumber party." Lily put the white wine in the fridge and poured the Zin.

"I've never been to a slumber party." Fisher held up her glass.

"To your first." Lily offered a toast. "We should go all out—paint our toes, watch scary movies, or would you prefer a romantic comedy?"

"Considering my love life, I think a scary movie would be more realistic," Fisher said.

"So, Cody doesn't know how you feel?"

"What's the point?" Fisher shrugged. "Especially since he's completely into you."

"The thing is, I'm just not into him." Because she couldn't get his brother off her mind. She let out a frustrated sigh.

"What about Carson?" Fisher must have sensed where her thoughts had gone. "He'd be a great catch."

"I'm not looking to catch a man," Lily insisted. "Besides, I don't think he's interested."

"He could be interested. But..." Fisher leaned forward, as if she was about to divulge top-secret information. "Carson would cut off his right arm for his brother. As long as he thinks Cody has a chance, he'll back way off."

"I never should have gone on that bike ride." Lily shook her head. "But I swear, I thought Carson was coming too."

"It would just be easier to give in to Cody," Fisher said. "Carson would never move in on his brother. Never."

"You'd think it would be easy." Lily reached for a second slice of pizza. "I mean, they look the same. They kind of sound the same. But I just don't react the same. It's weird, because it's a physical thing..."

"I know exactly what you mean." Fisher offered an all-too-knowing grin. "I admire and respect Carson. He's a great guy, and he'd be a terrific boyfriend. But...no one gets my blood pumping quite like Cody. Even though I know he's bad for me."

"A heartbreaker?"

"Yeah, except I know that deep down, he's a good guy, too." Fisher took a long sip of her wine. "He just doesn't know it yet."

"Sounds like he just needs the right woman to nudge him along." Lily gave Fisher a friendly shove.

"He seems to think that woman is you." Fisher focused on her last few bites of pizza.

"I doubt it." Lily decided to confess. "I'm going to have a baby."

"You're pregnant?" Fisher eyed Lily's wineglass suspiciously.

"Not yet." Lily lifted her wineglass in acknowledgement. "I'm going to use an anonymous donor. Hopefully by Labor Day I'll have a due date."

"Wow." Fisher sat silently for a moment, digesting the information. Then she smiled. "You have to admit, Cody would make pretty babies."

"He's not interested in being a father." Lily wondered if the same could be said for Carson. "And I'm not interested in putting that kind of pressure on any man."

"Cody's got issues with his own father, that's for sure." Fisher's lighthearted tone turned serious, and just a little sad. "He's never forgiven the man for abandoning them."

"I've heard bits and pieces about their childhood. How sad to lose their mother like that."

"At least their grandparents were there in the beginning."

Fisher helped clean up the dishes and they settled in the living room. She filled Lily in on the twins' early years. They'd lived with their mother's parents, until they got too old to care for them.

Lily gathered up her pedicure supplies—two plastic tubs filled with warm water, peppermint foot scrub and lotion, nail polish in several colors, and those little foam thingies to stick between their toes while the polish dried.

"You still up for a scary movie?" Lily brought up the menu of movies available for download.

"Sure. Unless you want to just hang out and talk." Fisher slipped her feet into the foot bath. "Tell me more about this donor thing."

"I have my first appointment the middle of June." Lily scrubbed her feet as if she could rub away the frustration at having to wait. "It's just a consultation. I guess they'll make sure I'm serious about becoming a single parent."

"Is this something you've been thinking about for a long time?" Fisher's tone suggested she wasn't quite sure how deep she should pry.

"My ex-husband was infertile. We'd been trying for years." Her words dripped with regret. "He was also unfaithful."

"What a bummer." Fisher sounded so sincere that Lily couldn't help but feel a kinship with her.

"Yeah, a real bummer." Lily sighed, lifting her foot and rubbing it with a towel. "But it would have been worse if he'd only been unfaithful."

"I guess you're right." Fisher was still soaking her feet, in no hurry to get to the next step. "No father is better than a lying, cheating, no-good... I'm sorry, I shouldn't judge someone I've never met."

"No, it's okay." Lily flashed her new friend a warm smile that came from feeling like she had a true ally. "I was thinking the same thing. Except I sometimes wonder if it's selfish of me. I'll always wonder if my child will be missing something."

"I was raised by just my Dad," Fisher admitted. "There were times when I wished more than anything to know my mother, but..." She shrugged, wiggling her toes in the footbath. "I always knew Dad was there for me. And at least I didn't have to spend all my holidays shuffled from one house to the other."

"I thought once my dad moved out, my parents wouldn't fight over me anymore," Lily said. "It only got worse."

She shuddered at the memories. But it was still better than having no parents at all. Poor Carson and Cody. Yet they had managed to build something special with their company. With each other.

"So tell me, how long have you worked for Swift River Adventures?" Lily desperately wanted to change the subject.

"Three years, now." Fisher pulled her feet from the water. She patted each foot dry before slathering them with lotion. "I planned on moving on once I got my masters, but I like it here. It's like being part of a family."

"And the fact you've got a thing for Cody?"

"Not a thing. Just..." Fisher reached for a bottle of nail polish—the bright pink, sparkly one. "Maybe if I was more girly, he might not see me as just one of the guys. Most of the time I'm cool with it. It helps when we're on the river, you know. I like being treated like an equal. But sometimes I wish he'd realize I have actual feelings. And, you know, *needs.*"

"I'm too often treated like a delicate flower." Lily reached for the soft shell pink, then traded it for the drop dead red. "Like I need to be sheltered or protected. Carson actually asked me if Cody was bothering me. Like I couldn't handle a little flirtation."

"Maybe he's jealous."

"No. That's not it." Lily smeared her nail polish and wiped it up with her thumb. Her concentration was definitely not on the job at hand.

"He's used to seeing Cody get what he wants." Fisher concentrated on her pedicure. "And we all know that Cody wants you."

"Then I think we need to work together to change that." Lily worked on her other foot. "I'll continue discouraging him. And you, my friend, should let him know how you feel."

"I couldn't do that." Fisher said. "Besides, I've been trying to help him get closer to you. I can't just backpedal and put the moves on him myself."

"Sure you could." A devious plan sprang to Lily's mind. "Or you could give him really bad advice, the kind that would make any woman run the other way. Then you could be there to pick up the pieces."

"I couldn't lie to him." Fisher twisted her long braid, uncomfortable with such trickery. "I just couldn't."

"No, I don't suppose you could. But you could teach him how you would want to be treated. Maybe even offer to let him practice with you."

"I wouldn't know how to do that either." Fisher stared down at her toes, a flush creeping up her skin that had nothing to do with the wine. "I mean, how do you tell a guy after three years that you've changed your mind—you do want to sleep with him?"

"We'll come up with something." Lily wasn't sure what she wanted more, to get Cody off her back or to get him to see what a gem Fisher was. "We've got all summer, right?"

* * * *

Carson sliced up some chicken breast, bell peppers, and onions for a quick fajita dinner. He needed to get a few things off his chest and Cody always listened better when he had a full belly. Staying home would minimize the distractions they'd have if they went out.

"Dinner's just about ready." Carson added a squeeze of lime as the finishing touch. "You want to grab a couple of beers and we'll eat outside?"

"Sure. Smells good." Cody pulled two bottles from the fridge, grabbed the salsa and a bag of tortilla chips, and took them out to their deck.

Carson pulled the warm tortillas from the oven and set up a fajita bar on the kitchen island. He set the pan with the meat, onion, and pepper mixture on a trivet, even though the guy at the home improvement store had told him he could set hot pans directly on the engineered stone. He and Cody had built the house together; each had made their mark on the design. Cody had insisted on a large deck and plenty of room for entertaining. Carson's only requirement was that they each had their own bathroom. He didn't want to worry about walking in on some woman in the middle of the night.

They dished up their plates to take out on the deck. Carson wasn't sure if he should lead off with the problem Lily found on the books or with his planned trip to Utah. A trip that was now in serious jeopardy.

"How was your trip?" he asked as Cody sat down. When had they become an old married couple?

"Fine. Not much to report." Cody spooned extra salsa on his fajitas before taking a bite.

"Meet anyone interesting?" Carson really did sound like a suspicious wife.

"Not really." Cody didn't seem to remember not to talk with his mouth full.

"Any single women?" He could only hope. For Lily's sake.

"I didn't ask." Cody swallowed, then took a slug of beer. "Not interested. Any woman I meet on a day trip would be like mining for pyrite. I'm holding out for the real gold."

"Lily?" She was no get-rich-quick scheme, that was for sure.

"Don't worry, I'm not just looking to dip my oar—"

"I wasn't going to lecture you…"

"Really? Because I was hoping you would."

"Can't we have a conversation without you getting all defensive?"

"Not lately." Cody took another big bite.

"Look, there are some things we need to talk about." Carson tried to keep his voice neutral. To not sound judgmental.

"I'm not going to discuss Lily with you," Cody said between bites. "So you can just lay off."

"Wouldn't you like to know what she found?" Carson knew he wouldn't be able to resist finding out.

"As long as it wasn't the birthmark on your left thigh," Cody joked. As usual, it had sexual undertones. "I don't really care what you two have been putting your heads together about."

"Even if it's your money too?"

"What money?"

Now he had his attention. This could be worth whatever amount was stolen or moved or whatever if he could get Cody more involved.

"Lily found some suspicious entries in the bookkeeping." Carson kept his voice steady, not letting on that he was really worried.

"No shit?" Cody's voice lacked the usual joking note. "Like embezzlement?"

"Maybe." Carson's fajita sat like a huge boulder at the bottom of his stomach. "She's still looking into it."

"Wow. That was quick. I was pretty smart to hire her, wasn't I?"

"No. I hired her." Carson couldn't quite remember the details, though. It had come about kind of fast. They had just come off the river. Fisher had told them about Heather bailing. Lily offered her services and…maybe it was Cody who'd jumped on it first. Like he wanted to jump on her.

"You just assume I don't do jack around here." Cody licked sour cream off his fingers. "But I do plenty."

No comment.

"Well, depending on what Lily finds, we may both need to pay closer attention to details," Carson said. He'd tried like hell to ignore the details he'd been paying close attention to all morning. The cut of Lily's blouse. How her neckline gaped when she leaned over and he could see the lace of her camisole. The subtle scent of her shampoo. The way her hair fell forward when she was deep in concentration and she kept tucking it behind her ear.

"…Lily's tits." Cody's voice penetrated his thoughts. The chair shot out from under him and if the table hadn't been in the way, his hands would have been around his brother's neck before he had a chance to think.

"Just seeing if you're paying attention." Cody laughed, amused at catching him off guard. "But it looks like your mind was on Lily's tits."

"They're called breasts." The words could barely escape Carson's firmly clenched teeth. He managed to return to his seat now that he'd realized Cody was just messing with him.

"Whatever you call them, I see you can't stop thinking about them." Cody found far too much to smile about. "Wondering if they're as firm and as soft and as luscious as they look."

"Cool it, would you?" Carson warned. "Lily's our accountant."

Immediately his mind conjured up the image of Lily leaning on a mahogany desk. A tight pencil skirt—charcoal gray wool. The kind that was just a little bit scratchy as he rubbed against it. A silky, flimsy, see-through white blouse tucked into the waistband. Her hair held up off her neck by a sharpened number two pencil. No, make that a pair of number two pencils, the pink erasers miniature replicas of her taut nipples. The only thing missing were the wire-rimmed glasses.

Damn, he was the sick one, not Cody.

Carson had never met a woman who got to him like this. Sure he liked women. Enjoyed giving them pleasure when he could. But he'd never met anyone he wanted to make a permanent or even steady part of his life. Shit, he was as bad as Cody.

"We're through discussing Lily." Carson stood, taking his plate into the kitchen.

"I don't think we are." Cody followed right behind him. So close that if he'd stopped, Cody would slam right into him. "I think we're just getting started. She really floats your boat, doesn't she?"

Carson didn't respond to the master of clichés.

"She does. She really pumps you up." Cody dumped his plate in the dishwasher. "You are in deep, my brother."

Carson rinsed his plate before placing it next to Cody's. He resisted the urge to rinse Cody's plate, too. It would just piss him off. "Lily works for us, remember?"

"I'm not stupid."

"Yeah, well it would be stupid to believe that either one of us has anything to offer her." Carson felt a pang on the left side of his chest. "It's not like we have any idea of how to treat a woman."

"I think we both know how to please a woman." Cody grinned. "And I would bet that Lily wouldn't mind finding out for herself."

"I'm not talking about in bed." Carson tortured himself enough with thoughts of Lily in his bed. "I'm talking about a relationship. A real, solid, grown-up relationship. What kind of examples have we had?"

"You don't learn how to swim by watching someone else. You have to get in the water and just do it." Cody actually had a point.

"Yeah, well, I already saved her from drowning once." Carson gathered the rest of the dishes, dumping the leftovers into the trash.

"You really care about her, don't you?" Cody grabbed a dishcloth and wiped down the counters.

"I feel responsible for her. I don't want to see her get hurt."

Because that was the real reason he'd never allowed himself to get close to a woman. He didn't know how to protect them. Sure, he could be the big strong manly man. Fend off wolves or whitewater or whatever physical dangers a woman might face. But when it came to protecting her heart, the only way he knew how to protect her was to stay away.

"Lily's tough," Cody said. "She's soft where she's supposed to be, but deep down, she's got some spunk."

"She's pretty smart," Carson said. "She hasn't slept with you."

"Not yet." Cody laughed. He sounded just a little bit evil with that laugh.

"Don't." Carson's voice had an edge.

"Sure, I'll have to work at it. But I've never been one to back away from a challenge." Cody put on his cockiest grin. "You ever notice that the trout who fight you the hardest taste the best? Or the blackberries in the deepest of thorns are always the sweetest? The hardest earned victories are the most satisfying."

"Lily isn't some prize to be won." Carson's voice steadied. He was working hard at control.

"She's the prize; she's most definitely the prize." Cody licked his lips. "The question for you, my brother, is do you want to play along?"

"This isn't a game." Carson stalked out of the kitchen and up to his room.

No. It wasn't a game. The stakes were too high. Lily had been through enough with her divorce. She didn't need Cody sniffing around, acting like he was ready to settle down. If anything, she'd be better off if Cody offered what he usually offered. One night. Two at the most. At least she'd know what she was in for.

And what did Carson have to offer her? Not much more than Cody. Especially if he was able to make the trip to Utah.

Chapter 9

"Good morning, ladies." Cody was standing on the porch to the guides' house when Lily and Fisher arrived the next morning. "You two sure know how to brighten up my day."

The two women looked at each other and broke into a conspiratorial laugh. They had been talking about him for most of the night. Lily was convinced that Fisher would be good for him. And he'd be good for Fisher. As long as he was good *to* her.

And if Cody was busy with Fisher, then that would leave Carson free to pursue Lily. If he truly was interested.

If he wasn't then at least she'd know. And she could go along with her original plan.

"Oh, Cody, you're such a ladies' man." Fisher tapped him on the shoulder as she walked past him. "I think my heart just might break if you ever settle down with one woman."

She glanced over her shoulder at Lily and winked.

Cody hesitated before following Lily and Fisher into the guides' house.

"So what you got there?" Cody eyed the cups of hot coffee longingly. "And why didn't you bring me any?"

"It's coffee." Fisher shot him a funny look. "What's the matter, still don't know how to make a cup of Joe?"

"You know, Carson already left the house and it seems silly to brew a whole pot for just one person." He sounded whiney and a little desperate.

"Oh, you are so pathetic." Fisher motioned for him to follow her into the small kitchen. "I'll make a pot. The rest of the guys will want some when they get up."

"Thanks, Fisher, you're the best."

"Don't you forget it." She flashed a quick smile before turning to fill the coffee maker.

"I never do." Cody leaned against the counter, watching her work. His need for coffee seemed to override his desire to flirt, since he'd ignored Lily until he was assured his caffeine fix wouldn't be too far off.

"So what are you two up to on such a fine morning? Did you meet for coffee?" Cody seemed a little unsure of himself. Or maybe he just really needed a caffeine fix.

"No, we had a slumber party at my place," Lily said.

"So what did you guys do?" Cody closed his eyes, almost as if he was trying to picture the two of them in their jammies.

"You know, naked pillow fights, rubbing lotion on each other." Fisher stared him down, just waiting for his reaction. "Girl talk."

"And what did you girls talk about?" Cody actually blushed at the mention of lotion.

"You know, politics, the weather, sex." Fisher was clearly messing with him. Good for her. "Mostly sex."

"So you shared your ideas for peace in the middle east." Cody took slow sips of coffee, trying to keep his breathing steady.

"Yep, that and the solution for global warming." Lily kept out of the conversation as much as possible. This was Fisher's chance to make some progress. Lily looked around at the homey touches Fisher had brought to the place. She'd told Lily that she was currently the only woman living at Swift River. She had her own room while Tyler, Luke, and Ross shared the upstairs loft. Aubrey lived with her parents, just a few miles away. When the college kids got out of school for the summer, they'd pick up a few more housemates.

For a house full of mostly young guys, the kitchen was clean. Dishtowels hung neatly over the oven door handle, instead of wadded up on the counter or lying on the floor. A cheerful jar contained the cooking utensils and a bright blue vase held a collection of wildflowers. Most certainly Fisher's doing.

"Thanks. You're a lifesaver." Cody nearly moaned when he took his first sip of coffee.

"Yes, I do have Red Cross training." Fisher studied him while he sipped the warm rich brew. Yeah, the girl had it bad. "Oh, come on, you know we were talking about you. And Carson."

"Oh, I can't imagine why," Cody said. "Unless it was to gush over what great bosses you two have."

"Yes, that's it. We were talking about benefit packages." Fisher dropped her gaze to the front of his shorts, her tongue flickered between her lips for a millisecond, and then she broke into a fit of giggles. "You are so one-track-minded, it's not even funny."

"What? You're the one who laid that track, sweetheart."

"Well, I should get going." Lily felt like she should leave the two of them alone. Fisher was certainly holding her own in the flirting department. Maybe her pep talk was doing her some good. "I've got a lot of work to do."

"Oh, yeah." Fisher blushed, as if she'd forgotten her friend was there. "Thanks for the slumber party."

"Thank you for coming over. I had a great time." Lily meant it. "See you later, Cody."

With that she slipped out the door and headed over to the office. Still a little groggy from staying up too late last night, Lily gratefully sipped her double-shot mocha latte. It was worth it, though, since she not only had an ally, she had a plan. Fisher would distract Cody by pretending to give him advice, and Lily would figure out a way to either get Carson into her bed or get him out of her head.

First, she had to figure out what was going on with the duplicate entries in the books. If she could find the source of the problem, then maybe she could find the solution. Or at least enough evidence to pursue legal action, if necessary.

Lily found it harder than normal to be objective. She wasn't just helping a client, she was helping a man. A good man. An attractive man. A man she cared about. And someone had been messing around in his accounts. She had been messing with his business. His livelihood. His life.

Lily was going to stop the bitch.

Sliding into her desk chair, Lily booted up the computer. She ran detailed reports, hoping to find a clue in the numbers. Then she compared the bank statements to the computer reports and the tax returns. They didn't all add up. The tax returns matched the payroll reports, but not the financial statements she'd printed from the software. There had to be a separate file somewhere. The computer showed a record of regular backups, but Lily had no idea where to find the hard copies of the files.

After feeling like she was slamming her head against the wall, she realized she needed a break. To step away for a moment to clear her head. Some mindless task would take her focus off the problem just long enough to get back on track. She glanced at the electric pencil sharpener across the room. Perfect. She reached for the pencils in the cup. All three were already perfectly sharp. Opening the desk drawers, Lily searched for a box of spares. The top drawer contained sticky pads, staples, and paperclips, but no writing instruments. She checked the next drawer down.

A box of blue fine point pens, another in red, and several highlighters took up the front half of the drawer. Maybe in the back. She pulled the drawer out farther, and found a box of tampons. Odd. She'd think Heather would have kept them in the bathroom. There was plenty of drawer space, and it wasn't like there were dozens of other women to swipe her supplies. Lily was about to close the drawer when she felt an odd flutter in her belly.

She reached for the box and took a calming breath before lifting the flap. "You crafty little devil you." Sure enough, the box contained a flash drive. In the last place a man would dare look.

"We stock those in the store, if you, uh, run out." Carson had come in while she was busy investigating the contents of the box, looking about as uncomfortable as a man could be.

"No, these aren't what you think." Lily triumphantly shook out the contents of the box. "I believe these are the missing files."

"Oh." A slow smile spread across his face as he realized what she was holding. And what she was not holding. "I never would have looked there."

"I'm sure she counted on that." Lily felt the excitement of solving at least a portion of the mystery. "Which leads me to believe that this drive contains information she wanted to hide."

"Let's take a look." Carson leaned over her shoulder while Lily inserted the drive. Her hand trembled as she reached for the mouse. Was it in anticipation of what she'd find on the disk or something more primitive?

It took every ounce of her concentration to open the file. He was too close. She could feel his breath flutter against her neck. She could practically hear his heartbeat against his chest. Was it because he was afraid of what she would find? Or because he, too, felt the room get smaller, the air get heavier, the more time they spent together?

* * * *

"Maybe I should step back." Carson couldn't breathe and it had nothing to do with discovery of hidden files Heather had stashed in a tampon box of all things. It was all Lily.

He'd tried to stay away from her as long as possible. He'd finished repairing the last cabin's roof. The fences were all straight, and he'd filled in the gravel on the road so there were no more potholes. Short of digging up and replanting every tree, shrub, and wildflower on the property, Carson couldn't come up with anything else to stay busy. When he'd walked in on her holding an embarrassing box and talking to herself, he almost went to get the shovel. But there was something about her posture that made him stay.

She had discovered a hidden cache of files. A cleverly hidden cache of files. He wasn't sure he wanted to find out exactly what was on them, but Lily was determined. And he was standing too close for her to do her job. He could feel the electricity humming through her, causing her muscles to tense and making her movements less than smooth.

"I've got some e-mails to check." He took a step back, noticing her body relax ever so slightly. "Let me know if you find anything interesting."

"Sure. It might take a while. I want to go through each file and compare it against the current file. Hopefully I can find the original entry."

"Take your time." Carson slid into his chair, banging his knees on the underside of the desk. He felt like he had in high school, when the combination of his rapidly growing frame and his newfound interest in girls made sitting in math class more than a little awkward. "Just let me know if you need anything."

Anything at all.

"Sure." Lily looked up from her desk and smiled. It was a genuine smile, a hit to his chest just left of center. Carson had to remind himself to breathe and tear his gaze away from her.

He should leave. Let her work in peace, without having to be conscious of him staring at her. Because he couldn't help but watch her as she scanned the files, her eyes squinting, brows furrowed in concentration as she dug deep into the files.

But he had to know what she found, when she found it. He couldn't walk away until he knew just how bad things were. Then he'd have to come up with a way to fix it. He might be able to walk away from the business, but it was all Cody had.

It didn't take long to plow through his e-mails. He eliminated the junk mail and spam, and carefully read the customer responses. He selected a few quotes to add to the website, pending their permission.

After checking the online reservation system and confirming they had the staffing to cover all the upcoming trips, he stretched his arms overhead. His stomach growled, signaling that it was past lunchtime.

"I'm gonna go grab a sandwich. Do you want anything?" He stood, arching his back.

"Oh, is it that late?" Lily glanced down at the corner of her screen. "Wow, one-thirty already?"

"You hungry?" Carson knew asking her to lunch would only be giving in to temptation.

"I brought my lunch." Lily let him off the hook. "Besides, I feel like I'm getting close."

"Yeah, okay." His disappointment ran deeper than it should have. "I'm just going to grab something from the store. Would you like a soda, or something?"

"A diet soda would be great." Lily rubbed her temples. She had been working hard. If he had to guess, he'd say she had been sitting at that desk six hours without a break.

"Coke or Pepsi?"

"Coke, please." She flashed a quick smile before turning back to the computer.

Carson left shaking his head, wondering why he felt such pleasure in knowing they shared the same soft drink preference. Cody often teased him about drinking Diet Coke, calling it a girly drink, but there were times when he needed a pick-me-up and he didn't like all the added sugar in regular soda.

He grabbed a couple of energy bars, some trail mix, and two Diet Cokes. He took his time going back to the office. Until he could figure out why Lily seemed to get to him more than any other woman, he figured he should keep his distance. He'd give her the soda and convince her to go home at a decent hour.

When he stepped back into the office, Lily's face lit up with the kind of smile that had him looking for canary feathers and listening for a purr. She'd been up to something. Something good.

"You found it." Carson set her diet soda on the desk and knelt down next to her.

"Yup." Lily brought up two screens, side by side. "Remember Project Green-light?"

"Fisher convinced us we could save a lot of money by going solar." Carson wondered what that had to do with anything.

"Right, and to prove it, you had your bookkeeper set aside the exact amount you paid for electricity each month."

"We were able to put a down payment on the system within six months." He took a swallow of soda.

"Then you transferred the average electric bill payment for another six months." Lily brought up the register.

"Yeah, we were able to pay off the solar panels and close the account." Carson said.

"But the account was never closed."

Lily scrolled down, showing eighteen months' worth of transactions. But this time instead of electricity payments, the duplicates were disguised as tax payments. A little bit with each payroll. He wouldn't question tax payments.

"But how did I miss the fact that the account was still open?"

"She changed the contact info. She had this account's statements sent to her e-mail address." Lily had figured this all out in the time it took him to down half a soda and two energy bars. "Fortunately she also kept a password list, and I was able to access it."

"So, how much did she get away with?" Carson was grateful he hadn't had a real lunch. His stomach churned and burned enough without it.

"That's the weird part." Lily clicked on the bank's website. "It's all there. I figure either she chickened out about taking the money or she's waiting until enough time passes that she won't be an obvious suspect."

"The money's still there?" Carson blinked. Twice. But the numbers on the screen didn't change. Nearly twenty-three thousand dollars. If it wasn't for Lily, he would have lost twenty-three thousand dollars.

In his relief, Carson reached out and hugged her. Just a quick, sideways, casual kind of hug. An expression of gratitude, nothing more.

Except his left hand grazed her breast. Again. He should pull away. Just let his hand fall to the side. He should even apologize. But he was frozen in place. The signal from his brain did not reach its destination.

Lily turned toward him. Her hand came up to the side of his head. Carson held his breath as he braced for the indignant slap across his face.

Instead, her touch was gentle, affectionate. The look in her eyes that of longing, not anger. She drew him toward her, her lips just a whisper from his. She'd come this far, it was up to him to go the rest of the way.

He closed the distance between them. Claiming her with his mouth. Or was it the other way around? She gave as good as she got. This was no tentative, caught by surprise kind of kiss. Lily clung to him, pulling him closer, closer. Too close. God, he could drown in her. Just let her surround him and pull him under until the outside world faded completely away.

Gasping for air, he tore himself away. No wonder he couldn't get her out of his head. His body had taken control.

"I have to go." He staggered to his feet.

"To the bank?" Lily smoothed her blouse. "Yeah, I guess you should get that account taken care of sooner rather than later."

"Yeah. That, too." His heart was hammering too hard. He couldn't breathe. "I have to…go… Now."

"Carson." Her voice was strained. Pleading. "You don't have to run away from me."

"From you?" He shook his head. "No. It's not you. I…I guess I am running away. But not from you."

A look of confusion flashed across her face. Of course. She didn't get it. He wasn't making sense. She didn't know about his plans. Plans that he wasn't even sure about any more.

"I need a break." Carson started to explain.

"Of course, it's been a long day." Lily rolled her neck side to side.

"No. That's not what I mean." If he couldn't express how he'd been feeling to his brother, who he'd known all his life, why did he expect it to be any easier to talk to Lily? "I've been the responsible one my whole life. Just once, I'd like to only have to worry about myself. To be in charge of nothing more than the boat I'm floating down the river."

"That sounds nice, but… Aren't you a little young for a midlife crisis?" Lily had a real good point.

"Yeah. You'd think I would be." Carson backed out the door. "I'm sorry, Lily. I just need some space."

"Okay." Lily turned her attention back to her computer. "So what next?"

"I guess I should give you a raise."

"I meant for you." She smiled. A half-smile, like she knew this was a good news, bad news situation. "You obviously had some plans that you can get back to."

"Right." He was torn. He needed to leave. But Lily made him want to stay. "I guess I did. I was planning on leaving town. At the end of the month."

"A vacation?" she asked, but there was doubt in her voice.

"Six weeks," Carson admitted. "I've committed to six weeks. Then who knows?"

"So your 'running away' from home involves a six-week commitment?" It did sound kind of funny when she put it that way.

"I have a friend, he's got an outfit in Northeastern Utah. He could use a hand." He owed her an explanation. "The river's only runnable for six weeks in the summer. I figure that's enough time to get a feel for freedom. But not too long that I can't come back if things fall apart."

"Freedom?" Lily shook her head ever so slightly. "Good luck with that."

Chapter 10

Lily worked for another hour, making a good-sized dent in her in basket. But her mind was far from on her work. There was a reason why kissing your boss was usually a bad idea. Although Lily got the impression the boss/employee thing was not the reason Carson had pulled away. He didn't want to get too close. He was a man looking for fewer ties, not more. The knowledge didn't keep her from wanting him. It did help prevent any fantasies about being one big happy family, despite Fisher's observation that they would make pretty babies together.

She had to get out of there. The office was too small. His scent still lingered and Lily couldn't breathe. She needed some fresh air. This was supposed to be a part-time job, and if she stayed much longer, state law would require overtime pay.

After straightening her desk, properly labeling the backup files, and shutting down her computer, Lily stepped outside. She should just go home, but it was such a lovely afternoon, she decided to take a walk down to the river.

Just sitting on the bank listening to the sounds of the water soothed her. It was almost impossible to remember that she was once afraid of the river. Carson had helped her get over it. He'd made her get right back out there and face her fear. And it worked. She could sit here by the river without even a twinge of panic. She could even envision wading out into the current, letting the water swirl around her ankles, maybe even up to her knees. She wanted to go rafting again. Maybe even try kayaking, if she had the right guide.

She knew exactly who that guide would be. She just needed the courage to face him. Carson hadn't let her give up on the river. She wasn't going to give up on him. She just had to convince him that she was okay with a temporary arrangement. No, he had to think she was more than okay with it. He had to believe that she needed it. That the only way she would recover from her divorce would be to engage in a short-term affair.

She stretched out, hoping to figure out how to persuade him that she needed him. Her contemplation was interrupted by the approach of three rafts. Cody was in the lead boat, followed by Fisher and Ross. She stood to greet them.

"Looks like you had a good trip." Lily watched the interaction between Cody and Fisher, looking for signs that her new friend had made at least some progress on letting him know how she felt.

There was a lot of playful banter, more brother and sister-like than anything. Lily just hoped Cody wouldn't flirt too wildly with her. She didn't want Fisher to get hurt.

"Oh yeah. Couldn't ask for a better day." Cody grinned, leaning toward Lily enough so that she didn't need to see behind his sunglasses to know he was indeed checking her out.

"Well, I'm off for the day." She stepped back, trying not to encourage him. "If you see Carson, tell him…"

"Tell me what?" Carson had approached from behind. His voice settled around her like a thick beach towel after a long swim.

"I'm just on my way out." Lily wanted to wrap him around her, to snuggle up close, but she knew she'd need patience. She didn't have a lot of time, but she couldn't push him too hard or too fast. "And I wanted to be sure you got everything straightened out at the bank."

"Yeah. It's all taken care of."

"Good." Lily managed a half-smile, a pretty good one, considering how awkward their interaction had become. "I'm glad."

Before they could spend too much time standing there as awkwardly as a couple of teenagers on their first date, a commotion erupted just downstream. Two teenage boys ran toward them shouting something about a flip and a missing kid.

Carson was the first to speak to the teen boys. His voice steadied them enough to get the details of the location and a description of the missing boy. Cody, Fisher, and Ross all stood ready to help. They looked to Carson to organize the search and he took on the role of leader with practiced ease.

"What can I do?" Lily felt useless, not knowing a thing about river rescue other than being on the receiving end.

"If you could take the coolers and the smaller gear back to the boat barn, that would be a big help." Carson's voice was calm. Too calm. "Just take what you can carry. We'll deal with the boats later."

"Okay. Sure." She wanted to say something more. She wanted to tell him to be careful, but she knew he would do what he had to do. He would save that boy.

Several of the passengers helped Lily gather the life jackets, paddles, and loose equipment. The boat barn was well organized, and now that she had a better understanding of what the various items were it was easy to find where everything went. Once they got the gear stashed, except for the heavy rafts, and Cody's paddle, all they had left to do was wait.

* * * *

Carson sent Fisher and Ross to help the kids with their raft. Cody was preparing ropes and getting ready to hit the water at his command. The missing kid's name was Nate. With light brown hair and green eyes, he stood about 5'9" and weighed around 120 pounds. A skinny kid without a lot of body fat wouldn't last long in the cold water. If they didn't find him in thirty minutes, someone would need to call Search and Rescue.

Cody rowed them as close to the spot of the flip as he could without danger of being carried past it. Carson studied the current, trying to determine the path it would have carried an unsuspecting swimmer. A hidden boulder about two thirds of the way across the river split the current, sending the majority of the force to the left, but there was a chance the kid caught the smaller current to the right side. He thought he saw a flash of color, a faded orange that could be a life jacket. Hopefully it had done its job.

Without hesitation, he dove into the water, swimming with the current to the spot where a tangle of blackberry bushes could have snagged the kid. Carson grabbed one of the thicker vines and pulled himself up into the direction in which he saw the orange. Ignoring the cuts from the thorny bush, he listened. He thought he heard a sound, like someone crying.

"Nate!" Carson called. "Nate Smith, can you hear me?"

"Go away!" The kid was sniffling. "Please don't come any closer."

"Nate, it's going to be okay." Carson tried to keep his voice as calm as possible while preparing for anything. The kid could be in bad shape if he didn't want anyone to see him. "I'm here to help. Just stay where you are and I'll get to you."

"No. Don't," the kid pleaded.

This could be bad. But at least he was talking. He sounded scared, his voice a little squeaky. But at fourteen, that was normal.

"I need to know the extent of your injuries, so we can get help." Carson inched his way closer. Not an easy task considering the overgrown vines. "There are plenty of people here who can help you."

"Don't bring anyone else. Okay." Nate's voice sounded a little stronger. Like he was reaching deep down to find his strength.

"Let's just see what we're dealing with here." Carson could feel solid ground beneath his torn knees.

"No. Don't look," Nate insisted. "I'm naked, okay!"

Carson bit back a chuckle. The kid must have lost his shorts.

"And you're afraid I'll feel inferior," Carson teased as he popped his head through the clearing. The kid was huddled beneath the torn life jacket. Half of it clung to the thorns where the kid had crawled out of the water, and the other half barely covered the shivering body of poor Nate. But the kid did crack a smile at his little joke.

"Are you hurt?" Carson plopped down in the dirt next to the boy.

"No. Just stupid." Nate shook his head, wiping his eyes with the backs of his hands. "I can't believe I lost my shorts."

"Happens all the time," Carson assured him. "It's happened to me more times than I'd like to admit." So he'd lied to the kid. He'd lost more than his share of hats, a few pairs of sunglasses, even a sandal or two, but never his shorts. "It's kind of like an initiation. You're now officially a brother of the river."

"Yeah?" Nate offered a tentative smile. He still had the problem of getting back to the other side of the river. No guy wants to walk through thorns without protection.

"As a matter of fact, in order to graduate from guide school, you have sacrifice an article of clothing to the river gods." Carson wanted the boy to feel comfortable, but there was still the problem of wardrobe. He would have gladly given up his own shorts, but there was no way they'd fit. The kid was even skinnier than the description given to him.

Carson took off his wet shirt and offered it to kid. He turned his back so Nate could have some shred of pride. Being fourteen was hard enough.

"Okay, I'm ready. I look like a dork, though." Nate stood there, dripping wet, with the shirt worn over his hips. "It looks like I'm wearing a skirt."

"No, man, a kilt." Carson did his worst Scottish accent. "Like a warrior. You ever see that movie, *Braveheart?*"

"Yeah. Sure." Nate's smile was barely visible beneath the flush of embarrassment that covered his adolescent face.

Carson found an easier path to the river bank. He shouted at Cody on the other side where his brother waited with the boat. By the time he navigated across the current, the kid had almost recovered his sense of humor.

Cody brought the raft alongside the shore, and tossed the bow line to Carson. He held the raft steady while Nate stepped into the boat. Cody offered his life jacket since Nate's was shredded. There was no way for the kid to refuse. There were few things Cody was anything but lackadaisical about—safety was one of them.

A quick ferrying across the river reunited Nate with his group. They had been on a private trip. One of his buddies had an older brother who was a guide, and they'd thought they could just figure it out from watching YouTube videos. Not too smart.

"So guys, you thought you'd have a little fun on the river today." Cody looked each boy in the eye. "Well, let me tell you something. The river is like a woman."

This could get interesting. Carson just hoped his brother would keep the conversation rated PG-13.

"You've got to show her respect. Always." Cody had them hooked already. "You may think you can control her, but a smart man learns to work with her. Now that doesn't mean you're totally at her mercy. You guys take geometry in school?"

"Yeah," they all kind of grumbled about it.

"Well, geometry is important in running the river," Cody explained. "You have to understand which angles you want to take when approaching an obstacle, like that rock back there."

The boys were riveted to his every word.

"But there's physics, too. You have to understand force and motion." Cody the professor. Who would have thought? "But mostly it's about being in tune with the river. Understanding her flow. Her moods…"

Carson had to admit, his brother had a way with people. He wouldn't be surprised to see all of them signed up for the next junior whitewater school.

No. He wouldn't see them. Thanks to Lily, he knew the business would still be standing when he returned. And seeing how Cody rose to the task today, Carson was starting to feel better about his brother being able to take on more responsibility. He was the kind of guy who would just go with the flow, until he was needed to step up. Maybe he just wasn't being challenged enough.

He left Cody in charge of educating the youths, and herded poor Nate up to their store. A new T-shirt and some shorts, if they had anything small enough, would help the kid restore his dignity. He could use a change of clothes himself.

He met Lily on the way. She looked relieved to see the kid was all right. She'd made a lot of progress since her own adventure in the river. He hoped this wouldn't open that fear back up for her, because he wouldn't be here to help her regain her confidence.

* * * *

Lily's heart flipped at the sight of Carson. His hair was wet and plastered to his head, his shorts were torn, and he had cuts all over his back, chest, arms, and legs. Had he pulled the kid from the claws of a mountain lion? "Oh, Carson, look at you, you're a mess!"

"You should see the other guy," he joked. "That blackberry bush didn't stand a chance."

"We should get you cleaned up." Lily envisioned a hot bath and hours to spend kissing each and every scratch. Yeah, right. The only way that would happen would be if he was unconscious.

"Nah, I'm all right," Carson insisted. "I need to take care of this guy first. I figure if I outfit him head to toe in Swift River gear, it's like free advertising."

"Good plan." Lily tried not to look at the smeared blood from all the scratches and cuts. She felt a little lightheaded. What kind of mother was she going to make if she couldn't stand the sight of a few boo-boos? "What can I do to help?"

"Hey, Nate," Carson called the kid over from where he was looking through the racks of shorts with little enthusiasm. "Come meet a good friend of mine. Lily's probably a much better judge of fashion than I am."

Lily shook the boy's hand and noticed he blushed from his forehead to his knees. He was wearing Carson's wet T-shirt and a beach towel wrapped around his waist. She could sympathize with the kid for feeling a little foolish for having to be rescued. But she couldn't think of a better man for the job.

"Let's get you outfitted." Lily took Nate to pick out a T-shirt while Carson headed toward the staff bathroom to clean himself up. "I'm thinking with your green eyes, this one will look really good on you." She pulled out a faded olive T-shirt with the Swift River logo on it and held it up to him. She found a tan pair of shorts with a green abstract leaf pattern. "These will go with the shirt. What do you think?"

"They're okay." Nate took the shorts but shook his head. He put them back and pulled out a different pair. He glanced in the direction that Carson had disappeared. "These are kind of like Carson's."

"Then they're definitely cool." Lily sensed a bit of hero worship coming from the boy. Yeah, she could relate to him on that one, too. She noticed a few scratches on the kid's face and arms, but he didn't look quite as cut up as Carson. "So what happened to the two of you? Did you wrestle with a barbed-wire covered bear?"

"No. Just blackberry bushes," Nate said. "I fell out of the boat and got caught in the bushes. I lost my shorts and shoes. Then I tried to climb out of the water, but my life jacket got caught in the thorns."

"So did Carson find you in the water?"

"No. I made it out of the river." Nate dropped his voice to a near whisper. "But I was kinda scared. And naked."

"I know the feeling." Lily wanted to reach out to this kid, pat him on the shoulder, and feed him milk and cookies. "Hey, why don't you go try those on? The changing rooms are back there."

As Nate went to get dressed, Lily went to check on Carson. The employee bathroom was coed, so she just walked right in and found him at the sink, rinsing his cuts and swearing under his breath.

"Here let me help you." She took a paper towel, wet it, and started to dab his forehead.

"No. That's okay. I've got it." Carson pulled away. This time she wasn't going to let him get away with it.

"You have no problem jumping in to help a stranger." Lily pressed gently on the cut above his eye. "You'll dive into freezing cold water, climb through thorns, but when it comes to letting someone help you… Why, you're just a big coward."

"I am not." Carson said defensively. "I just don't need…"

"Yes, you do." Lily blew gently across the wound. His eyes flickered shut, and it was all she could do not to press her lips against his skin. But she backed off. "I'm going to get some antibiotic cream."

"I'll just take a shower when I get home." Carson opened his eyes, but he didn't look at her directly.

"Yes, but if I know you, it won't be until you're sure Nate is safe and sound and dressed and fed." Lily grabbed the first aid kit from under the sink. She washed her hands again before tearing open a packet of antibiotic cream. She dabbed ointment on each cut, starting with his face, and moving to his neck. He winced, and Lily wondered if it was from pain or from the fact that she was touching him and he couldn't escape.

Lily couldn't understand why he was being so difficult. He was a big man, a strong man. He could tame a wild river, fix a wayward fence, and he didn't think twice about rushing into a raging river or barreling through a tangle of thorns, yet the prospect of getting close to her made him more skittish than a squirrel in the middle of a country road.

There was a large gash on the back of his neck. He groaned as she applied the ointment. But it didn't sound quite like pain. The hairs stood up and oh, how she wanted to taste him. Touch him. Take care of him. She took a bandage out of the first aid kit and placed it over the cut.

"I'm sure that's not necessary." Carson's voice was far from his normal confident tone.

"Why don't you let me be the judge of that." Lily wasn't going to back down. Not this time. "You can't even see how deep the cut is. But it's not as bad as the one on your calf."

Lily knelt down to examine his leg. So muscular, tanned, and perfect except for the gash in his left calf.

"I think you might need stitches," she said, pressing a piece of gauze against the cut.

"No. I'll be fine. Just leave it."

"I don't think so." She grabbed two butterfly bandages from the first aid kit. "We'll try this."

She pulled the paper backing from one side of the bandage, applied it to the cut, and stretched it across the wound. "Hold still." She exposed the rest of the adhesive of the bandage. One down and maybe two more to go. She opened the second bandage and repeated the process at a slight angle from the first. She reached for a third bandage but Carson pulled away.

"Why are you so afraid of me?" Lily asked. "Do think I'm going to seduce you right here in the employee restroom? Some guys wouldn't mind being used for sex."

"You don't want me." Carson pulled away from her. Again.

"You know, I'm sick and tired of people telling me what I want." Lily slammed the first aid kit closed. "Like I can't figure it out for myself."

"I didn't mean…"

"Hush." Lily shoved the box under the sink. "I know what I want." She turned and glared at him.

"I want you." She bit her lower lip. "I want you, Carson. I want sex."

He closed his eyes, then let out a breath. "You deserve better."

"You're right. I do deserve better. I deserve someone who isn't afraid to touch me. Someone who wants to be with me."

She stormed out of the bathroom, choking back tears.

Damn him. He was the most difficult man she'd ever known. Brian had been selfish and controlling. Her father had been weak and passive. Carson was just infuriating in his inability to admit that he had needs. And despite her relative inexperience with men, she had a pretty good idea of what he needed from her. If only he'd let her.

She barreled right into Cody as she headed back toward the store.

"Hey, Lily. Where are you off to in such a hurry?"

"Oh, sorry." Lily stepped back, shook her head, and let out a heavy sigh. She'd been a million miles away, not looking where she was going, and Cody was the last person she wanted to deal with right now.

"Hey, you okay?" he asked.

"Yeah. Fine. I was just on my way home. Now that everyone is back, safe and sound."

"Hey, I invited a bunch of people over for a party at our place tonight. We'll throw some meat on the grill, knock back some brew."

"I don't think so. It's been a long day."

"Oh, come on," Cody pleaded. He flashed his most dimpled grin. "Please? It won't be any fun if you're not there."

"Right." Lily cracked a smile. She wasn't totally immune to his charm. "Like you need me to have a good time."

"I need you to keep me in line." Cody dropped his voice so she would have to stay close to hear him. "You have no idea what kind of trouble I might get into otherwise."

"Oh, I can imagine." Lily laughed.

"Please say you'll come." Cody was practically begging. "That way Carson won't have to worry about me."

She bit her lower lip at the mention of Carson's name. She wanted him. But he wouldn't let her get close.

"I'll think about it." Lily backed down the porch steps toward the parking lot. "Maybe I'll bring a salad."

"Make it a big one." Cody grinned. "It's going to be some party."

* * * *

Carson was at the counter buying Nate a whole new wardrobe. Hat, shirt, shorts, and sandals. He considered it a business expense, since word would spread fast, and chances were the story would grow by the end of the week. So would their business. Who wouldn't want to come down the river with a hero?

"Hey, bro." Cody nodded, then shook his head after getting a good look at him. Man, he must be a mess. Probably looked like he'd tried to break up a cat fight. Between seven or eight cats. And most of his cuts were shining with ointment.

Lily.

Didn't she know how much harder she was making this? How the more she cared for him, the more he wanted her? The more he wanted to stay?

"So I invited Lily to the party tonight." Cody seemed oblivious to the turmoil Carson was going through. "Who knows, maybe she'll finally realize what she's missing. I think I've waited long enough."

"Hey, Nate, why don't you go grab yourself a Gatorade or something?" Carson ignored him completely. "Then you should probably catch up with your friends."

"Yeah, okay." Nate grinned up at Carson, all traces of fear gone from his expression. "Hey, next time I'm coming with you guys."

"Sure, we'd be happy to have you." Carson gave the kid a pat on the shoulder. "See you soon."

Carson told the clerk to put anything else the boy wanted on his tab and then headed back to the office. Cody followed.

"So what's your deal?" he asked. "You're not speaking to me for some reason?"

"Are you really that needy?" Carson asked. "If you're not the center of attention, you think something's wrong."

"No, I just don't know why you hate me all of a sudden." Cody crossed his arms over his chest and leaned against Lily's desk.

"I don't hate you." Carson opened a filing cabinet and went rifling through the drawer. He needed to get his head on straight. Stop thinking about Lily and all the things she made him feel.

"If it's because of Lily, don't worry," Cody said. "I'm not going to use her. I think... I think I'm falling for her."

Carson slammed the metal drawer shut, cursing under his breath.

"I know I joke around and all, but..." Cody let out an exaggerated sigh. "She's really special. I think she could be the real thing."

"Good for you." Carson brushed past him, leaving Cody alone in the office. Maybe Lily would be good for Cody. Maybe she'd instill the kinds of feelings in his brother that she'd stirred in him. Longing for something more. Something real.

Chapter 11

Lily almost hadn't come to the party. What if Carson blew her off again? She didn't think she would recover. But then she thought of Cody. How he kept coming back for more. Rejection didn't stop him. He was like that cartoon coyote. Maybe he could offer some pointers. Teach her how it was done.

Speaking of tutors. Fisher hurried down the stairs of Carson and Cody's house. Had she come from Cody's room?

"Hey, Fisher." Lily approached her to see if she'd made any progress on the Cody front. They'd talked about letting him know how Fisher felt about him. A party would provide a great opportunity to take action.

"Oh, hi." Fisher's eyes were red around the rims, mascara smeared down her cheeks. "Sorry, I didn't know you were here."

"What's wrong? Did something happen between you and Cody?" Lily put a protective arm around her waist, leading her to the back deck.

"Oh, yes. And no." Fisher wiped her eyes then stared at the back of her hand. The black marks were foreign to a woman who rarely wore makeup.

"Let's get a drink and talk about it." Lily reached into the beer cooler and pulled out two bottles.

"Thanks. But I'd rather not." Fisher grabbed the beer and downed a long swig. "Talk about it, that is. The beer, I could use."

"So I heard you were the one to rescue the raft from that flip this afternoon."

"Thanks for changing the subject." Fisher gave an appreciative smile. "But tell me about you and Carson. Any progress there?"

Lily took a long pull on her beer. She didn't quite know how to answer that.

"I get the impression he's more interested in his freedom." A sigh escaped; she couldn't hold it back.

"What is it about men and freedom? They think they need it and... Oh, listen to me, I'm going to start singing "Desperado" here pretty soon. And trust me, *no one* wants to hear me sing."

It nearly broke her heart to see Fisher so downhearted. All dressed up, wearing makeup and everything. It was almost enough to make Lily want to find Cody and knock some sense into him. But she wasn't here to find Cody.

"Have you seen Carson?" Time to get on with it.

"Not recently." Fisher shook her head. "If he isn't around, you could try down by the river. There's a path around back. I'll bet you find him skipping rocks or something."

"Thanks for the tip."

"Anytime." Fisher finished her beer and tossed it in the recycling bin. "See ya."

Lily waved to her friend and went to look for Carson. He hadn't been inside, as far as she could see. He didn't appear to be out on the deck, either. There were plenty of people there, most of them talking about the rescue, and it was clear that Carson held the respect of most of his friends and neighbors.

Lily didn't want to hear about how great he was. She wanted to see for herself. She smoothed her skirt, clutched her purse to her side, and marched toward the river.

A clever little path wound its way to the water. Large stones had been set here and there, where a step was needed to make the journey safer. Carson would have done that. Funny, for a guy who was so intent on leaving, he'd sure put a lot of himself into the place. The house belonged to both of them, but it felt more like Carson. The kitchen especially. It had a warm, open feeling. Functional and inviting with its smooth stone surfaces, sleek stainless steel appliances, and warm maple cabinets. The homey feel spoke of Carson more than Cody. Not that she expected Cody to decorate the place like a college dorm room or fraternity house, but she couldn't see him putting so much thought into the selection of materials.

The sand volleyball court down by the water, now, that had Cody written all over it. He'd see any excuse to spend time with girls in bikinis as a solid investment. Still, it was an interesting touch. Lily removed her sandals so she could walk across the sand. It was almost like being at the beach. They must have trucked the sand in, and she wondered why it didn't extend all the way down to the water. It would be much more comfortable to walk on than the granite stones and broken slate lining the banks.

Lily stopped when she saw Carson at the river's edge. He stooped to pick up a small stone, and examined it carefully before skipping it across the water. It skittered across the smooth surface several times before sinking into the river's depths. He bent down and picked up another stone. Then another and another and another. The tension in his broad shoulders, the tightness in his long legs, and the fact that he hadn't noticed her standing there just a few feet behind him made Lily believe this was serious business. Those weren't just stones he gathered and tossed out into the blackness of the river. They were burdens.

The money Heather had attempted to steal. *Plip, plip, plip, plink.* The passengers on the upcoming trips. *Plip, plip, plip, plink.* The guides, the store clerks, and campground workers. *Plip, plip, plip, plink.* His brother. *Plip, plip, plip, plip, plip, plink.* The death of his mother. His grandparents. Maybe a pet he'd had as a child. *Plip, plip, plip, plink. Plip, plip, plip, plink.*

Lily realized that if she approached him, she would only add to his pile of rocks. It wasn't the thought of being cast away that bothered her, but rather the idea that he would feel obligated to pick her up in the first place.

She should turn away. Go back to the party. Maybe find Fisher and commiserate with her about the misery of wanting the one man they shouldn't want. But she couldn't leave him there. She watched him gather stone after stone after stone. It was almost as if he felt the need to clear the beach of every last bit of granite, slate, or quartz. Carson took care of everyone. But who would take care of Carson?

Lily dropped her purse to the ground. She kicked off her shoes and began to unbutton her blouse. She shimmied out of her skirt and slipped off her bra and panties. There was no way he could ignore her once she stepped naked into the river.

*   *   *   *

Carson skipped yet another rock. If he kept this up much longer, he'd change the course of the river. But he didn't feel like being part of the crowd. He didn't feel like replaying the events of the day. Everyone wanted to know about how he rescued the kid. They wanted to treat him like a hero. He wasn't a hero. Just someone who happened to look in the right direction.

He bent down, grabbed a smooth flat piece of slate. He cocked his arm, ready to fling it across the water, but he stopped himself just in time to avoid hitting Lily.

She'd waded into the river, the moon highlighting the fact that she was completely naked.

Maybe she hadn't noticed him there. She was skinny dipping, and he should leave her alone. He started to leave, but he couldn't tear himself away.

"Lily." He stepped forward, catching her attention. "You really shouldn't be out there. Anyone could see you."

"What are you going to do about it?" She stood her ground. A goddess standing waist deep in the river.

"Lily, I…" He started to protest. To give her all the reasons he shouldn't. Wouldn't.

Oh hell. Who was he kidding? The only thing he couldn't do was resist. He couldn't just leave her there. Alone in the river. He tugged his shirt over his head, slipped off his shorts, and entered the water. If he was going to go under, he was going to go all the way.

"Carson." Lily shivered. He'd just have to warm her up. The best way to do that would be skin to skin. Wrap his arms around her and do his best to provide enough body heat.

They came together. Two bodies colliding with the force of nature. Gravity, erosion, the water cycle. All of those seemed minor compared to the power of their attraction to each other.

Lily wrapped her arms around his neck. She buried her head in his chest and he seemed to gain strength with each breath they took together.

Closer. He wanted her to get closer. Needed her to get closer. The only way to do that was to let go. All the way. To just surrender in every way.

He started with a kiss. Tentative, shaky, and oh so desperate. But she welcomed him. Consumed him. She wrapped her legs around his waist, and then started to slide lower, to the point of no return.

"Lily, wait." His voice sounded foreign. A traitor. "We could be swept away."

"Would that be so bad?"

"If we end up naked on the shores of Folsom Lake, yeah." Carson struggled for control. For sanity. "Besides, we don't have any protection."

"In my purse," Lily whispered, and it took every ounce of control to pull away from her.

"Are you sure?" It was a little late, but he still had to ask.

"Yes." He followed Lily to the shore.

Lily gathered her clothing and fumbled with the zipper on her beaded handbag. Thankfully, she was more prepared than he was.

She held up the square packet with a triumphant grin. He had just enough brain cells working to grab his T-shirt and lead her to the soft, sandy volleyball court. He spread his shirt on the ground so she wouldn't get sand where it didn't belong.

Lowering her to the ground, he asked one more time, "Are you sure?"

"Absolutely." Lily pulled him on top of her. "Don't worry, Carson. I'm not going to fall in love with you."

If she meant to lighten the mood, her comment had the opposite effect. Somehow, it felt more significant. He hesitated, like he wasn't sure where to begin.

"Touch me, Carson," she whispered. "Touch me everywhere."

She guided his hand to her breast and moaned. He followed with his mouth. He circled her perfect breast with his tongue. She shuddered as he drew her nipple between his teeth. Finally. He'd wanted her like this since he first met her. Since he first touched her.

Carson moved down her body, trailing soft kisses across her smooth skin. She tasted like the river. Like Lily. Like heaven. He watched and listened and sensed. She let him know when to slow down, speed up, use more or less pressure. He read her body like he'd read a current. He'd never felt so in tune with a river, though. He'd never felt so in command and out of control at the same time. And it had never felt so vital that he make sure they arrived at their destination at the same time.

"Carson." His name on her lips as she came surged through him. A powerful flood of emotion ripped his own climax from him.

"Are you okay?" He withdrew, careful to keep his weight off her while still covering her, shielding her from potentially harmful lunar radiation. Or curious onlookers.

"Yeah." She laughed, a shy, almost timid kind of laugh. Funny, considering how brazen she'd been in seducing him. "Are you?"

"Of course." He was a man. "Why wouldn't I be?"

"I don't know." Lily sighed, long and satisfied. "It just felt more…"

"Intense?" How did she know that this was different for him, too?

"That too." Lily reached for her blouse. "It was also so much more… I don't know? I guess we'll have to do this again sometime. So I can figure out the right words for it."

Her words came out so casually. *We'll have to do this again sometime.* Like it was no big deal. Or at least that's what she wanted him to think. But he'd heard the question, the doubt, the oh-my-gosh-is-he-going-to-call-me?

"It may take several attempts." Carson hoped to reassure her. "To get the right words. But I'm up for it. Or I will be in about twenty minutes."

She laughed for real this time. The sound settled somewhere in his chest.

"We should get dressed." Lily wriggled out from underneath him. "It's too bad you have a house full of people."

"Yeah. Too bad." Carson realized he didn't want to share her with any of them. 'I hope we didn't have an audience."

"You can't see down here from the house." Lily pulled her blouse over her head and slipped her skirt over her hips. "Believe me, I wasted a good half hour looking for you."

"Really?"

"Yes. Really." Lily smoothed her skirt over her knees. She seemed shy all of a sudden. "I came here for you. For this."

Her cheeks darkened. Even in the moonlight, he could see she was flushed. Half embarrassment, half the natural result of what they had just done.

"You came here to get sand in your hair?" He smoothed her silky strands, brushing the grains his T-shirt hadn't been able to keep away.

"I should get going." Lily laughed. "Don't you have to work tomorrow?"

"Yeah. I have a long day on the river." He wanted her to know his absence in the office tomorrow didn't mean he was avoiding her.

"Maybe you could come to my place…" The uncertainty was back in her voice. "We could have dinner."

"I'd like that." Carson caressed her cheek. "I don't know if I'll make dinner though. I'll be on a full river run. Won't get off the river until almost dark. Then I have to unload and make sure everything is dry before putting it away."

Not to mention there was the matter of getting by Cody.

"Then come by late." Lily looked at his shoulder, his ear, anywhere but in the eye. "My kitchen closes at midnight, though."

"And your bedroom?" He leaned in for one more kiss. "What time does your bedroom close?"

"When you leave for your grand adventure." Lily gathered her purse and planted a quick kiss on his forehead. Then she walked away, into the night.

Carson had a feeling it wouldn't be so easy to walk away at the end of the month.

Chapter 12

"Hey, are those the passenger release forms?" Cody indicated the stack of papers in Carson's hands. He had stayed up entertaining the last of the guests long after Carson had gone to bed, but didn't seem to suffer the effects of a late night.

Then again, Cody hadn't tossed and turned, thinking about Lily all night long.

"Yeah, we've got a youth group from Prospector Springs Community Church."

"Great." Cody must have come by looking for an excuse to go into the office, forgetting it was Saturday and Lily had the day off. "So that was some party last night."

"I guess." Carson shrugged, but a small smile crept across his lips. "Did Fisher have a good time?"

"Nothing happened." Cody jumped to her defense. "Fisher's a great girl. Whatever you think you saw, it's not that."

"Sure."

"Look, things got a little...heated between us. But we cooled things off. We both realized that we shouldn't mess around with our friendship."

"Fisher's great. I'd hate to lose her."

"So would I," Cody said. "She's the best. Besides you and me, of course."

"If she sticks around, I think she'd make a good assistant manager."

"Why would we need an assistant manager?"

"You don't seem to be interested in management." Carson had come to accept the fact. Cody's skills were with the customers. There were others who could take on more responsibility in the office. "And if we want to keep Fisher, we'll eventually have to offer her something more than a Senior Guide position."

"And I'll need to keep my hands to myself, right? Isn't that what you're really saying?" Cody shook his head. "Don't worry, I'm not going to hook up with Fisher. I'm not stupid. Besides, that would really mess up my chances with Lily."

"You still think you have a shot with Lily?" Carson clenched his jaw. "You don't."

"Wanna bet?"

"No. I don't think I do." He didn't want to fight over Lily. She'd made her choice. What happened last night was personal. Private. Besides, he had to get ready for his passengers.

A full river trip always made for a long day. Most people did the upper stretch one day, camping or staying at one of the Swift River cabins, and tackling the lower half of the river the next. But occasionally a group would take on the whole river, from Chili Bar to Folsom Lake in one trip. Fortunately, the teenagers were eager to participate and they paddled quickly through the slow spots. They covered more miles this way, but there wasn't much time to sit back and take in the environment. It was more like taking the interstate versus a two-lane country road.

By the time they stopped for lunch, Carson was ready to take a breath. But the task of feeding twenty-two teenagers fell to all four of the guides. Fisher seemed to avoid Cody, working closely with Ross instead. He'd have to keep a close eye on the situation. They definitely couldn't afford to lose her. He was serious about offering her an assistant manager position. But it wouldn't do her any good to have anyone think she'd slept her way into the job.

Once the kids were fed, Carson took the opportunity to chat with Fisher. Something had happened with her and Cody. He wasn't sure what, but there was a vibe between them. "You okay?" He helped her clean up the sandwich makings.

"Yeah, sure. This is a great group of kids." Fisher replaced the caps on the condiments and placed them in the cooler. "Everyone seems to be having a good time."

"There's something going on between you and Cody."

"No. There isn't." She sounded a little too defensive. "We're. Just. Friends."

"Sure. So, why are you avoiding him?"

"I'm not avoiding him. He's just working the crowd." She pointed to where Cody was entertaining a group of girls. They were giggling and blushing and enjoying the attention of a handsome older man. "It's nice to see him use his powers for good."

"His powers?"

"You know, his charm." Fisher smiled like she was one of the teenagers. "They seem to gravitate to him. You know the bus ride home will be full of girlish sighs."

"And half the guys will be begging their parents to sign up for guide school." Carson had to admit that Cody was a people person. All the women wanted him and the guys wanted to be him.

"We both know that Cody is never going to be a business man." Fisher seemed to understand that better than he did. "I think it's a good thing you have Lily. In the office. I'm sure she'll be better than Heather."

"So you heard?" It surprised him how quickly information got around Swift River. It was even smaller than the town of Prospector Springs. "I can't believe Heather tried to steal from us."

"She tried to steal what?" Fisher must not have heard.

"A little more than twenty thousand."

"Dollars?" Fisher turned to him in disbelief. "I just thought Heather was kind of a flake. I had no idea she was a thief."

"Well, she didn't get away with it. Thanks to Lily."

"So how are things with you and Lily?" Fisher gave him a knowing smile.

"She's a great addition to our team." Carson wasn't quite ready to discuss the details of his budding relationship with Lily. He wasn't even sure the exact nature of that relationship.

"So she's just a teammate, huh?" Fisher looked like she knew something else was going on.

"You like her, don't you?" Carson was pleased to know that the two women had become friends.

"Not as much as you do." She gave him a friendly pat on the shoulder and went off to start loading the food back on the boats.

It was that obvious? He just wished he knew what to do about it. Sure, they were great together, physically. Lily had made a point of telling him she was just using him for sex. She'd also told him she wouldn't fall in love with him. But he wondered if she'd just been saying what she thought he wanted to hear.

It should be what he wanted to hear. That he didn't have to worry about hurting her when he left, but it wasn't that simple. They had connected. Really connected on a level he'd never experienced before. If their lovemaking had been a river, it was Class IV, maybe even a Class V adventure.

He was in deep. Deep, deep, *deep* trouble.

But he didn't have too much time to think about it. He had to get these kids back on the river. Then he had to get Cody settled before he could head over to Lily's place tonight. He'd woken this morning thinking he would try to cool things off with Lily. Wasn't going to happen. He'd end up at her place tonight, no doubt about it. From the moment she stepped naked into the river, he'd been done. Hell, from the moment he jumped in the river the first time, he'd been sunk.

* * * *

As much as she wanted to see Carson, Lily was glad to have the day off. He was on the river all day, and she needed time to process what had happened between them. She decided to explore Prospector Springs. Her cabin was only eight miles east of town, and she wanted to get to know her new community.

She'd driven through town, bought groceries at the Golden Harvest Market, and pumped gas at the 49er Fuel Stop, but she'd never really taken a close look at the old mining town. She parked in the Gold Pan Alley lot, free parking for the first three hours, and decided to play tourist. She passed the post office, Empire Theater, and a couple of antique stores. The General Store had been in operation since the 1860s, as had the *Prospector Springs Sentinel*. The newspaper office also housed a newsstand where all the latest magazines and several obscure journals could be found. They also sold local guide books and maps and pamphlets on gold panning techniques.

After crossing the street, Lily ducked into the Golden Era Soda Fountain for a treat. In addition to ice cream and fountain drinks, they had an old-fashioned candy counter, homemade fudge, and handmade chocolates. Yum. Lily had a mini scoop of praline dream ice cream and picked up some dark chocolate-covered hazelnuts for later.

A Good Read bookstore was on the other end of town, but Lily was in no hurry. She licked her ice cream cone while window shopping. The Mother Lode Fabric Store also took in your dry-cleaning. The Goldsmith Jewelers, established in 1862, had a fine selection of bling in the front window. Next door to that, Lily found herself staring at the display window of Beverly's Bridal and More.

Simple, elegant, and refined were the words that came to mind as she studied the dress in front of her. It couldn't have been more different than her own wedding dress. She hardly remembered the girl who had chosen the poufy, beaded, over-embellished gown her mother had talked her into.

"Is someone planning a wedding?" A kind voice startled Lily into almost dropping what was left of her cone.

"Oh, goodness no." Lily felt the color rise in her cheeks. "I was simply admiring the dress."

"Certainly." The saleswoman was about her age, but her subtle accent made her seem more worldly. "Although, you do look like a woman in love."

"Me?" Lily blushed deeper. "Oh, no. We've just met. Really we're in the exploring each other stage."

Had she really shared that much information with a stranger?

"In that case, we do have a rather nice lingerie selection." The woman's smile deepened. "If you're interested in exploring something lacy or silky."

"Let me finish my ice cream, and I'll take a look." Lily polished off her cone and stepped inside the bridal boutique. Half of the store was dedicated to brides and their attendants, but the other half offered a selection of formal and semi-formal dresses, shoes, and accessories. And the back corner held a fairly decent selection of lingerie. They had everything from bridal white bustiers and garters, pale cream baby dolls and slips, to racy red push-up bras with matching thongs.

Lily selected a cranberry-colored slip with ivory lace trim and a pale pink push-up bra with matching panties. She was almost tempted by the leopard print bustier, but she wasn't ready to walk on the wild side just yet. She wasn't even sure if Carson would show up tonight. She stuck with her more practical selections. She could sleep in the slip, and the push-up bra would be comfortable enough to wear on a daily basis.

"Just to let you know," the saleswoman said as she rang up Lily's purchases, "we are a full-service bridal shop. Besides the gown and bridesmaid dresses, we offer tuxedo rentals, limo service, stationery, and party favors. We have connections with local caterers, florists, and photographers."

"That's lovely, but I already tried the fairy tale wedding. It was more of a horror story." Lily didn't want to even let her mind wander down that aisle. "Besides, I've only known Carson a little over a week."

"Carson Swift?" The woman's eyes opened wide. "Now there's one man I wouldn't mind fitting for a tuxedo."

"Do you... I mean, were you ever...?" Lily couldn't seem to form the words.

"Goodness, no." She blushed, shaking her head. "We went to Prospector High together. He was a senior. He was *the* senior, while I was a lowly freshman. Braces, bad skin, a complete geek. He wouldn't have noticed me anyways. He had a girlfriend. Everyone thought they'd get married, but... Listen to me, going on and on about ancient history. I'm Emily, by the way."

"Nice to meet you." Lily offered her hand. Small town, she remembered.

"I'd have you tell Carson hello for me, but..." Emily tucked a lock of hair behind her ear. "He wouldn't remember me. Especially not after seeing you in this outfit." She held up the slip. "Sorry. You'd think I was still that awkward teenager mooning over her first crush, not a twenty-eight-year-old world traveler and successful business owner."

"So Beverly's Bridal is yours?"

"Beverly is my grandmother," Emily explained. "She lives over in Golden Years Retirement Village. She's still active, playing bridge every week, but the business got to be too much for her. So I quit my job in London, and moved back home."

"I thought you had a bit of an accent," Lily said. "Did you live there long?"

"Seven years," Emily said. "I thought I wanted to get as far from Prospector Springs as possible, but it's nice to be home."

"Yes, this seems like a really special community." Lily warmed to the woman after an initial stab of jealousy.

"It is." Emily smiled back. "And you're with Carson? That's great. He's a great guy." She fanned herself with a bridal brochure.

"I'm not sure if I'm 'with him,'" Lily said. "I'm helping him out with his bookkeeping."

"Yeah, I heard Heather skipped town." Emily shook her head. "I wish I could say I was shocked, but she did get her wedding dress from one of those giant chain stores."

The horror.

"I'm sorry." Emily sounded a little embarrassed. "I shouldn't judge. We do offer a wide variety of dresses here. In a wide range of prices. It's just that I never cared for her. There was something just a little... I don't know. I've been in this business long enough, I can tell right away when a woman is in love and when she's faking it."

"I guess that's a good skill to have in your business." Lily wondered if Emily would have been able to warn her before she married Brian.

"Unfortunately, I can't refuse service to customers I feel are only looking for a wedding."

"Oh, I don't know, you might get more business if you could guarantee your work."

They exchanged a few more words of small talk while Lily waited for her credit card approval. She smiled to herself when she thought of being able to pay it off with her own money next month.

Yes, things were definitely looking up. She loved her cabin on Hidden Creek. The sound of rushing water was so much more soothing than busy traffic noise. Now that she wasn't afraid anymore. She could thank Carson for that. And for the job. And for the spectacular sex that apparently gave off quite a glow. Imagine, Emily thinking she was in love. Maybe it was just her natural salesmanship. The woman did make a living off the idea of true love. Why else would any woman in her right mind spend hundreds, even thousands of dollars on a dress she would only wear for a few hours?

Lily wondered if she was moving too fast in buying the lingerie. Just because Carson had given in and had sex with her, didn't mean he was going to do it again. She hoped. Really, really hoped he would. But there were no guarantees. No promises. Except for her assurance that she wasn't going to fall in love with him. It wasn't a lie if she believed it at the time, was it?

No, she really needed to focus on her plan. In a way, she was glad he'd be gone when she went to her appointment at the fertility clinic. It wasn't exactly the best pillow talk, discussing the state of her ovaries and whether or not she was a good candidate for artificial insemination.

And she definitely didn't want to peruse the donor catalog with him. She couldn't imagine how it would go over if she happened to pick someone with similar physical traits as him.

It was best if she stuck with her plan. Just like he was going to stick to his plan. They would have fun together while it lasted and then…?

Two doors down from Beverly's Bridal was a shop called Once Upon A Child. Cautiously, she stepped inside the children's boutique. Her heart seized up at the tiny little outfits, each more precious than the last.

Poufy pink dresses, adorable overalls, and oooh…the cutest little fisherman outfit for a little boy. It had a little plaid shirt, cargo pants, and a tiny little fishing vest with the words, "Mommy's Lil' Catch" embroidered on the chest.

Lily could picture her own child wearing the outfit, complete with the miniature hiking boots on display nearby. But she could also picture a man kneeling down to help her son hold a small fishing pole. That man was Carson.

She turned to leave the store before she was tempted to buy something. Near the registers, a double stroller held two little boys, about two. One of the boys reached over and grabbed his brother's stuffed monkey and threw it toward her, causing the other boy to wail.

Lily picked up the monkey and handed it to the mother, who had finished her purchase.

"Thank you." She handed the toy back to her son, but his brother grabbed it from him again.

"I swear, they came out fighting." She sighed. "They have two of everything, but they each want what the other has."

"You sure have your hands full." Lily wondered if the woman could hear the envy in her voice.

"Yeah. But as much as they fight"—the mother made sure both boys had their monkeys, or their brother's—"whenever I separate them, they're miserable."

"Must be a twin thing," Lily offered.

The woman smiled and then pushed the stroller out the door.

Lily wondered how Carson would really feel once he left his brother behind.

Chapter 13

"I suppose you want to head on over to the Argo." Carson helped Cody put away the last of the gear. They had been on the river all day and he knew his brother would most likely want to throw back a couple of beers to help loosen up his muscles.

"Nah. I think I'll just head home. Relax a bit. Maybe catch up on a few episodes of *Deadliest Catch* on DVR." Cody rubbed his temples like he had a headache.

"Drink some water." Carson didn't mean to nag, but he'd seen the effects of dehydration and it wasn't pretty. Even in a pretty boy like Cody.

"This isn't my first time on the river." Cody shot him a look that said he was tired of being treated like a kid. "I know how to take care of myself. I even manage to feed myself now."

"I didn't mean…" Carson just shook his head. When Cody was in one of his moods, the best thing was to leave him alone. "Do you want me to bring you anything?"

"No. I'll heat up some leftovers." Cody twisted the top off his water bottle and drained the remaining few ounces. "Maybe I'll go to bed early. I guess I'm not as young as I used to be."

"Well, I might be out late." Carson had debated going to Lily's tonight. He figured he would have to entertain Cody, but now… "Don't wait up."

"Sure." Cody started to walk off, but then he stopped. "Do me a favor. If you see Fisher, keep an eye on her."

"No problem." There was definitely something going on between those two. Not that it was his business, except for how it might affect his business. He was one to talk; he was sleeping with their bookkeeper. And he didn't intend to stop anytime soon.

After a quick shower and change of clothes, Carson jumped in his truck and drove straight to her place. He didn't even stop for dinner. Food could wait. He had more pressing needs. The need to touch, taste, and hold Lily again. He'd tried to resist her, he couldn't even remember why, but she wouldn't give up. Didn't give up. And now, he wanted to spend as much time with her as he possibly could.

It was just dark when he pulled into her driveway. The porch light was on. For him. His heart swelled at the realization. He should have brought something. Flowers. A bottle of wine. Whipped cream and chocolate sauce. He'd been in such a hurry to see her, he didn't think. He'd just have to give her the kind of gift that couldn't be found at the Golden Harvest Market.

He smoothed the collar on his shirt. A short sleeved button-up shirt that brought out the blue in his eyes—the shirt he wore when he wanted to make a good impression. He had no reason to be nervous. Lily had made it very clear that she liked him. She'd sought him out and responded to his touch with an enthusiasm he'd never seen before. She'd invited him over tonight, making it very clear that they would end up in her bed. So what was he still doing sitting in his truck?

It's just sex, he told himself as he climbed her front steps. Just the best sex he'd ever known. He was about to knock when the door swung open.

* * * *

"Hey there." Lily tried to sound casual. Like she hadn't been waiting all day for his arrival. But the instant she heard the gravel crunch beneath his tires, she'd raced to her bedroom and slipped into her new lingerie.

"Wow." Carson took her in, the look in his eyes pure lust.

"You like?" Lily did a quick pirouette, giving him the full effect of her new purchase.

He answered her by pulling her into his arms, claiming her with his mouth, his hands, his insatiable desire. He devoured her with his kisses. Like he was starving and she was the only nourishment he would ever need.

They stumbled together into the living room. Without taking their hands off each other or breaking contact of their lips, they tumbled onto the couch. His hands skimmed the soft satin of her slip, inching the fabric over her hips. He slipped his hands beneath the waistband of her panties, sliding them down her hips with one quick motion. Instinctively she lifted her hips, giving him more access. His fingers found her center, stroking her to near ecstasy. But it wasn't enough. She wanted him inside her. Now.

She grabbed the front of his shorts, yanking the button open and tugging at the zipper. She shoved his shorts and boxers away and reached for him, guiding him to where she needed him most.

He groaned as he thrust deep inside her. Their joining was frantic, urgent, almost desperate. Lily gasped, her climax coming on so sudden, so fierce. She drew a breath and Carson thrust once more, harder, deeper, and more intense than ever. He stilled, tension filing his body.

"I'm so sorry." His voice had an edge, a frantic quality to it that Lily couldn't understand. Unless he thought she hadn't...

"No, you were great." He had nothing to apologize for.

"I've never lost control like that." Carson hadn't moved; he was frozen in place.

"You should lose control more often." She was still trembling all over.

"I wasn't wearing anything." His eyes were wide with something like fear.

She looked him over. He still wore his shirt, his sandals, and his shorts were wrapped around his ankles. Her slip was pushed up to her ribs, one strap dangling from her shoulder.

"Oh." She understood why he was so concerned. No, so outright terrified. He hadn't worn a condom. They had been so hot for each other, they'd skipped that step. "It's okay. I'm not ovulating. I can't get pregnant. Not right now."

Maybe not ever.

"How can you be sure?" Yeah, that was sheer terror in his voice. While she might be ready to be a parent, it was very clear Carson was not.

"Trust me, I know my cycle." Lily felt a stab of disappointment. "I've spent years figuring out the optimal time for me to conceive and tonight is not even close."

He stroked her hair, looking deep into her eyes for the first time since his arrival. He wanted to believe her, that much was obvious. But he was shaken.

"Have you had dinner?" He was still inside her. His fear was so immobilizing that he hadn't moved.

"No. I came straight here." He withdrew slowly, causing Lily to feel empty the moment their connection broke. "I wanted to see you. I needed to be with you."

"Why don't you get cleaned up? I'll fix you something to eat." Lily smoothed her slip down her thighs. "I made a pot roast."

"That sounds great." Carson fumbled to pull up his pants. Lily watched him wander down the hall to the bathroom. She reached for her panties, slipped them on, and made her way into the kitchen, wondering if he would come up with some excuse not to stay.

She reheated the pot roast, mashed potatoes, and gravy. After tossing a quick salad, Lily opened a bottle of wine. She poured two generous glasses and waited for his return.

"Something smells wonderful." Carson looked more like himself as he slid into the chair she'd pulled out for him.

"I made extra." Lily had hoped he would make it in time to join her, but she hadn't held her breath. She realized she was holding her breath right now. Wanting more than he could give.

Carson leaned back into the chair, weariness showing in every line of his body. His shoulders, his neck, even his hair seemed weighted down with worry. Lily scooted closer to him, picking up the fork, stabbing a piece of pot roast, and bringing it to his lips. He closed his eyes and accepted her offer of nourishment. A soft murmur of enjoyment escaped his lips. She continued to feed him, encouraged by his appreciation of her cooking. If only… No she couldn't let herself start to fantasize about anything domestic. Or permanent.

"That was delicious." Carson swallowed the last bite and reached for the wine. "I can't remember the last time someone made me a meal."

"You do all the cooking?" Lily's heart broke just a little at the thought. Carson took care of everyone. There was no one to take care of him.

"Sure." He shrugged. No big deal.

"There's something you should know." Lily took his empty plate, dropped it in the sink, and took a step toward the refrigerator. She plucked the appointment card off the door. "Maybe I should have told you before, but…" She sighed. "I didn't want to scare you away."

She dropped the card on the table in front of him. "I'm going to have a baby."

He reached for her glass of wine. It was purely instinct; she took no offense. He protected. That's just what he did.

"I'm not pregnant." Lily took her wineglass from his hand and took a long swallow. "But I'm going to be." She tapped the card. "June seventeenth. I go in for a consultation. And then hopefully, in a few months' time, I'll return for prenatal care."

He stared at her blankly. Lily felt a rush of relief that neither Cody nor Fisher had told him about her plans.

"I'm going to use an anonymous donor." Lily felt the need to explain. "If that doesn't work, I'll take the next step. In vitro."

"You're serious about this." It wasn't a question. It was more an absorption of her news.

"I've wanted a baby for so long." Lily tried not to think about what it would be like to have his baby. "And this is the best way."

"Really?"

"Yes." Lily avoided his gaze. "I'm not getting any younger. And I have no plans on getting married again, so…"

"Interesting." She could feel Carson's gaze on her. She couldn't bring herself to lift her eyes. She wasn't sure if she wanted to know what she'd see in his eyes. Judgment? Repulsion? The overwhelming need to escape? "So you really are just using me for sex?"

She dared a glance in his direction. He was smiling. A dimple appeared on his right cheek. Of course, he would have dimples, just like his brother. Only Carson didn't use them as a weapon. He saved them for a special occasion.

"Yes. Just sex." Lily felt her cheeks flush, and heat spread throughout her whole body. "Lots and lots of sex. I bought the jumbo box of condoms. It's in my bedroom."

"Maybe we should stash some in every room of the house." Carson leaned forward, his eyes filled with lust. With need. "I can't guarantee I won't lose control again."

"Let's hope not." Lily felt her nipples tighten. "I kind of like it when you lose control."

"Me too." He pulled her to her feet, kissed her hard, and led her back to the bedroom where the full box of condoms awaited.

* * * *

Carson woke shortly before dawn. He hadn't planned on spending the night, but he couldn't tear himself away from Lily. She was everything he could want in a woman. If he allowed himself to want what she could give.

They'd made love again after dinner. It wasn't at all like the first time. Or the second. They'd taken it slow, exploring each other as if they had all the time in the universe. Then they'd drifted off into a contented sleep. She'd snuggled against him, wrapping her arms around him as if they had been made to fit together.

He needed to go. As much as he wanted to lie there and watch her sleep, to wonder if the smile that curved her lips was because of him or some dream she was having. He couldn't think when he was this close to her. And he really needed to think things through. To get his head on straight. To figure out why, when she told him it was nearly impossible for her to get pregnant last night, he'd felt disappointed instead of relieved.

He dressed quietly, not wanting to wake her. She looked so peaceful sleeping there in the bed where they'd made love. A lock of hair curled across her cheek and Carson couldn't resist the urge to brush it away. Her eyes fluttered open and she smiled warmly.

"Good morning." Lily's voice was groggy with sleep. "At least I think it's morning. What are you doing up so early?"

"I have to get home," Carson admitted. "Go back to sleep."

"I wish you could stay." Lily grasped his hand. "We could spend the morning making love. Maybe have a picnic lunch, and then…"

"I really have to go." Carson interrupted her by brushing a kiss across her forehead. He pulled away, the weight of her expectations crushing him, making him feel trapped.

"Relax, Carson." Lily sat up, letting the sheet fall away, leaving her exposed. "This is supposed to be fun, remember? As much as I would like to spend the day making love with you, I know you have work to do."

"Yes, I have passengers waiting for me." Carson let his gaze fall to her bare breasts. They'd captivated him from the first and he'd since discovered they were as firm and luscious as he'd anticipated.

"And I have plenty to keep me busy." Lily lifted the sheet, covering herself, to his disappointment. "Maybe you shouldn't come over tonight."

"Oh?" Was she telling him she was bored with him already?

"Then when we see each other next, we might not be able to resist tearing each other's clothes off." Lily gripped the front of his shirt, threatening to pop off the buttons.

"You tempt me." Carson reached up to cup her face, stroke her cheek, and offer a goodbye kiss. "But I really have to get to work."

"Do you ever take a break?"

"I'm interviewing for a few more guides on Monday. It turns out we can afford to add to our staff, thanks to you."

"I just came along at the right time," Lily said, dismissing her role in saving his business.

"Yes, you did." Carson stood. The right time to catch a potential thief, the absolute wrong time for her to capture his heart.

* * * *

Lily waited until she was sure Carson had gone. She dressed in a robe and went in search of coffee. She couldn't go back to sleep, so she might as well start her day. She found the coffeepot already set up. All she had to do was push the start button. Carson had left at dawn, but not before making her coffee. Tears stung her eyes. It was such a simple gesture, and yet it meant so much to her.

Once the coffee finished brewing, Lily poured herself a cup, stirred in a scant teaspoon of sugar and a generous amount of half and half. She took a long sip and felt the earth shift. It was a lot like being out on that rock. She could feel herself falling and had no way to stop it. But instead of into the river below, this time Lily realized she was falling in love.

Carson had swept her into his arms, giving her a second shot at life, and now love. But he couldn't know. Not yet. The last thing she wanted to do was add to his burdens. His sense of responsibility. Maybe sharing her plans for motherhood had been a mistake. But she had been afraid he'd find out from either Cody or Fisher. She'd wanted to let him know she had plans of her own. That she wouldn't be sitting around pining for him when he left next month.

Could she be content to love him for a month—less than a month—and then let him go? Could she wait for him to get a taste of freedom before...? Oh, who was she kidding? He wasn't going to be content to be free for six weeks and come back and tie himself to an instant family.

No, he could never know the extent of her feelings. She had to convince him that she was only with him for sex. To have a little fun before she tied herself down with a baby.

She could pretend for a little while. Hell, the last few years of her marriage had been one big sham. Only this time she would be doing it not for her own sake, or for appearances, but to protect Carson. She wouldn't put any more pressure on him than he already felt.

When he left, he'd have nothing but good memories to take with him.

Chapter 14

Cody sauntered into the office shortly after Lily had arrived. She wondered if he knew about her and Carson. If he had been up before dawn, awaiting his brother's arrival.

"Good morning, Lily." Cody leaned against her desk like a man without a care in the world.

"Good morning." Lily hoped she didn't sound too cheerful. Too much like a woman in love. "Are you on the river today?"

"Nope. I thought I'd hang around here." Cody picked up her stapler, turning it over in his hands, as if he wasn't sure of its use. "Maybe you could show me what you do."

"Sure." Lily glanced at him and smiled. "What do you want to know?"

"Well, since you found out that Heather was trying to steal from us"—Cody leaned over, to look at her computer monitor—"I thought I should keep a closer eye on things. Only I don't have any idea what to look for."

"Why don't you pull up a chair?" Lily offered. "We'll start with the basics."

They spent about an hour going over the various accounts, balance sheets, and income and expense reports. Lily was encouraged that Cody seemed so interested in the business side of the company. Carson would be pleased to know that Cody wouldn't let things slide while he was gone.

"Why don't I just watch you work?" Cody suggested. "That way I can see what it takes to keep this operation afloat on a daily basis."

"Don't you use rubber rafts?" Lily joked. "Life jackets, too?"

"Yes, to keep afloat." Cody let a slow grin spread across his face. "I like your sense of humor. I like everything about you."

"Even the fact that we can never be anything more than friends?" Lily's words wiped that grin off his face in a hurry.

"Oh come on, Lily." Cody tried one more time. "Don't you know how good we'd be together?"

"So are you sitting in on the guide interviews with Carson?" Lily was done discussing any potential relationship with Cody. She was with Carson. For however long it lasted.

"You know, I think I might." Cody scooted the chair back. "I need to make sure he doesn't hire another Heather."

She detected the slightest hint of contempt in his voice. Or maybe it was jealousy. Maybe she should tell him that she and Carson were together. But he might ask questions she wasn't yet prepared to answer.

"Well, Cody, what a surprise." Carson stepped into the office before she could think of a response. "I thought you'd be off...somewhere."

"No. I'm here. Lily was giving me the rundown on the bookkeeping. Then I thought I'd help you with the guide interviews. And I was hoping this afternoon we could go back over the raft inventory. If we need to order any new boats, I'd like to get them in before Memorial Day."

"Great." Carson barely hid his surprise. "I'd love to have you sit in on the interviews. But I already ordered the new boats. We even paid cash. Thanks to Lily."

He shot her a look of gratitude.

"So how many guides are we looking at?" Cody asked. It took a few seconds for Carson to tear his gaze away from Lily and acknowledge Cody's question.

"Um, I have six interviews lined up." Carson was clearly distracted. "If we can pick up three guides, we'll be in good shape."

"Sure."

"So do you have résumés I can look over before we meet with the candidates?" Cody was trying. Lily was happy for that. She really hoped they could patch things up before Carson left.

"Sure, I'll print out copies for you." Carson booted up his computer but he never took his eyes off Cody. It was as if he didn't trust him.

Cody walked over to the printer to grab the first résumé that Carson printed. He scanned the contents, and picked up the next.

"So where are we conducting the interviews?" Cody asked after reading the third résumé. "It might get a little cramped in here."

"I can get out of the way," Lily offered. "There's nothing here that can't wait until this afternoon. I could pick up lunch. Bring it back here."

"That would be great." Carson smiled at her, his eyes caressing every inch of her. "How does that sound to you, Cody?"

"Delicious." Cody sent a smoldering look at Lily and she swore Carson was about ready to jump across the desk and grab him by the neck.

"I'll run a few errands." Lily reached into the drawer for her purse. "And I'll see you boys later."

She left without looking back at either of them.

* * * *

"What the hell are you trying to pull, here?" Carson had walked in on Cody once again trying to put the moves on Lily. His Lily.

"I'm just taking more of an interest in our business." Cody dropped into the chair Lily had just vacated. "Isn't that what you wanted?"

"You're just taking an interest in Lily." Carson glared at him.

"Lily is an interesting person." Did Cody know he'd spent the night with Lily? Was he just messing with him, trying to get him to admit it? "She has a way of making even the most boring of subjects absolutely fascinating. In fact, I think I'll spend the next few days really soaking in all the bookkeeping information Lily has to share with me."

"Stay away from Lily." Carson's mouth didn't move as he said the words. His jaw was clenched so tight he'd need a jack to get it open.

They were interrupted by a light knock on the open office door.

"Excuse me, I'm looking for Carson Swift." Their first interview was early. "I'm here about the guide job."

"Welcome to Swift River Adventures." Cody stood to shake her hand.

A petite brunette with great shoulders. He could tell she spent a lot of time outdoors. Not just from her physical build, but the confidence she carried as she approached the two of them. He liked her immediately.

They got through five interviews in four and a half hours. One guy was a no-show. They ended up with four pretty good candidates. Carson was glad Cody had taken part in the process. Mostly. He had a nagging suspicion that he was only trying to impress Lily.

When he walked into the office this morning and saw Cody sitting so close to Lily, he'd felt something bordering on rage. His heart rate had jacked up, his blood had begun to boil, and he'd been about three steps from grabbing Cody by the back of his shirt before he'd realized they were just working. Cody was talking to her about balance sheets, not trying to talk her into his bed sheets.

He was doing what Carson had asked. Cody was taking responsibility for the business side of their company. He should be happy. He would be, if he didn't think that the only reason for Cody's sudden interest in being in the office was their new office mate.

Hell, he should just tell Cody. That he and Lily were... What were they exactly?

"I brought burgers and fries." Lily arrived with two bags of food. "I can grab a couple of drinks from the store."

"I'll grab the drinks," Cody offered. "What's your pleasure?" He looked at Lily and although Cody was asking about drinks, Carson could see her blush.

"I'll take a Diet Coke, please." Lily turned her attention to unpacking the burgers.

Carson held his breath until Cody left the room.

"So how did the interviews go?" Lily asked, seemingly unaware of the tension between the brothers.

"Good. Real good." He stretched his neck from side to side. Whether she was aware of it or not, the tension was there.

"And Cody was a big help?"

"Actually, yes." Carson wanted to reach for her, to take her in his arms, to do that clothes-ripping thing she'd mentioned this morning.

"I'm glad." Lily unwrapped her burger and sat down at her desk to eat. "I think he feels like he's not good enough. Or that you think he's not good enough."

"Why would he—" Cody came back with the drinks before he could finish the question.

"Here you go, Lily, your Diet Coke. Not that you need it. You're perfect." Cody set the can in front of her. He handed the same diet soda to Carson and popped open a can of root beer for himself. He dug into the burgers and sat on the edge of Lily's desk. "No onions, huh?" He raised an eyebrow toward Lily but she was busy enjoying her lunch.

She did a damn good job of ignoring Cody's obvious attempts at flirtation. God, he loved her for it.

He about choked on a french fry. Carson grabbed for his soda, washing it down. He saw Lily's look of concern over the top of her computer monitor.

"I guess I should try chewing before I swallow." Carson made the joke, letting her know he was okay. Physically at least. But he wasn't sure about his emotional state. He couldn't be in love with her. They'd only known each other a short time. They were just having fun. A temporary connection that had no place to go. He was leaving in three weeks. A little less now that everything was under control.

And Lily? Lily had plans of her own. Plans that didn't involve him. Just an anonymous sperm donor. He wasn't exactly sure how he felt about that. Only that he had no right to judge. Not when he had no intention of sticking around and giving her a baby the old fashioned way.

"So you have some good candidates?" Lily asked, and it took Carson a moment to realize she was talking about the guides. His mind was still on her plans. He wondered if she had any candidates picked out yet.

"Yeah, a couple of good guys." Cody was the first to answer.

"And women," Carson added, wondering if Lily would be jealous. Not that she had any reason.

"So, it comes down to the bikini test?" Lily flashed a playful grin.

"Yeah, if a guy's not willing to put on a bikini, he's not for us," Cody joked. He tossed her a smile, but it seemed to be wasted.

"I meant the women." Lily ignored Cody, focusing her attention on her lunch instead.

"Well, if any of them look half as good as you..." Cody started to move closer. Carson took a deep breath, waiting for Lily's response.

"Please." Lily waved him off with the back of her hand. She kept her eyes on Carson the whole time. He felt the tension drain from his shoulders. She wasn't going to fall for Cody's charm. "Just eat your burger."

"We'll have the finalists come back for a hands-on interview." Carson relaxed into his chair. "That way we can see what they're able to do on the river."

"So there will be bikinis involved." Lily grinned. "I figured as much."

"We only require our bookkeepers to show up topless," Cody said.

Lily shot him a look that could castrate horses.

"Too far?" Cody backed up, nearly falling off the edge of the desk.

"Yes." Lily wadded up the burger wrapper and tossed it into the trash. Two points.

"Well, you know me." Cody stood, picked up his trash, and started for the exit. "I can't be trusted to say the right thing." He shot a look at Carson. "Or to do the right thing. I'll be going now. I guess I should stick with what I do best—beer, babes, and being an ass."

He stormed out of the office.

Lily waited a few minutes before saying anything. "Aren't you going to go after him?"

"Why?"

"He's your brother. And he's trying." Lily stood up and came around to his side of the desk.

"He's trying to get into your bed."

"He's too late." Lily rested her hand on his arm. "I chose you."

Carson looked up. Her eyes were warm with emotion as she lightly stroked his arm. He wanted to pull her onto his lap and never let her go.

"I chose you to share my bed." Lily's voice dropped to almost a whisper. A sexy, seductive whisper. "I'm not interested in anyone else."

Carson still wondered how that had happened. Most of the time he ended up with Cody's rejects. Or at least the women his brother had found less attractive than others. Whether they met a pair of females or a group of them, Cody zeroed in on his prey and Carson was left entertaining her friend. All too often, he ended up with a woman by default.

But Lily had picked him.

"I do think you should cut him some slack." Her voice was mostly teasing. She didn't know Cody like he did.

"Who? Cody?" Carson shook his head. "He's a jerk."

"You're jealous." Lily laughed even as she fingered the blond hairs on his arm. "You actually think I would... Don't you trust me?"

"Of course I trust you." The hurt look on her face stung. "It's just that I don't trust him."

"You think he has some kind of super power over women?" Lily pulled her hand away. He'd pissed her off somehow.

"No." Carson hated that she saw him like this, petty, pissed off, and powerless. "You don't understand. I've spent my whole life watching him get everything he's ever wanted."

"Not everything," Lily crossed her arms across her chest.

"Right, he hasn't had you."

"No. That's not what I'm talking about." Lily exhaled sharply. "He doesn't have your respect. *That's* what he wants more than anything."

She walked out the door.

Carson was afraid she was going to go after Cody. He was even more afraid that she was right.

* * * *

It's really none of my business. Lily had been afraid of coming between the twins from the beginning, but she realized that the rift had been there before her. They were close, but there was an underlying friction.

Sure, Carson was a little jealous. It was only natural; Cody did have a way of communicating that looked an awful lot like flirting. His cockiness only masked an underlying insecurity. Cody was very likely also jealous of Carson, and it had nothing to do with her.

No, they had established their roles a long time ago. Carson was the responsible one, the protector, the designated driver. Cody had somewhere along the line been labeled the fun-loving, free-spirited life of the party and he didn't quite know how to live it down.

She didn't need to get involved. But she cared about Carson. No. She loved him. And she cared about Cody, too. They were brothers. Twins. They had a connection that ran deeper than any other relationship. If one of them hurt, they both hurt. If she could heal one, she could heal them both.

Lily made it all the way to her car before she realized she still had work to do. She had been so caught up in the tension between the two men, she'd forgotten about the stack of bills in the inbox that needed her attention. And one hour's training wasn't going to give Cody the skills to handle her job, especially since he didn't want it.

Lily came back through the store. She picked up a bag of peanut M&Ms and grabbed another Diet Coke from the cooler. Sure, Carson would think she'd only left the office because she was thirsty.

Carson was busy on the computer when she returned, his brow furrowed in concentration. Lily wanted to wrap her arms around him, ease his troubles, make it all better. Instead, she sat down at her workstation, opened the accounting program, and got back to work.

"So you didn't go after Cody." There was a hint of fear in his voice. Like he really thought she'd trade allegiance so quickly.

"He's not my type." It was a good thing they weren't serious. This jealousy thing would get old.

"Oh really?" Carson's voice held just a hint of amusement. "Why not?"

"He's not you," Lily said simply.

"What have I got that he doesn't?"

"Me." Lily walked over to his side of the desk and put her arms around him. He pulled her into his lap and kissed her. He kissed her hard. He kissed her deep. He kissed her like he was a drowning man and she'd just thrown him a rope.

He pulled away, breathless. "You really do make me lose control."

"That's a good thing." Lily smoothed her hair, worried about someone walking in on them. "I like the way you lose control."

"Yeah?" Carson moved his hands up her sides, sending shivers down her spine.

"Oh yeah." Lily waited for his hands to reach her breasts. Her nipples were already tight with anticipation. "Carson…"

He stopped, his hands hovering just inches from her skin. "We can't do this." His breath was ragged. "Not here."

"You're right." Lily felt more than a little disappointment. "Maybe you can come over tonight."

"There is no maybe." Carson dropped his hands to his sides. "I'll be over as soon as I can."

"You should talk to Cody." Lily rose and perched on the edge of his desk. "You two need to clear the air."

"I don't want to share this with him." Carson leaned back in his chair and closed his eyes. "I don't want to share you."

"Sorry, but I'm not into that." Lily let out a nervous laugh. "I prefer to only sleep with one of my bosses."

"No. That's not what I meant." Carson opened his eyes and met her gaze. "I've never had anything that was only mine."

"You've never had a girlfriend?" Lily wondered about what she'd heard at the bridal store.

"Yeah. But that was a long time ago." Carson steadied his breath. "I dated this girl in high school. Cody dated pretty much all of her friends."

"Did you love her?" The question slipped out before she could stop it.

"No," he said after a long pause. "Not really. We were more study partners than anything. She's the reason Cody made it through pre-calculus."

"So they didn't..." Lily wondered why she even asked, but it would explain a lot.

"No," Carson answered quickly. A little too quickly. "I don't think so. But he was always there, hanging around. Sometimes I got the feeling she wished she'd hooked up with him instead. He was more fun."

"I think you're plenty of fun." Lily flashed a reassuring smile.

"Yeah, well, you're the only one," Carson said with a heavy sigh.

"So how old were you when you were labeled the 'responsible one'?"

"Eight or nine."

"And Cody was the 'fun one'?"

"Yeah. I guess."

"But it doesn't have to be that way." Lily reached out and touched his arm. "If you give Cody a chance, I think he'll take on more responsibility."

He shot her a look that said "In your dreams."

"And I happen to know for a fact"—Lily gave him a teasing smile— "that you know how to show a girl a good time."

"Oh yeah?" His face relaxed into a partial smile, as if he believed her.

"Oh. Yeah." Lily slid off the desk and leaned over him, offering a clear view of the new bra she wore under her blouse. "I can't wait for you to come over later and show me a real good time."

"I could do that." Carson sounded so cool.

"Good." Lily straightened. "You and Cody have dinner. Talk. Or however you two communicate. Then come see me. I'll leave a key for you. Under the heart-shaped rock in the flowerpot on the porch."

"You really shouldn't leave a spare key outside." Carson had slipped back into protector mode. "Anyone could find it. I hate to think of you all alone out there."

"Then don't let me be alone for long." Lily used her most seductive voice. A voice she hadn't even known she had until recently. Until Carson.

"I'll get there as soon as I can," he promised. "I just don't want Cody to get suspicious."

"So we're sticking with the sneaking around thing? Okay. Makes it a little daring. Naughty even. See, I knew you had a wild side."

She had seen that wild side. Up close and personal.

Chapter 15

Carson found Cody on the deck of the Argo, watching the sun set over the river. He didn't notice his brother's approach, he was busy flirting with the waitress.

"Another shooter? Or some hot wings?" The way she tossed her hair and licked her lips made it clear she was on the menu as well.

"I think I'll switch to a Gold Rush." If Cody had been doing shots, he'd need a ride home. Something else Carson would have to worry about when he left. "And I will take you up on the wings."

"Coming right up." She hesitated just long enough for Cody to take her up on the secret menu choice of herself, if he was interested. Sure, she was sexy in her low-cut, too-short T-shirt and super-tight jeans. Stacked, tattooed, and heavily made up, she gave off a bad-girl vibe. She'd been around long enough to know what she could expect if Cody took her home. More importantly, she'd know what not to expect. When Cody didn't say anything more, she shrugged before heading inside to fill his order.

After she walked away, Cody looked up and acknowledged Carson's presence with a slight nod. "There you are," Carson said. "You left before we had a chance to talk."

"Talk? Sure. Tell me some more how I'm not good enough for Lily. I love hearing all about it."

"I wanted to get your input on the guides we interviewed today." Carson ignored the sarcasm and sat down on the bar stool next to him.

"Why? So you could pretend my opinion counts for something?"

"It does."

"We both know you're going to make the final decision." He continued to whine.

"It doesn't have to be that way." Carson flagged the waitress and ordered a pulled pork sandwich and a beer. Cody signaled for another beer. "We're partners," Carson said. "Equal partners."

"Yeah? So why do I get the feeling that you don't want me in the office? Especially with Lily around."

"This has nothing to do with Lily."

"Right."

"You forget it's an office. A place of business." Carson knew he was being a hypocrite. "Not your personal playground."

"I was trying to work. Until you came in there, making it very clear I was honing in on your territory. You might as well have started pissing on the office furniture. Lily was just trying to show me how things are run."

"It's just too much of a coincidence that you suddenly start showing an interest in the business the minute Lily started working there." Carson picked up the salt and pepper shakers, as if he needed to inspect them before his food arrived. Anything to keep from looking at Cody.

"Don't worry." Cody's slurred speech indicated that he was pretty drunk. "I'll behave. Unless you think Lily would be into spanking."

"Fuck off." Wow. He'd hit a nerve. All of them.

The waitress arrived with Carson's sandwich and two more beers. She gave Cody a look of resignation. They all knew Cody would be going home with his brother tonight.

He wondered, not for the first time, what would happen when they got to be old men. A couple of crusty, washed-up bachelors reminiscing about their conquests and fighting over whose turn it was to buy the prune juice.

Cody stared at his half-empty beer. It should be his last. "I don't know what it is about her," Cody wondered aloud. "But Lily is really special."

"Yes. She is." Carson looked out over the river, memories of what he and Lily had done just upstream flooding him.

"Sure she's got a great body. That rack, mmm-mmm-mmmm." Cody was up to his usual antics, trying to get a rise out of him. "But there's something else."

"Yes. She's something else." Carson felt his chest tighten.

"She'd make a good mother." Cody sounded wistful. But he had an excuse. He was drunk. "Don't you think?"

"Yes. She'd be a really good mother." Carson took a bite of his sandwich, looking at the view as he chewed. Carson had never liked to talk about what happened to their mother. The one time they'd come to blows was an argument over whose fault it had been that she'd died.

"She wouldn't let her kids get away with crap." Cody chuckled softly. "She'd be firm. But loving. You know, so they wouldn't want to screw up. They'd want her to be proud of them."

"Our mother would've been proud of us." Carson hoped.

"She'd be proud of you." Cody drained his glass. "She'd know I was a screw-up."

"You're not a screw-up." Carson's response was automatic. Without feeling. They both knew he wasn't telling the whole truth.

"Sure I am." Cody actually sounded serious. "I've never had a relationship that lasted longer than a long weekend. Hell, most of them lasted as long as my relationship with mom." Cody heaved a sigh. "Twenty-seven minutes."

Carson flinched. Officially, the cause of her death had been ruled medical error, but each of the twins believed they had been the cause. Cody had often complained that the reason Carson was so hard on him was because he blamed Cody for their mother's death. Their father's abandonment. If he only knew that it was guilt that drove Carson to be so protective.

"I think I need another drink." Cody half-heartedly raised his hand to flag the waitress.

"I think I need to take you home." Carson stood, threw some money down on the table, and jingled his keys.

"Yes, Mommy." He let Carson lead the way, preferring to stagger behind, instead of in front of his brother.

"I expect you to be in good enough shape to go down the river with the prospective guides tomorrow." Carson held the door open.

"No problem." Cody worked at staying steady. "They're not meeting us until ten."

"Be ready by nine." Carson watched him stumble over to the truck.

"Yes, sir." Cody gave him a mock salute.

Cody had often compared him to a drill sergeant. Usually when he was pissed off about not getting his way about something. If he thought Carson was tough on him, he would have been in for a surprise if they'd joined the military instead of guide school. Maybe it would have been good for him.

* * * *

It didn't take long for Cody to drop off into a deep, if drunken, sleep. Carson hoped he'd be able to meet the prospective guides the next morning, but he had his doubts. He'd seen him drunk before. That wasn't the problem. It was seeing his brother look so...defeated that bothered him most.

He was worried. Sure, he could have chalked it up to Cody feeling sorry for himself. He'd always been a sore loser. But he couldn't know about him and Lily. They'd been discreet. Besides, he would have said something. He would have made a snide comment or a crude joke to cover up his disappointment.

Instead he'd gone on and on about how Lily would be a good mother. And then he'd started in on their mother. It was just... He needed someone to talk to. To sort out his feelings of frustration over having to babysit his older brother.

Lily's light was still on. He didn't even need to search for the key in the flowerpot. Not that he was comfortable with the idea of anyone being able to get into her house. But what right did he have to say anything? They were just lovers. Short-term lovers. She'd made it clear that she didn't mind that he was leaving soon. It was just sex. Or so she claimed. She didn't want anything more.

He didn't have a right to anything more.

"Carson, come in." Lily took in his appearance with a look of concern. "What do you need?"

The question stunned him. He hesitated before crossing her threshold. He couldn't ask too much of her.

"Do you want to talk?" Lily reached for his arm, leading him gently inside. "Do you need a drink? Or do you want to just get naked and lose ourselves in the pleasure we can give each other?"

Carson felt a smile crack through his stone-faced façade.

"Can I have all three?" He'd been weighed down for so long, until Lily came by and released the anchor.

"Sure." She led him into the kitchen. "Do you want wine or beer?"

"Either's fine." Carson didn't want to be too much trouble. "Whatever you prefer."

"Would you like a glass of wine?" Lily asked again, slowly, as if he hadn't heard her the first time. "Or would you like a beer? I'm sorry I don't have anything stronger, but I can get something, whatever you want. For next time."

"Oh, that's okay." Carson tried to remember the last time someone had cared about what he wanted. "I'll take a beer. Please."

"See, that wasn't so hard." Lily offered a warm smile, but she looked a little sad, too. "It's been hard for me to get used to asking for what I want. But it gets easier. Trust me."

"I do." Carson took the beer she offered. He trusted her more than he wanted to.

"So do you want to take these outside?" Lily took a long sip of her beer. "Or should we just get right to it?"

Carson stood there in her kitchen, wondering where to begin. He wanted to talk, but now that he was here, he didn't know what to say.

"You do want to get naked, don't you?" Lily put her arms around his waist, pulling him close, looking up at him with those mysterious eyes. Gold. Brown. Copper. All those shades mixed together. But it was what he saw behind those colors that nearly brought him to his knees. She wanted him. More than that, she wanted to take care of him.

"Oh, Lily." It took him three swallows to finish his beer. Then he set the empty bottle on the counter, lifted her in his arms, and carried her to her bedroom. He lowered her to the bed and began taking off his clothes.

"Wait." Lily sat up. "Let me undress for you."

She shoved him on the bed and switched on the bedside lamp before slowly undressing. She lifted her T-shirt over her head, letting it fall to the ground.

"You like my breasts, don't you?" Lily turned slightly, so he could get a better view.

"Yes. I do." He loved her breasts. And everything else about her.

"They like you too." Cupping her hands beneath her breasts, she lifted them, showcasing the supple curves.

She hooked her thumbs into the waistband of her pajama shorts, inching them down as she shimmied her hips, letting them fall to the floor, leaving her standing there in a tiny scrap of pink satin.

He groaned and started to reach for her.

"No, you stay there," she ordered. "I want to do this for you."

She wanted to torture him?

"Take a good look." Finally, she slipped off her panties and stood there, perfectly naked. "This is for you. All for you."

Slowly, she turned around. Letting him see every curve, every inch of her smooth skin. He'd touched every inch. Tasted every inch. But he'd never stopped to look at her this closely. The first time he saw her naked, he'd been too worried about getting her to safety. And making sure she didn't think he was some kind of creep. And every time they'd made love, he'd been so busy feeling that he hadn't stopped to look. To really appreciate how beautiful she was.

"Tell me what you want me to do to you." Lily stepped closer.

"Take off my clothes." Carson's voice was a harsh whisper.

Lily slowly removed his T-shirt, sliding it over his head. She trailed little kisses down his chest as she reached for his shorts. It seemed to take forever for her to undo the button and slide the zipper down. He was so hard he thought he might shatter if he didn't get relief soon.

She grasped his penis, stroking him tenderly. Inspecting it as if she'd just discovered some curious artifact, rare and priceless. Barely touching the sensitive skin, she traced her fingers along the entire length. She licked her lips and then lowered her mouth, brushing her lips over the tip before sliding her tongue down his shaft. Tentative, yet curious, she tasted him, drawing him deeper into her mouth.

He was pretty sure she'd never done this before.

"Lily, stop." The urgency in his voice brought her head up. He was so close to losing it.

"Am I doing it wrong?" The uncertainty in her voice just about broke his heart.

"No, baby. You're definitely not doing it wrong." He lifted her up so that she was lying on top of him. Her body lined up with his. "Kiss me."

She complied. And there was nothing tentative about this kiss. She kissed him hard and hot and hungry. When she came up for air, she smiled a devilish grin, and then moved her hips over him, drawing him inside. She started rocking back and forth, riding him. Determined to make this good for him. Wild. Uninhibited. Too fast.

Carson grabbed her hips, holding her in place.

"Slow down, baby." His breathing was ragged, so close to losing control. "Please."

She stilled. Then she shuddered, a low moan escaping her throat. He could feel the pulsing of her inner muscles as she climaxed.

Slowly, he began to thrust upward, with just the smallest movement. She squeezed, pulling him deeper. Time seemed to stand still as they moved together in slow-motion. Micro movements that suddenly burst into the most powerful orgasm he'd ever had.

She collapsed on top of him, both of them out of breath and unable to move.

Finally, she spoke. "I'm sorry."

"For what?"

"I wanted this to be special. I wanted to give you more than you gave me." She sounded like she was on the verge of tears.

He could barely breathe. "It was special." He wrapped his arms around her. "You're special. What I can't figure out is why you picked me."

"Isn't it obvious?" Lily rolled over, spooning against him. She took his hand and placed it over her left breast. "See, perfect fit."

Yes. She was a perfect fit.

He held her. Just held her. There was so much he wanted to say. So much he needed to say. He just didn't know where to begin.

How could he describe the way she made him feel? How could he tell her he loved her when he was planning on leaving in a matter of weeks?

* * * *

"You okay?" Lily didn't want to push, but he'd been so tense when he arrived. Something was bothering him. Something weighed on him like an anchor. She wanted to relieve the pressure. She wanted to comfort him. To take care of him. She wanted to love him with everything she had.

The beer had loosened the lines around his mouth. Sex had relaxed his body. Now she hoped he would talk.

"I can't move." He pulled her even closer. "I don't think I'll ever leave your bed."

"That would be great." She snuggled against him, wishing he could stay. "Until I'm arrested for kidnapping."

"I wonder how long it would take Cody to miss me?" Carson laughed softly and sighed. "He'll probably want coffee. He'll need a lot of coffee."

"What happened tonight?" Lily asked. "I take it you didn't get a chance to talk."

"He was drunk." Carson rolled over on his back, threw his right arm over his head. "He's been drunk before, of course, but this was different."

"How so?" She wanted to encourage him without prying.

"He was really down." Lily felt the tension return to his body. His muscles tightened and she could feel him withdrawing. "I think I might have made a mistake in coming here. In being with you."

Lily couldn't breathe. Was he breaking up with her? She'd known this was only temporary, but she wasn't ready to give him up just yet.

"Cody doesn't deal with disappointment very well," he continued. "I knew he wanted you. I should have stepped aside."

Lily found her voice. "It wouldn't matter. I wouldn't have slept with Cody. If you'd turned me down that night, I wouldn't have gone looking for a substitute."

She scooted away from him, put one foot on the floor, before he grabbed her arm.

"Lily. I'm sorry. I didn't mean…" He took her hand. "Please, don't go."

"This is my house. I'm not going anywhere."

"Please, Lily." He looked so desperate, so worried. "I don't have anyone else I can talk to"

"So what do you want to talk about?"

"I'm worried about Cody." She could tell it took a lot for him to admit. "He's taking your rejection harder than he should. I don't understand it."

"I never led him on." Lily tried to think of anything that she could have done differently.

"I think he's drawn to your nurturing side." Carson let his hand fall to her chest, just above her heart.

"Oh." Lily felt her head spin. "I want a baby. Not a man-child."

"That's right." Carson shifted, just enough for her to notice he was less than comfortable with the subject. "You want to have a baby."

"Yes." Lily wondered if this was a deal breaker. Not that they had made any kind of deal.

"And you're going to…" He couldn't even say the words. Was he was so repulsed by her plan?

"I'm not willing to wait." Lily could only tell him the truth. "It wouldn't be fair to start a relationship with you, or anyone else, knowing that I hope to be a mother within a year."

He didn't say anything so Lily kept talking.

"That's why this is so perfect." She hoped he wouldn't run screaming from her bed. "We can enjoy each other's company. No pressure, no demands. Just great sex."

"Really great." Carson ran his finger along her curves, sending waves of arousal throughout her body. How was it possible that she had been so completely satisfied just minutes ago, and now she was dying for his touch?

"If Cody finds out about us…" Carson tensed, his loyalties torn. "I think it will destroy him."

"So are you saying we should stop seeing each other?" He held her heart in his hands. A heart she'd never meant to give him, but it had happened anyway.

"No." He turned her, so they were facing each other, and fingered a strand of her hair, examining it as if it was the finest silk. "I just think we need to be careful that he doesn't find out. At least not until he finds a distraction."

"Or until you leave?" She brushed her lips across his chest.

He held her, stroking her skin, setting her on fire. Making her want more. Making her want to give more than just her body.

But for tonight, this was enough.

She'd worry about tomorrow, tomorrow.

Chapter 16

Carson slipped away from Lily's bed before dawn. He hated leaving her like this, but he didn't know what else he could do. He couldn't let Cody find out about them. Not like this.

He couldn't stay away from her either. He'd never known anyone like Lily. She asked nothing of him. She simply opened her arms and let him in. In her arms he'd found something he'd never had before. Give *and* take.

He prepared the coffeepot, pouring the grounds in the filter basket, adding the water and leaving a clean mug on the counter. All Lily had to do was turn it on when she got up. Maybe someday he could actually share a cup of coffee with her. Someday they could laugh together over breakfast. Someday he wouldn't have to sneak into his own home.

Maybe someday he could live his own life, without worrying about how it would affect Cody.

After quickly showering in his own bathroom, making coffee, and depositing his breakfast dishes in the dishwasher, Carson went across the road to get ready to meet with the potential guides. Maybe training new guides would give Cody something to focus on. Two of the candidates were women. Both had the right training, but Brooke seemed the more experienced of the two. She would make a good addition to the team. And she wouldn't be too much of a distraction.

Hillary on the other hand, she could be trouble. She was built, not like a raft guide, but more like a model. There had been some sparks flying between her and Cody. Not enough to dismiss her outright. She'd have to prove herself on the river. They'd all have to prove themselves on the river.

It was a little after nine and still no sign of Cody. Great. He'd have to take all four candidates out on his own. It would be nice to have a second set of eyes to observe the little things, like how each candidate did when it wasn't their turn to act as guide. Some had a hard time giving up control. They would try to guide from the front of the boat rather than wait for commands from the rear. They needed to find out who could be a team player and who would let ego get in the way. It was important to choose guides who understood that the river was ultimately in charge. A good guide would always respect that.

Carson rolled one of the rafts out to the concrete pad, silently cursing his brother for living up to his expectations. He'd hoped, but he hadn't actually expected him to actually show up this morning.

"Hey, bro, let me help you with that." Cody sauntered over around nine-fifteen. His hands were wrapped around a travel mug, presumably filled with coffee.

"You're late." Was it on purpose?

"Yeah, well. I'm here now." Cody sipped his coffee like he had nothing better to do.

"Help me get this boat in the truck," Carson ordered. "Or are you too hungover?"

"I'm a little slow, but I'll manage." Cody drained his cup before pitching in to help. "I think she gave me double shots last night, instead of singles."

"She was just trying to get into your pants."

"Yeah, I figured that." Cody gave him a crooked smile. Like he could use his charm to get away with anything. "She's cool and all, but I just couldn't."

"Yeah, there comes a point where too much alcohol defeats the purpose."

"No, man, that's not what I meant." Cody grabbed the other side of the raft and together they lifted it into the truck. "I could have; I just didn't want to. She's hot, but I don't know. She's a little too easy."

"You've been with plenty of women like her before." Carson went back for the second raft.

"Yeah, but I've raised my standards."

"Since when?"

"Since when?" Cody shook his head, like the answer was obvious. "Since I realized there's something better out there. Someone better."

Lily. He had to be referring to Lily.

"Look, I know you don't think I'm good enough for Lily." Cody put his foot on top of the rolled up raft. "But I could be."

Oh please. If he wanted to prove anything, he wouldn't have gone to the Argo alone and started doing shots—singles or doubles.

Maybe this was the time to come clean. Confess. Admit that he and Lily were lovers. Maybe even in love.

Brooke, one of the potential guides, appeared while they were loading the raft into the back of the truck. "Hi. I know I'm a little early, but I wanted to see if you needed help getting ready for put-in. I know there's a lot more to being a guide than paddling down the river."

He had to give her points for enthusiasm. And for helping him delay the conversation he really didn't want to have.

Cody took charge. A refreshing change. "Sure, let me show you the equipment shed."

The three of them had the truck loaded in plenty of time to meet the other guides who would compete for the job. They could get away with hiring two more guides. Three would be better. But if they really liked all four, they could manage. It would depend on how many hours they were all looking for, and what kind of schedules they were willing to accept. Flexibility was important.

With the sudden increase in temperatures, business had picked up fairly quickly. One advantage of their location was that they booked quite a few last-minute trips. If the weather heated up, people started thinking about getting out on the water. They could check the website for availability and make plans as short as one day in advance.

If he wanted to do a private trip on the Grand Canyon, he'd have to enter a lottery. Same thing for the Yampa in Utah. If he wanted to raft either of those rivers, he'd either have to wait or pay to go on a commercial trip. Or he could commit to work for Epic Adventures in Utah. If he really liked the change of pace, he could transfer to another river. Epic had outfitters in Utah, Colorado, and Idaho. If Cody could keep things running here, Carson could do whatever he wanted. Wherever he wanted.

He just wasn't sure that's what he wanted anymore.

Brooke took the first shift acting as guide. It was weird being a passenger, and letting someone else be in charge of the raft. The last time he'd sat back and let someone else guide had been on the trip with Lily. Back when all he'd wanted was to help her overcome her fear. Yeah. Right. That was all he'd wanted.

Carson needed to focus on the job at hand, not start wondering how things would play out with him and Lily.

Brooke was a skilled guide. He was able to relax and not feel the need to jump in and give directions. She navigated the first two rapids with ease.

"What can you tell me about this last rapid?" Cody asked. The question was aimed more at Brooke, but Hillary answered him first.

"It's a Class Two rapid?" She didn't seem too sure of herself.

"Class Two rapids are classified as having moderate difficulty." Brooke chimed in. "The rapids are usually pretty straightforward, easily maneuvered without need for scouting."

"Great." Carson was impressed with her knowledge and confidence. "Next up we have a Class Three rapid."

"Oh, I know this. It's considered difficult." Hillary wasn't about to be ignored. "Except for experienced guides like you two. You probably could run a Class Three in your sleep."

"Class Three rapids contain difficult passages, requiring scouting unless the guide is very familiar with the river under the same conditions." Brooke continued to impress with her expertise. "Most of the passengers will find these rapids exciting, but not terrifying. They will remember these as the big ones. These are the rapids they tell all their friends about."

"True," Cody agreed. "What about the designation of the American River?"

"The American River is considered a Class Three," Hillary answered. "But the guides, and especially the owners of Swift River, are in a class by themselves."

"Now where did I hear that?" Brooke couldn't quite keep the sarcasm from her voice. "Oh, yeah, the website."

Okay, ladies. Time to put the claws away.

Brooke maneuvered the rapid with ease. She was good, but she might want to rein in the sarcasm. Some days, the toughest part of the job was dealing with tourists who wanted to know if the water was recycled after each trip.

"Okay, Hillary, you're up." Cody extended a hand to the blonde, while Brooke seamlessly took the other woman's position at the front of the raft.

Hillary took over the guide's position at the back of the boat. She was a little too quiet in giving the commands, but Brooke and the other guides seemed to anticipate the directions so they made it through the first rapid, a Class Two, without incident.

The next rapid was more of a challenge. A large rock split the river right down the middle. It wasn't easy to sit back and let her determine if she would take the right or left passage. If she didn't make a decision soon, they would head straight for...

Whap. They hit the rock dead on. Brooke flew from the raft and Hillary started to panic.

"Oh-my-god. Oh-my-god." She stood up and would have fallen in the river too, if Cody hadn't dragged her back into the boat. He grabbed his paddle and took charge of the raft. They were lucky they hadn't wrapped. But she'd managed to hit the rock and bounce off. "I'm so sorry. I'm so sorry."

"Brooke will be fine." Carson saw her swimming toward the eddy and Cody steered the raft toward the bank so they could pick her up.

"Well, that was refreshing." Brooke laughed as she climbed back into the boat.

"I am so sorry." Hillary sounded on the verge of tears.

"Hey, it's cool." Brooke got situated. "Now I can relate to the passengers better if they get dumped."

"You've never fallen out before?" Cody asked.

"Not since the first day of guide school." Brooke undid her ponytail, squeezed the excess water out of her hair and then put it back up. "When was the last time you took an involuntary swim?"

"I honestly don't remember." Carson hoped he hadn't just jinxed himself.

"It's been awhile." Cody had never been dumped, but no guide wanted to test their fate by acknowledging their luck. They never said they hadn't wrapped or flipped or popped a tube. If pushed, they'd say they hadn't done it…yet.

Hillary didn't have a lot to say after that. She was rattled, and even more timid in her commands on the next rapid, which fortunately was barely a Class Two. The raft would have practically steered itself if the six of them weren't paddling along.

Cody excused Hillary and one of the other guide candidates took over for the next few rapids. Gavin was competent, confident, and congenial. He threw out enough corny jokes along with his commands that Carson was feeling pretty good about adding him to the team.

Jake was the last to take command. He was pretty laid back, and he had plenty of experience. Carson hoped Cody would be willing to give Brooke, Gavin, and Jake the job. With all three of them working this summer, they would have plenty of coverage, and Carson would be free to leave.

The second to last rapid was the big one. The one everyone talked about. The one the photo shops set up their cameras by to sell action shots of each of the rafters as they went by.

Cody took over and gave them a good ride. Hillary squealed like a game show contestant who'd just won the big prize, and Brooke stood up to give him a high five at the end.

They got to take out at the end of the river and Brooke immediately got to work unloading and dragging gear out of the way. Gavin and

Jake weren't about to be shown up by a woman, so they also did their share. Hillary held back, as if she wanted a private word in with Cody. Carson pretended to be busy with the boat, so he could listen in on what she had to say.

"Look, I know I messed up back there," Hillary said. "But maybe we could discuss it over dinner."

"I don't think so." Cody didn't sound at all interested. This was new. "Besides, I need to discuss any final hiring with my brother. And we'll get back to you in the next few days.

"Oh, okay." She sounded disappointed, as if she knew she wasn't going to get the job.

She walked off, without helping bring the boat or any of the equipment up. Carson definitely wasn't going to reconsider.

"So, that was fun." Brooke sounded like she was holding her tongue. He could tell she hadn't been impressed with Hillary even before she'd tossed her into the river.

"You did a great job." Cody helped her drag the boat up to the grassy area where they would let it dry before deflating and rolling it up for storage. "You'll need to see Lily in the office. She has some paperwork for you to fill out. You'll want to come back this evening and meet Fisher. If you decide to live onsite, she'll be your roommate."

"Cool." Brooke sounded a little surprised. Like she expected Hillary to get the job instead. "I mean, thank you. I'm really excited to be working here. Truly."

"Good." Cody flashed his lopsided grin. The one that made Hillary giggle. "Welcome aboard."

He pointed her in the direction of the office and finished gathering the equipment.

"So you just offered her the job right on the spot?" Carson agreed with the decision, but couldn't help but give his brother a hard time. "What about the others?"

"Either of the guys will be fine." Cody shrugged. "But I don't think Hillary is Swift River material."

"I think you're right about that."

"Wow. Did I just hear you say I'm right about something?" Cody placed his hand over his chest, as if he was faking a heart attack. "And with no witnesses around."

Carson just rolled his eyes. Not that Cody would notice, since they were both wearing sunglasses. "So why not hire both Jake and Gavin?"

"Sure. The more the merrier." Cody acted like he didn't care. "I'll have Lily print out three copies of the hiring paperwork."

He headed for the office before Carson could stop him.

* * * *

"Hey, have you seen Cody?" Carson had just come in off the river. Sun-kissed, a little sweaty, he looked sexy as ever.

"You just missed him," Lily said. "He was in making sure I got the paperwork on the new guides you hired. Trying to help out a little more."

"I guess." Carson shrugged. "It will be good for him to train a few new guides. It's what he does best."

"You still want him to do more, though," Lily guessed.

"Well, there's so much he doesn't even think about." Carson stretched his neck and shoulders.

"Maybe you should make a list." Lily stood and reached up to rub his shoulders. "Sometimes it's more helpful to be specific about what you want. Instead of saying 'you don't help around the house enough,' it's better to specifically point out that putting dirty socks in the hamper makes it easier to wash them."

"So your ex left his dirty socks on the floor?" Carson teased. "That's it, I'm going after him."

"This isn't about me." Lily dropped her hands. "Or my ex. It's about you communicating with your brother. If he doesn't do enough around here, you need to tell him. Or find someone else who can do the work."

"I do tell him." Carson sat down on the desk. "But he doesn't get it."

"Well, maybe he needs to focus on what he's good at." Lily hoped she wasn't crossing a line here. "Let him take care of the customers, and let the rest of us worry about the rest. I'm serious about you making a list. Write down everything that needs to be done around here. I'll take on what I can. I'm sure Fisher would be willing to help out."

"Thanks." Carson grabbed a pen and walked over to the copier to pull a piece of paper from the tray. He sat down at his desk and started on his list.

"Wow," he said after about fifteen minutes. "Even I had no idea how much was involved in running this place."

"It's a lot of work." Lily smiled to herself. "Would you have gone into this business if you'd known what was involved?"

"It was an opportunity I couldn't pass up." Carson looked up from his list. "One *we* couldn't pass up. Can you picture Cody working in some corporate office? Or even working for someone else?"

"Not really." Lily could see him in sales maybe. "But I can't picture you working as a suit either. What did you really want to be when you grew up?"

"The usual. A professional ballplayer. Cop." Carson sounded so casual, almost too casual. "Maybe join the Marines."

"I could see you as a Marine. Serving your country." Lily smiled. "You'd look great in the uniform."

"Do you think they'd still take me?" He sounded like he was only half joking.

"I'm sure you'd pass the physical." Lily couldn't help but run her hands across his shoulders. "You're in great shape."

"I work hard." Carson shrugged. "Comes with the territory."

"So why didn't you enlist?" Lily asked. "Did you fall in love with the river and give up your dream?"

"That's part of it," Carson said. "But I couldn't leave Cody behind. He never would have made it past boot camp."

"No, I can't picture him in camouflage." Lily perched on the arm of his chair. "Tie-dye is more like it."

"Are you calling my brother a hippie?"

"No." Lily ran her fingers through his hair. "But his hair is about a quarter of an inch longer than yours."

"You've been running your fingers through my brother's hair?" Carson tensed. A little bit jealous?

"No. I was trying for a joke." Lily patted his hair. "You don't need to worry."

But worrying was what he did. He could wander to the far corners of the earth, but that wouldn't keep him from worrying about those he cared about.

Chapter 17

The last two weeks of May flew by. Carson managed to take care of all the needed repairs and routine maintenance. Barring any unforeseen accidents or natural disasters, there was no reason for him to worry about Swift River Adventure Company and Resort. Lily took care of all the clerical and financial details of running the business. She also had a way of getting Cody to chip in. He had taken on daily garbage and recycling collection, making the weekly Costco run to pick up supplies and store inventory that wasn't on the delivery schedule.

Carson should be thrilled that Cody was taking a more active role in the day-to-day operations. He would be thrilled, except for the nagging suspicion that he was only doing it because Lily asked him to.

He struggled with the desire to tell Cody to back the hell off—Lily was his. But if Cody knew that, he might start slacking off again. Carson didn't want the extra work to fall on Lily's shoulders. She'd done enough already.

Like every night the last few weeks, Carson waited for his brother to go to bed. When he was sure Cody was asleep, he snuck out and drove over to Lily's. She'd given him a key so he could let himself in. Tonight, like many nights past, she was already in bed. Waiting for him.

He undressed by the light of the moon streaming through her windows. Since she had no neighbors, she preferred to leave the windows bare. She'd told him about the decorative security bars on her house in Sacramento, the heavy drapes installed by her decorator, and the electronic alarms on all her windows. She gushed about the privacy and freedom she got from living out in the woods. He would prefer she had a security alarm, especially since she had the habit of sleeping in the nude.

"You're late." Lily rolled over as he slid naked between the sheets.

"Sorry. Extra innings." Carson pulled her into an embrace. "Cody wouldn't go to bed. He was pretty pumped up."

"We could just tell him about us." Lily pressed her body against his. A perfect fit.

"I know." Carson felt the burden. The secret had grown, threatening to suck some of the pleasure from his relationship with Lily. "But then he'd stop working so hard to please you."

"He's working to please you." Lily had been fine with keeping their affair a secret in the beginning, but he could tell her patience was starting to wear thin.

"I don't want to talk about Cody." Carson stroked her skin, touched her in the way he'd learned she liked. "I just want to make love to you."

"No." Lily rolled over, offering her back to him.

"No?" His heart seized up. His throat could barely get the word out.

"Not unless you plan to stay." Lily turned around to face him. "Stay past sunrise. Stay for breakfast."

"Okay." Relief washed over him that it wasn't their relationship that was stagnating. Just the routine.

Lily sat up, a big smile on her face. "Really? You'll stay? We'll have breakfast together?"

"Yes. I'll stay." Carson knew it was time. He had to offer her more than just sex. "I'd love to have breakfast with you. Anything but pancakes."

"Why not pancakes?"

"It's just something I used to make for Cody's overnight guests. It was sort of my specialty."

"Why didn't he make them?" Lily asked. "I mean, pancakes are pretty easy. Anyone can make them."

"Yeah. Unless you're trying to avoid someone. Then you send your brother into the kitchen."

"Wow," Lily said. What could she be thinking? "So did Cody make pancakes for your dates?"

"No. I could take care of my own guests." But he didn't take care of her. Not in the way he'd like.

"That's why you set up the coffee before you leave?" Lily's voice held a note of bitterness. "Because pancakes would get cold?"

"I don't like leaving you." Carson felt his world slipping away. "I hate leaving you. I do. I just don't know what to do. I don't know how to break it to Cody."

"Wow. I feel like I'm in the middle of a threesome, only..." She was going to send him packing.

"I love you." His words slipped out. Part desperation, part relief at finally being able to admit it. "I know this was supposed to be a casual thing, but I've managed to fall in love with you."

Silence.

Carson thought his heart would stop. Or the world would stop turning. Or all the air would be sucked from the atmosphere.

"I've managed to fall in love with you, too." Lily placed a soft, gentle kiss on his forehead.

That kiss led to another, not so gentle, not so innocent. It was the kind of kiss that would lead to other things. And it did.

* * * *

Carson woke up to the smell of bacon cooking. He'd slept in. And no wonder, they'd made love once, twice, three times throughout the course of the night. Each time more intense, more meaningful than the last.

He pulled on a pair of shorts and stumbled to the bathroom. After cleaning up and brushing his teeth with the toothbrush she'd given him that second night, he went into the kitchen to help with breakfast.

"Smells delicious." Carson wrapped his arms around Lily's waist. "What can I do to help?"

"You can crack the eggs." Lily was busy dicing potatoes. She had a hot skillet ready with onions already sautéing over a medium-high flame.

They worked together, preparing a hearty breakfast, with laughter and kisses and playfulness that Carson had never experienced before. This was what it was all about. This was the life he'd never known he'd wanted.

He went to the fridge to retrieve the orange juice. His eye strayed to the appointment card tacked to the door with a fruit shaped magnet. The card was from Foothills Fertility Clinic. Her appointment scheduled for June 17. He'd be gone by then. And when he returned, she'd be ... He couldn't think about it.

"Carson, are you okay?" Lily put her hands on his shoulder.

"Yeah, I guess I forgot what I came over here for." He shook his head, trying to clear the disturbing image of her lying on a table, feet in stirrups, awaiting insemination. "Orange juice, right?"

"Yeah." Lily wrapped her arms around his waist. "You do like orange juice?"

"Sure."

"Look, if you're worried I'm going to beg you stay, don't." Lily reached around him and grabbed the carton of juice. "I mean, I'll miss you. I'll miss you like crazy, but I understand you made these plans before you even met me. I can't just expect you to change your mind because of me."

"So, you want me to leave?"

"No." Lily poured the juice into two short glasses. "But I won't make you choose. I understand that you need to complete this journey. I just hope we can pick up where we left off when you get back."

"Lily. You're amazing."

"Stop."

"No, it's true," Carson said. "You're so amazing, and wonderful, and I love you."

"I love you too." She sounded a little scared. Like she knew he was going to drop something heavy on her and shatter this little domestic bliss they were sharing.

"You're too good for me." Carson pulled her against him. "You are so giving and strong and you haven't asked one thing of me, except for this breakfast. Which is perfect, by the way. Just like you are. And I'm going to sound like a completely selfish Neanderthal."

Lily didn't say anything. She simply stood there. Letting him hold her. Letting him touch her, as if for the last time.

"Lily." He turned her around and placed his hands on her flat tummy. "I love you. I love you so much."

"I love you too." Lily's words held just an edge of sadness. An edge of fear.

"I can't believe how lucky I am to have found you."

"But?" Lily started to tremble.

"I can't do it." Carson wrapped his arms tighter around her waist. "I can't think about some other man's sperm inside you. Another man's baby inside you."

"Oh, is that all?" She let out a nervous little laugh.

"Look, I know you made plans before you met me. And you've had this dream." Carson felt a lump rise in his throat. "It's not my place to ask you to give that up. It's not even my place to ask you to wait for me."

She leaned against him. Was her heart breaking, too?

"The thing is..." Carson turned her around. He had to look into her eyes. "I don't know what scares me more—losing you, or being a father."

* * * *

This was exactly the kind of situation Lily's plan was supposed to avoid. Her decision to use a donor was supposed to simplify things.

"We don't have to decide anything right now." She led him to the table. "We do have to eat. I finally get to have breakfast with you. I don't want it to get cold."

Carson sat.

"It's simply a consultation." Lily wanted to ease his mind. And hers. "I'm just going to go over my options."

"What about my options?" He took a bite.

"You're leaving in what? Two? Three days?" Lily forced herself to eat. "Let's enjoy these last few moments together. The future can wait."

"How long?"

"I don't know. But taking some time apart will give us both time to think about it. I didn't expect to meet you. I didn't expect to fall in love with you. And I certainly didn't expect to include you in this decision."

"Well, I'm included." Carson's voice had an edge. Bitter. Angry. Frustrated. "Whether we expected it or not. I either have to go along with you, or get out."

"You make it sound like it's my way or the highway."

"Well, you're not going to suddenly decide you don't want children, are you?"

"No." Her heart started to break. What if he didn't? Ever? "But I don't need to have them today. Or tomorrow. Or even next week."

"These potatoes are delicious." Manspeak for subject is closed.

They finished their breakfast, making small talk, discussing details about work. She almost wished they had stayed on the topic of Cody. At least she knew where she stood where he was concerned. Sure, Carson was jealous of any time she spent with him. But that was nothing compared to the possessiveness she felt when Carson put his hands on her abdomen. He was almost territorial. Like a wild animal. The kind that would eat the young of another male.

What did it all mean? Would his biological urge to spread his seed overrule his reluctance to settle down? She knew he had some issues with his father. She wished they could talk about it. But she couldn't push. He was getting ready to leave. If she wasn't careful he wouldn't want to come back.

"It seems like a waste to take two cars." Carson stood in the doorway, keys in hand. "Do you want to ride with me?"

A peace offering. Lily had never been more relieved in her life.

"Yeah, sure." Lily grabbed her purse. "Why waste the gas?"

He leaned over and placed a kiss on her cheek. They were still okay. For now. She'd have six weeks to figure out what she wanted more. A baby? Or Carson? In a perfect world, she'd have both. But if it came down to making a choice, what would she choose?

* * * *

Carson took the last curve before the entrance to Swift River Resort slow, like always. His eye strayed to the fence he'd repaired several times over the last several years.

"See the fence there, right before the turnoff?" Carson pointed to where the wood was new. "Cody took out that section the summer before our senior year."

"Really?" Lily said. "Were you in the car with him?"

"No. He'd been partying along the river upstream and took that last corner too fast. Plowed right into the fence." He hadn't thought about that night, except when some teenager or tourist took that same corner too fast. "Cody called me to come get him. He knew our dad wouldn't help. I went to pick him up, hoping I could get there before the cops and pass the sobriety test for him. But Travis, the former owner of the resort, made us an offer we couldn't refuse. He let us work off the damage."

"Why did you do the work if Cody was the one who wrecked the fence?"

"Because he's my brother. I wanted to keep an eye on him. Make sure he didn't screw up." Carson pulled into the long driveway and made his way to the parking area behind the boat barn. "I didn't know it at the time, but that night changed our lives. We fixed the fence, did maintenance around the property, and eventually made our way to the river.

"Cody loved the action, the adrenaline of braving the rapids."

"And what about you?" Lily asked. "What do you love about the river?"

He didn't even have to think about it. "It felt like home. It's where I belong."

Lily didn't ask why he needed to leave the one place that felt like home, and he was grateful for that. At the moment, he couldn't answer that question. He just knew he hadn't been happy. He hadn't been happy for some time and it was easier to blame Cody than to look in the mirror and find out why. It was easier to blame Cody because it was convenient. He was always there.

And then all of a sudden, Cody was there. He'd marched over to the truck. Grabbed the driver's side door handle.

And dragged his brother from the vehicle.

"What the...?" Carson stumbled to the ground.

Cody's fist connected with Carson's jaw.

A direct hit. He cocked to hit him again, but Carson ducked out of the way and Cody spun around. Carson's fist landed squarely on his nose. He heard a horrifying, yet satisfying crunch and Cody stumbled backward crashing into the side of the truck. He wiped his forearm across his face. Blood dripped out of his nose. Broken? Must be. Cody dove for Carson, but he dodged him again.

In the distance, he heard a female voice begging them to stop. Lily's concern distracted him and Cody rushed at him, slamming Carson into the truck. He got off one or two good punches, in the gut. Carson hit him again, but he avoided his face this time.

Cody reared back, ready to strike, but he was hit with a blast of cold water. Fisher stood behind Carson with the hose aimed straight at him.

"You too, Fisher?" Cody shook the water out of his eyes. "I thought you, at least, were on my side."

"I am." She stopped the spray, but held the hose at the ready. "I don't want either of you getting hurt."

Too late.

"I'm outta here." Cody stormed over to his truck and yanked the door open. "You can all go to hell." He hopped into his truck and without another word, he tore out of the driveway.

Carson ran his hand across his mouth. Blood smeared across his knuckles. From his mouth or his hand? He couldn't be sure.

"Oh, Carson!" Lily was at his side. "Are you okay? No, you're hurt."

"I'm fine." Carson licked his lip, tasting the sharp tang of his own blood. He was shocked. What the hell had provoked Cody to come at him like that? That kind of rage could only come from one place. Jealousy. No, it was more than that. It was primal. Animalistic. Territorial.

"You're bleeding. Let me help you." She reached for him, to wipe away the blood. To comfort him.

"You've done enough." Carson moved away, out of her reach. He grabbed for the door of his truck. With his back turned he said, "You slept with him, didn't you?"

"What?" Lily's voice cracked. "I can't believe you'd even ask me that."

"I can't believe you won't answer." Betrayal sliced through him. And here he'd thought she loved him. But she'd been playing him for a fool.

He hopped up into the cab, yanked the door shut, and started the ignition. He couldn't look at her, except to see that she'd stepped back enough for him to drive away.

He'd go after Cody. Maybe his brother would tell him the truth.

He'd already said enough. With his fists.

He wanted to know when? Where? How often? But most of all he wanted to know why? Why would she sleep with both of them? Had she been unable to resist Cody's charms? Or maybe she'd been using them both. He had no idea how much artificial insemination cost. Maybe she was hedging her bets. If she didn't know which of them was the father...

What was he thinking? Lily would never do that.

And yet, he'd accused her of sleeping with Cody. What if he was right? Could he look at her and not picture Cody making love to her? Could he touch her and not think about Cody's hands all over her? Could he love her even if she'd been with the one man he had to share everything else with?

But what if he was wrong?

He'd lose her either way.

* * * *

Lily stood in disbelief as she watched Carson drive away. Cody had come out of nowhere, angry and violent. It was a side she'd never imagined she'd see in either of them. Carson had done a fine job of defending himself. She would have thought he was defending her, too, except for the way he'd spoken to her after Cody took off. He made it sound like the fight was entirely her fault.

Maybe it was. She should have insisted Carson tell Cody sooner. She should have done more to get the two of them to talk.

Now they were both gone.

All she could do was wait. And hope that they had a chance to calm down before Carson caught up with Cody.

She hated this helpless feeling. The man she loved had been in a fight. A no-holds-barred fistfight. She'd never seen anything like it. The blood. The rage. The primal nature of the fight. Two male animals competing over a female. She was the female.

"You okay?" Fisher wound the hose and stood next to Lily, shaking her head.

"Thanks for getting the hose." Lily was grateful for her quick thinking. "Who knows what would have happened if you hadn't blasted them."

"Can you believe those two?"

"No." Lily was pretty shaken up. She'd finally been able to share a breakfast with Carson, and it was about ready to come back up. "Tell me they fight like that all the time. That they'll be back in a half an hour, laughing, with their arms around each other."

"I don't know." Fisher put her arm around Lily's shoulder. "I've never seen either one of them like that."

"Great." Lily's heart sank. She leaned against her friend. At least she knew if she fell over, Fisher was strong enough to pull her back up.

"Hey, it'll be okay." Fisher gave her a quick squeeze. "They're guys. I'm sure they'll get over it."

"I hope you're right." Lily straightened. "I really hope you're right."

"Until then, it looks like it's up to us women to hold things together." Fisher got right to work. She took charge of the guides while Lily went into the office to keep things running.

Chapter 18

It wasn't until late afternoon that Carson returned. He barely glanced at Lily as he slid into his office chair, a look of weary resignation on his face.

"Fisher and the new guides got off without a hitch," Lily informed him, hopeful the news would relieve some of his burden. "I think they'll be able to cover until Cody gets back."

"Sure." Carson booted up his computer, drumming his fingers on the desk as he waited for it to come to life.

Lily could only imagine what Carson must be feeling. But he didn't need to tell her he was worried. It showed in every line on his face, in his posture, and in his complete lack of emotion.

"The invoice for the new boats came in." Over seventeen thousand dollars. Money that was sitting securely in the bank account, and not in the hands of the former bookkeeper.

"Go ahead and pay it in full." Carson didn't even glance up from his computer.

"I can do that." She clicked on the icon to pay the invoice. After loading the check stock in the printer, she ran the day's payouts.

She wanted to do more. To put her arms around him and assure him that everything would be all right. But every time she approached him, he would back away. Did he honestly believe she'd slept with Cody? Or was he just so worried that he couldn't let anyone in? Either way it frustrated Lily to know that the time when he needed her most, he shut her out. That hurt even more than the accusation that she'd been with Cody. A lot more.

Lily placed the checks in front of Carson, ready for his signature.

Carson flexed his right hand and groaned.

"Does your hand still hurt?" Lily noticed the scratches on his knuckles. The faint bruise under his left eye.

"I'm fine." He shook his hand and reached for a pen to sign the checks.

"Sure." Only a few scratches, an almost-black eye, and maybe some bruises on his ribs where he'd been thrown against his truck. But Lily was more concerned about the injuries she couldn't see. He was hurt by his brother's actions, even more so by his disappearance.

Carson cursed under his breath.

"I'm sure Cody is fine, too."

Carson looked up at her then, with a look of pure anguish on his face.

"He's probably off somewhere licking his wounds, and when he gets back the two of you can talk."

"I have nothing to say to him."

"Really? You think that will help?" Lily wanted to grab him. Shake some sense into him, but he'd been physically assaulted enough for one day. "Maybe if you'd talked to him, told him about…"

"He didn't want to hear it. Cody's used to getting his way. And when he doesn't, he throws a fit. He's such a child."

"Yeah." She didn't say it, but Cody wasn't the only one behaving like a child.

Lily stuffed the payments into the envelopes, ran them through the postage meter and placed them in the outgoing mail tray. "Well, I'm done here for the day. Let me know if you hear from Cody."

"Unless you hear from him first." He flexed his hand again. Was it still hurting, or did he want to hit something else?

With a heavy heart, Lily walked out of the office. It was only once she got to the parking lot that she realized she didn't have her car. Well, she wasn't going to go back to ask Carson for a ride. She'd just have to wait for Fisher to get off the river, and hope she would be willing to drive her home.

* * * *

The weekend passed without any sign of Cody. Tahoe was the obvious choice, but that had been a bust. Carson couldn't imagine where he could have gone. Vegas, maybe, but the only way to track him for sure would be if he used company cards for gas. He'd log on to the bank's website when he got into the office.

Carson parked his truck and made his way inside.

"Any word?" Lily surprised him by already sitting at her desk. She'd surprised him by not walking out on him, too, after he'd accused her of sleeping with Cody.

"No. I was thinking he might have used a company card for gas." Carson approached his desk with caution. He'd been a fool. If she had been with Cody, she wouldn't be here now. She'd be off with him, wherever. She certainly wouldn't be here, saving his ass, despite the way he'd treated her.

"I already checked." Lily shook her head.

"Not surprising." Carson ran his fingers through his hair. "He always took pride in the fact that he could pay cash for most things. Or with his debit card anyway."

"Does he get his bank statements through the mail?" Lily asked hopefully.

"I think he accesses everything through his phone."

"Maybe he didn't take it, maybe that's why we can't get a hold of him."

"I already searched his room. The whole house." Carson didn't have a clue to where Cody could have gone. The only thing missing was a duffel bag, a few T-shirts and shorts, and his life jacket, but it had probably been in his truck when he'd torn out of there.

"What can I do?" Lily asked.

"Nothing." Carson paced the room. "I feel so helpless. I've never gone more than a day without talking to him. Even when we fought…"

"I'm sure he's just cooling off." Lily stayed in her seat. "Maybe he's embarrassed about his behavior."

"I shouldn't have been so selfish."

"You're entitled to a life of your own." Lily sounded a little hurt. "And Cody's entitled to a life of his own. I think you knew that. That's why you planned your trip."

"Oh, no. I completely forgot." Carson stopped in the middle of the room. "They were expecting me. Great. One more person I've failed."

"I'll call them." Lily picked up the phone. "I'll tell them you had a family emergency. I'm sure they'll understand."

He gave her the number and walked outside. He couldn't listen to her make excuses for him. How could he have messed up so completely? All he'd wanted was a little bit of space. What had she called it? A life of his own. Now he had a missing brother, an estranged lover, and a soon-to-be-former friend short a guide for the summer.

                                    * * * *

"Epic Adventures, this is Kayla." A cheerful voice picked up on the other end. "How can I help you?"

"My name is Lily Price, I'm calling for Carson Swift."

"Oh my God, we just love Carson!" Kayla gushed over the phone. "From the minute he got here Saturday night, I don't think we've stopped laughing. He's going to be a great addition to our team. It's going to be really hard to let him go at the end of the season."

"So, Carson is there? Now?" Lily was confused. Until she realized that Cody had taken his brother's place. He must have found out about Carson's plans and that was what set him off.

"Yeah, he's out on the river right now, making final preparations for our first trip tomorrow. He'll be out of touch for five days. Did you want me to send a message to him?"

"No, that's okay. I'm glad to know he's arrived. He hadn't checked in with his brother, so I wanted to follow up." Lily hoped she didn't sound too flustered. "Thank you."

She hung up, relieved Cody was safe, but wondered how to tell Carson that Cody was pretending to be him. It could make the tension between the two brothers even worse.

How much worse could it be, though, than the two of them fighting, drawing blood? They'd both been so angry. And she'd never been so scared.

She hoped finding out that Cody was alive and well would make up for the fact that he was off on the adventure Carson was supposed to have taken.

Would he be relieved? Would not having to worry about his brother's whereabouts bring him back to her? The past few days had been miserable. He'd barely spoken to her, only when necessary to conduct business. She wondered if he'd eaten much since the breakfast they'd shared. It seemed a lifetime ago, when for one brief moment, Lily had been perfectly happy. If only it could have lasted a little longer.

Sure, she'd been ready for a separation, but it was to be a physical one. A temporary one. She'd been prepared to miss him while he was off finding himself in the desert. She wasn't prepared to miss him when he was in the same room.

At least she now knew where Cody was. Hopefully the knowledge would bring Carson back from where he'd shut himself up, hiding from her. Hiding from what they had.

She found him just outside the office, not far from where he had Cody had fought.

Please, let everything be all right.

* * * *

"Good news." Lily came up behind him and placed her hand on his arm, offering comfort he didn't deserve. "Cody is there."

"Where?"

"I talked to the gal at Epic. She said he got there Saturday." Lily sounded excited. Happy. Like everything was going to be just fine. "He's out on the river so he won't be able to call for five days. But he's safe. He took your place."

"But how did he...?" Cody must have found out about his plans. Somehow. "Did you tell him?"

"No. Of course not." Lily's smile faded with the accusation. "He must have found out some other way. But that's not important. The important thing is that we know where he is."

"Right."

"I'm sorry you didn't get to go." Lily touched him again. Her touch was so gentle. So caring. So undeserved.

"I shouldn't have made the plans in the first place. I shouldn't have kept it from him." Carson stepped away. He couldn't let her touch him. He couldn't take her comfort. "I meant to tell him the day we met, but I got sidetracked."

"I'm sorry for that," Lily said.

"No. You didn't do anything wrong. I'm the one who should be sorry. I messed everything up."

"Carson. Don't" Lily's voice was soft. Gentle. "There's nothing wrong with wanting to separate from Cody. I think he wants it too. That's why he left." She sighed. "Yeah, you should have talked about it. But you're both so...so...*male*. You couldn't say anything. So you fought. When he gets back, you'll make up. And everything will be fine."

"Everything will not be fine." How could she think that? Even as kids they'd never fought like that. Had never gotten physical to the point of drawing blood. "I've screwed everything up. Cody's not speaking to me, which is fine. But he's not speaking to Fisher either."

"He'll come around." Lily's confidence was unnerving. "He just thought she was on your side by breaking up the fight. He'll realize she was only trying to help."

"I think I broke his nose." Carson flexed his right hand, the memory still fresh in his mind. "I heard a distinct crunch."

"Then it will be easier for everyone to tell the two of you apart." Lily smiled, trying to relieve the tension. Trying to get him to smile.

"You didn't sleep with him." How could he even have thought that?

"No. Of course not." Her voice was soft. Understanding. Forgiving.

"Well, then I truly am an asshole."

"No, you're not." She reached for him.

"Yes. I am." Carson pulled away. "I don't understand why you're still here."

"You need me." She stood close to him, close but not touching. It was like she knew if he let her touch him, he'd be sunk. Unable to walk away.

"You could do better." Couldn't she see that?

"I disagree."

"Look, I appreciate all you've done." Why wasn't she running for the hills? Or the valley? She was so smart and talented and faithful.

"I'm not going anywhere."

"I'll understand."

"I'm not going anywhere," she repeated.

"You can give yourself vacation pay or whatever." Couldn't she see that he would only hurt her?

"I'm not leaving." He could hear the frustration in her voice as Lily turned to go back into the office. "You'll just have to deal with that."

He could deal with her leaving. He knew all about being left behind. He considered himself something of an expert. He didn't have any idea how to deal with her loving him. Standing by him. Continuing to come in and put their issues aside so their business could keep running.

No. It wasn't their business. It was his business. And he'd be sunk without her. She'd saved him more than once. And he'd repaid her with jealousy. Accusations. And by shutting her out.

* * * *

Fisher declared an emergency girls' night after finding out that Cody was safe and sound and offering his services on another river. She'd expressed both relief and anger, along with a need to blow off some steam and discuss what it was about men that drove all women crazy.

Lily offered to drive, she didn't feel like drinking much tonight anyway.

"I can't believe him." Fisher drained her beer in three swallows. "Where does he get off worrying everyone like that?" She turned her head to look for the waitress.

"Here, have mine." Beer just didn't taste very good to Lily for some reason.

"Thanks." Fisher took the glass from Lily and gulped down almost half of the drink. "I could just strangle him. He picks a fight, gets his ass kicked. I mean, did he honestly not see that you and Carson are together?"

"*Were* together." Lily reached for her water glass, and her stomach pitched at the realization that it was over. Even though he no longer thought she'd slept with Cody, he still blamed her for the fight.

"Oh, no. What happened?" Fisher set her glass down and reached across the table to pat Lily's hand.

"He accused me of sleeping with Cody."

Fisher shook her head. "Men can be such idiots."

"Then, when I told him I found Cody, he acted like he expected me to quit." The nausea flashed again, stronger this time. Lily grabbed a handful of pretzels and nibbled on them. "Like I could abandon him right now."

"His own brother did."

"Still." Lily felt a little better. Maybe she should have ordered a salad instead of a steak sandwich. The thought of red meat right now... "How could he think that after all we've been through, after I told him I loved him, that I could just leave?"

"His father left." Fisher reminded her. "When they were most helpless, the one person they had left, just abandoned them."

"I know. But how could he think that I would? That I could..." It became so clear. "Of course, he's never loved anyone who hasn't left him. First his mother, who died when he was born. Then his father. Even his grandparents."

"At least they had each other." Fisher said wistfully.

"Until I came along." Lily couldn't believe she'd caused a fight between the two of them. "I never meant to hurt Carson. Or Cody." She just wanted to love him. She wanted to love Carson and take care of him and instead she'd ruined his relationship with Cody.

"I know that." Fisher took another sip of Lily's beer. "You know that. Too bad they can't see it."

The waitress arrived with their food. Lily managed to pick at her sandwich, nibble on a few fries, but she'd lost her appetite. Heartbreak could be a real bummer.

"So what are you going to do?" Fisher had finished her meal and was sipping on her third beer.

"I guess I'll just have to wait him out." Lily couldn't see any other way. She'd pushed him into this relationship. Maybe before he was ready. She wasn't going to push him again. "I'll just have to show him that I won't give up on him. On us. But I'm not going to ask for more than he can give."

"I wonder if the same strategy would work for me?" Fisher was sounding a little tipsy. "Or maybe I should just jump Cody when he gets back."

"I don't know," Lily said. "I really don't know. But hey, you've got six weeks to think about it."

"Six weeks?" Fisher sighed. "I wonder if he'll miss me."

"I'm sure he does." Lily waited for Fisher to finish her drink, and then they paid the bill and walked out to Lily's car.

"You know, next time we should invite Brooke." Fisher slid into Lily's front seat. "She seems pretty cool."

"Yeah. I like her." Lily turned the key in the ignition. "It's a good thing they hired those three new guides. We'd have been in trouble this weekend without them."

"I still can't believe Cody just took off like that," Fisher said. "And that fight. Wasn't that something awful?"

"It was awful." Just thinking about the blood—the rage—made Lily's stomach lurch. She took slow, deep breaths to steady herself.

"But you know, I think it was a long time coming." Fisher leaned her head back against the seat. "Wow, is this leather? It's so soft."

"Yes, it's leather." Lily hoped Fisher wouldn't be sick. She wasn't as worried about her seats as she was in it starting a chain reaction. "Why do you say that? About the fight?"

"Oh, you know, it's not good for things to back up like that." Fisher let her eyes flutter closed. "They've been ready for something like this for a long time. It's like they just needed something to come along and shake things up."

"I shook things up all right." Lily gripped the steering wheel. She recalled the blood, mostly from Cody's nose, but Carson's lip, too. The nausea returned, but milder this time. She was glad she'd forced herself to eat at least half of her sandwich. The rest she'd have for lunch tomorrow.

"Hey, thanks for driving," Fisher said once they were almost back to camp.

"No problem."

"I'm just so glad Cody's okay." Fisher sounded almost like she'd been crying. "The stupid jerk."

"I'm glad he's okay, too." Poor Fisher. Cody had hurt her almost as much as he'd hurt Carson.

"I'm still mad at him, though."

"Me too."

"I'm glad you're here, though." Fisher sat up straight. Wiped her eyes. "It's nice to have a friend who isn't Cody."

"I'm glad we've become friends, too." Lily meant every word. "I don't think I could get through these next few weeks without you."

"Me either."

"I don't think Carson will let me back in until Cody returns." Lily knew even then it might be too late.

"Into the office?" Fisher asked.

"Into his heart."

"You know, I think you're right." Fisher shook her head in sympathy. "Cody has to accept that you're together before Carson will accept it."

"He won't let me love him if he thinks Cody will be hurt." Lily felt her chest constrict at the realization that Carson might pick Cody over her. Over them.

"Cody will be hurt," Fisher said. "He didn't start that fight because he knew he'd lost you."

"No?"

"No." Fisher grabbed the door handle, but didn't open it. "He wasn't fighting for you, he was fighting for Carson."

"That's what I'm afraid of."

"Well, it's a good thing we're women," Fisher said before exiting the car. "We're strong enough to fight for what we're afraid of."

Chapter 19

As the days flew by, Cody still hadn't called or picked up his phone. Lily was determined to hold everything together but it wasn't easy with Carson still shutting her out. It was as if he was just waiting for her to walk out on him one of these days. Man, he was being stubborn. What he didn't know was that she could be just as stubborn. Like Fisher had said, she was strong enough to fight. She believed in Carson. Even when—no, especially when—he didn't believe in himself.

He was hurting. Even though he no longer had the worry of not knowing where Cody was, he was still crushed by his brother's disappearance. Carson still wouldn't let her help him. He kept her at a distance that, although painful, also made her that much more determined to wait him out. He needed her—he wouldn't admit it, but he did.

So, she continued to show up. To be there. To prove to him that she wasn't going to let him down. Every other person he'd ever depended on had let him down. But she wouldn't. She couldn't.

"Lily." Carson nodded as he slipped into the office about twenty minutes after she'd arrived. His lips curved into a slight smile. Progress. His shoulders looked a little looser, too. He was still a man in need of a good massage. And then some. But she had to be patient. She couldn't pressure him. She couldn't add to his burden.

But damn, she missed him. She hadn't had a good night's sleep since the fight. Since he stopped sneaking into her bed. She'd been feeling the effects of more than sleep deprivation. She had basically put the rest of her life on hold, including her appointment at the fertility clinic.

Lily hadn't had much of an appetite either. She'd had to force herself to eat her oatmeal this morning. And she was too upset to even think about making herself a cup of coffee. It reminded her too much of all the mornings Carson had made her coffee before slipping out the door.

She watched him work, his brows furrowed, his shoulders hunched over the keyboard. Lily couldn't stand it anymore. She had to reach out to him. Had to touch him. She pushed her chair back, stood, and walked around the desk. She was two steps from him when she felt another wave of nausea. She'd been fighting this queasiness for weeks, but this time was a lot worse. She felt her face flush, her hands turn clammy, and the room started to sway. Oh no, not now.

Lily rushed into the hall, and just made it to the employee restroom before she lost what little breakfast she'd managed to swallow.

She waited for her stomach to settle, and the room to stop spinning, before venturing to the sink to rinse her mouth.

"You okay?" Carson had followed her. Had he heard all that?

"Yeah." She splashed cold water on her face and rinsed her mouth. "I don't know what came over me."

"Really? You have no idea?" His face broke into a wide grin. As pleased as she was to see him smile again, she didn't like that it was on her account.

"What's so funny?"

"You know, the river is always changing." Carson was making even less sense now. "The one thing I know for sure, the only thing I know for sure, is that the river changes."

"Okay." Lily had no idea what he was talking about. She was just glad he was talking to her again.

"You told me once that you knew your cycle like I knew the river."

Lily still wasn't sure what he was getting at. Why was he talking about rivers and cycles? Was it a full moon? The Summer Solstice?

"Lily, look at me." His face softened. He looked at her with concern, and an emotion she couldn't quite pin down. "Why didn't you tell me?"

"What, that I still love you?" She took a long deep breath. "I wanted you to figure it out on your own. I wanted you to see that I'm not going anywhere."

"And the baby?"

"What?" Lily felt a wave of nausea strike again. Only this time it suddenly made sense. "Oh my God…"

"Lily, you're pregnant." It wasn't a question or even an accusation. It was just a statement. A statement of high probability.

"Oh." Her legs felt weak, and he caught her before she slumped to the floor.

"You really didn't know?"

Lily couldn't speak. She just shook her head.

"How?" She couldn't wrap her mind around it. What if it was true? What if it wasn't?

"I think you know how it works." Carson's face lit up with amusement. How could he be so calm? So happy? "Come on, Lily, it's not like we were all that careful."

"There was the one time, but I swear…" Lily couldn't think. Couldn't string the words together.

"It wasn't just that one time." Carson took her hands in his. "Come on, Lily, if we used something half the time… I guess I was more ready than I thought."

"It could be a false alarm." Lily still couldn't accept the possibility. "It could just be nerves. The added stress of everything that's been going on."

"You could be pregnant."

"I don't know."

"We could find out."

"I can't." Lily's mind flashed back to all the times when she'd hoped. Prayed. Held her breath as her dreams had been crushed time and time again. She couldn't do it. She couldn't face another negative pregnancy test. Especially not now. Not when it was Carson's baby she'd be losing.

"Yes, you can. We can." Carson took her face in his hands. "We'll do it together. We'll pick up a home pregnancy test. You can do what you need to do, and I'll be there when the results come in."

"You want to be there?" She looked up at him, surprised and relieved that he wasn't angry at her. He didn't accuse her of doing it on purpose.

"Yes. I do." He placed a kiss on her forehead. "Like you've been there for me these last few days."

"But you don't want to be a father." Lily flashed back to the conversation they'd had the night before the fight.

"I said I wasn't sure." Carson pulled her into his arms. "I wasn't sure until right now. We can do this. Together. You and me."

"Are you sure?" Something that felt like hope sprung up inside her.

"I've never been more sure of anything in my life." He held her, stroking her hair, breathing her in.

"Then I guess we should find out." Lily straightened. Ready to face the truth. No matter what the results were. She could face anything as long as she had Carson by her side.

* * * *

They didn't stock home pregnancy tests at the store. They had condoms, feminine hygiene products, and personal lubricant, but no home pregnancy tests. No big deal. It wasn't like they were the only store in town. It was just that now that he was faced with the prospect of fatherhood, Carson wanted to know for sure. As soon as possible.

There was a pharmacy on Prospector Drive. He'd take Lily there, pick up the test, and drive to her place to confirm.

He was going to be a father.

Whether Lily was pregnant or not—and he seriously suspected she was—he was going to be a father. If the pregnancy test was negative, he'd do everything he could to change the result for next time.

Carson pulled up to the pharmacy and got a spot right up front. "Do you want to come in? Or would you rather wait here?"

She looked pale, afraid. No, make that terrified.

"I'll go in. You stay here." Carson wondered how many times she'd been disappointed. How many tests she'd taken only to have her dreams not come true.

"Okay." She nodded, still a little dazed.

"Do you need anything else?" Heaven? Earth? The moon and stars? He'd get it for her. For their baby.

"No, I can get this, really." She started to reach for the door handle.

"You wait here." He dropped a quick kiss on her cheek. "I'll take care of everything."

Inside the store, Carson didn't head straight for the pregnancy test section. He didn't know where to look, but being a man, couldn't ask for directions. And he had to come up with something manly to purchase along with it.

After grabbing some beef jerky, a stick of deodorant, and a can of shaving cream, even though he used an electric shaver, Carson found the right aisle. Who knew there were eighty-seven different home pregnancy tests? Maybe not that many, but there were seven different brands, plus the store brand. Each brand had more than one option. Digital, early detection, multipacks? If this was just the beginning of the choices he'd have to make, maybe he wasn't ready to be a parent after all.

He took a deep breath and selected the package that boasted a one-step, easy-to-use, 99% accurate test. On his way to the checkout, he picked up a carton of ice cream. Didn't pregnant women like ice cream?

* * * *

"There you are." Lily had tired of waiting and was heading for the front entrance. "I was just about to send out a search party."

"Sorry, I wasn't sure which kind to get." He looked a little traumatized.

"I should have warned you." Lily couldn't help but smile at the man who'd braved the pharmacy counter for her.

"I got some ice cream too." Carson flashed a half-smile, just barely showing his dimples. "But I wasn't sure what kind of pickles you'd like."

Lily threw her arms around him. "I've missed you." She leaned into his broad chest, feeling for the first time that it didn't matter what the results were. She already felt complete.

"I've missed you too." Carson walked her to his truck, held the door open, and helped her inside. "I can't tell you how many times I walked into our office, expecting you to be gone."

"I know."

"But you were there." Carson's voice was thick with emotion as he slid behind the wheel. "Every day, you continued to show up."

"I did."

"And every day, I shut you out." He gripped the steering wheel. "But you didn't let me down."

"I couldn't."

"I promise you, Lily, no matter what…" He turned to face her. "I will not let you down."

"I know." Lily felt a smile spread across her face. She was happy. Very happy.

"If you are pregnant, I'll be ready for that." Carson smiled back at her, his dimples deepening. "But even if you're not... I think we should get married."

"Married?" That was unexpected.

"Yes. I know I don't have a ring. And I've acted like a jerk these last few days. But…" He took a deep breath, let it out, and continued. "Lily, will you marry me?"

The look on his face said it all. Hope. Fear. Joy. Love.

"I can't." Lily's heart felt ready to burst.

"That's right. You said you didn't want to get married again." He bowed his head. Stared down at the steering wheel. "That's okay. I …"

"That's not it." Lily didn't know how to make this make sense. "I just don't think I can marry you until you make peace with your brother."

Lily knew how important his relationship with Cody was to Carson. Sure they needed to separate their lives a little bit, but being a twin was a big part of what made Carson who he was. The man she loved.

"It's not entirely up to me." Carson turned toward her, the look on his face was almost enough for her to relent. To say *Yes, I'll marry you no matter what.*

"Yes, but I know you won't be happy unless you try."

"But what if … What if he doesn't come back? Or what if we don't have anything to say to each other?"

"Let's find out." Lily took his hand. "Let's see what happens when you tell him he's going to be an uncle."

"That would be a good place to start." Carson relaxed, just a little. "If he's going to be an uncle, I should be the one to tell him."

"Yes. You should."

"What will I tell him about us?" Carson squeezed her hand, gently and firmly.

"Tell him that I'll only marry you if he agrees to be our best man." Lily smiled before leaning across the seat to kiss him.

Chapter 20

"Hey, I like the beard." Carson led the way down to Hidden Creek with Cody right on his heels. They had their fly rods, but fishing was the last thing on Carson's mind. He doubted Cody believed they were just here to drop a line in the water. They had unfinished business, and this was the best place to conduct it. "It gives you a rugged look."

"Takes away from my crooked nose." Cody had been gone for the full six weeks. He'd shown up yesterday, just as Carson was getting ready to head home to Lily. Instead, he'd helped his brother unpack and spent the night at the house. Cody had gone to bed early, having driven fifteen hours straight through. They didn't say much about the fight, or why he'd left. But then again, they didn't have to.

"Sorry about that." Carson would never completely forgive himself for breaking his brother's nose. For almost breaking Lily's heart.

"Hey, it's cool." Cody pinched the bridge of his nose. It was noticeably bent. Yet he could pull it off. It would probably make him even more of a chick magnet. "It'll make it easier for people to tell us apart."

At least he still had a sense of humor.

"Look, I should have told you about me and Lily." This was as close to an apology as he could get.

"Yeah. You should have." There was enough lightness in Cody's tone that Carson knew he wasn't going to hold it against him, at least most of the time. He could see it now, anytime Cody didn't get his way about something, he'd bring it up. And the broken nose. He'd never live down the broken nose.

"I know it's no excuse." Carson knew he sounded lame. "But I never expected to fall in love with her."

"So it's love, huh?" Cody stood there, stroking his beard as if he was thinking about what else he wanted to say. "Cool."

He turned, walking ahead of Carson. At first glance, it seemed like nothing had changed between them. They were just a couple of guys heading out for an afternoon fishing trip. But there was something different about Cody. Besides the beard. He just couldn't figure out what it was.

"So, how was the Yampa?" Carson still hoped to see it someday, but for now, he was happy staying right here. He'd moved in with Lily, unofficially. He still had a lot of his things at the house. The kind of useless stuff that tended to gather when you weren't paying attention. He'd brought the essentials to Lily's place. Including his tools. He had a lot of work to do, making improvements on her cabin. Baby-proofing. He'd shored up the deck railing, put in a sturdy gate, and was already planning on where to set up a play yard, where their child could explore his or her surroundings safely.

"The Yampa was good." Cody switched his rod case from one hand to the other. "The fishing wasn't so hot, but the rest of it was real good."

"The scenery?" Carson would have liked to have seen the sandstone canyons, the Native pictographs, and maybe even some dinosaur bones. But he was going to have a kid. Kids love dinosaurs. It would be even better to wait a few years and go as a family.

"The scenery was spectacular." The way Cody said it, Carson knew he wasn't talking about the sculpted cliffs or natural arches. He'd met someone. Most likely a few someones. He'd never gone very long without female company.

"So, you had a good time?" Carson was glad Cody had been able to take advantage of the situation.

"I did." Cody stopped. He took a deep breath. He was contemplating something. His tone was different, too. A little more serious. "I had the time of my life."

"That's great. Glad to hear it." Carson knew things would never be quite the same between them. It was no longer just the two of them. Still, he wanted his brother to be happy.

"It was totally worth it." Cody laughed, the same self-deprecating, yet slightly arrogant laugh Carson had come to associate with his brother. "Broken nose and everything."

Carson hadn't realized how much he'd missed Cody until just then. When Lily first requested he ask him to be their best man, he'd thought she was asking for trouble. But she must have known that it wouldn't be the same without him.

"She was that good?" She'd certainly put a smile on his brother's face, even weeks later.

"She was." Cody's grin was more crooked than ever. "She was damn good."

"You going to see her again?" He couldn't help but wonder about this mystery woman. Could she possibly be the one?

"Nah. Why ruin a good thing?" Same old Cody. Except for the hint of regret in his voice. That was new. She had obviously made an impact on him. Even if he wasn't going to admit it.

"I almost ruined a good thing." Carson might as well get this over with. He needed to tell the rest of the story. "I almost lost Lily."

"Because of me?" Cody stopped walking. His shoulders dropped a little.

"No, because of me." Carson knew it wasn't Cody's fault. "I almost didn't recognize what I had."

"I know what you mean." Cody sounded contemplative. Was he referring to this mystery woman he'd met in Utah? Maybe someday he'd share. But for now, it was just good to have him back.

"So things are good with you two?" Cody sounded like he had been afraid to ask.

"Real good." Carson braced himself. The rest of it was pretty serious. Permanent. Something that neither of them had prepared for. "Lily's pregnant."

"Is it yours?" Cody asked, but there was no teasing in his voice. "Or did she go with the sperm donor?"

"You knew about that?" Carson had learned that she'd rescheduled her appointment the day Cody disappeared. She cancelled it altogether after the pregnancy test came out positive.

"Yeah. I guess she figured if I knew she wanted to have a baby, I'd run for the hills." Cody laughed. It was a different kind of laugh. Less cocky. Yet he seemed a lot more sure of himself.

"Seems to have worked." Carson believed Cody would have never taken off if he hadn't been upset about him and Lily. Cody didn't like change. It was the main reason Carson had put off talking to him in the first place.

"You going to marry her?" Cody said it like he was asking about what they should order for take-out. Like it didn't matter either way.

"I asked her." Carson kept his own voice neutral.

"Don't tell me she said no." Cody sounded surprised. Concerned, even.

"Not exactly." Carson kept walking. The closer they got to the river, the more comfortable he'd feel.

"What's the deal?" Cody followed, like it was just another fishing trip.

"She wants us both in the wedding." This shouldn't be so hard. They were brothers. Best friends. It should be a given that they would stand up for each other when they each took the plunge.

"I don't think that's legal. Not even in Utah." Cody's voice held that teasing note that he'd known all his life.

"No, you dope. She wants you to be the best man." He couldn't help but laugh.

"And you thought I might say no?" Cody sounded a little hurt by the suggestion.

"I haven't spoken to you in over a month." Carson shrugged. Cody had made it very clear that he had Lily in his sights. That he was determined. And the last time they saw each other, he'd shown how he really felt about Carson and Lily being together. "We haven't had a knock-down, drag-out fight since junior high. No, not even then."

"You broke my nose." Cody could laugh about it now.

"And I know you had an interest in Lily." Isn't that what the fight had been about?

"I'm over it, bro." Cody turned, flashed his trademark free-spirited grin. "I'm happy for you. Really."

"So you'll be our best man?" Carson nerves were jittery, even more than when he'd asked Lily to marry him. Even more than when they'd waited for the results of the home pregnancy test.

"Do I have to shave my beard?" Cody stroked his chin.

"You'll have to talk to the boss lady." Carson felt a huge relief. Not that he worried Lily truly wouldn't marry him. Once they'd gotten past the initial shock of her pregnancy, they'd become more and more sure of their relationship. "But, I'm sure she'll be fine with it."

"Boy, have you met your match?" Cody chuckled. "I'm glad she picked you. I don't think I could deal with marriage and a kid."

"You think you can manage being an uncle?" He was trying to picture either of them holding a tiny baby. It terrified and excited him at the same time. But he was ready. Or as ready as a man could be.

"Will I have to change diapers?" Cody sounded genuinely worried. And a little bit grossed out.

"Sure. You man enough?" Carson tossed out the challenge.

"For Lily?" Cody said. "I could be."

"Don't even go there." Carson could only take so much.

"Just messing with you, man." Cody chuckled softly to himself. "You're really going to be a dad?"

"Yeah. I am." Carson was still a little unsure. Afraid he wouldn't be good enough.

"You know, I think you'll be good at it." Cody somehow knew the exact words he needed to hear. "You've got the nagging thing down."

"Oh really?" Carson should have known Cody would get a jab in. "You think I was too hard on you?"

"Sometimes." Cody said. "Most of the time. But look how I turned out."

That's what he was afraid of. Making the same mistakes with his own kid as he'd made with Cody. The only thing that kept him from being absolutely terrified was knowing Lily would be right there with him. She would keep them on the right path.

"So we're good?" Carson knew their relationship would never be the same. Maybe in some ways, it would be better. Maybe the space between them would actually bring them closer. Or as close as two guys would want to be. Maybe Carson finally getting a life of his own would convince Cody to want more out of his own life.

"We're good." Cody clapped his brother on the back. "Hey, are we still going to fish? 'Cause the last time we came down here, we never got the chance."

"We brought our rods, didn't we?" Carson had spent his whole life trying to make his brother happy. What was one more day?

"Hey, isn't that your bride-to-be?" Cody pointed upstream, where Lily stood waiting for them.

"Sorry for interrupting your fishing trip." Lily was talking to both of them, but she kept her eyes on Carson. "I just couldn't stand around waiting."

Carson came up behind her and put his arms around her waist. His hand immediately strayed to her belly. His child grew inside, and he couldn't help but feel protective.

"So, you two are good?" Lily snuggled up against him. "All made up?"

"You sure you want to spend the rest of your life with this guy?" Cody teased. "If you change your mind…"

"I won't." Lily placed her hands over Carson's, both of them subconsciously protecting their budding family.

"Oh, get a room." Cody groaned. "Are you two going to be all lovey-dovey all the time? I think I liked it better when you thought I didn't have a clue. At least I didn't have to see it."

"You'll just have to get used to it," Lily said. "Did Carson tell you you're going to be an uncle?"

"I can't wait." Cody grinned. It was his same old no-worries kind of grin. "I'll teach him how to fish, swim, climb trees, play pool. I'll teach him how to really impress the ladies."

"And if we have a girl?" Lily asked.

"Then I'll teach her all those things." Cody flashed a playful grin. "And more importantly, I'll teach her how to stay away from guys like me."

"Now that I know you two are good, I'm going to go back to the house." Lily turned to give Carson a quick kiss. But kissing her was never quick. He kissed her thoroughly, forgetting that Cody was there.

Cody cleared his throat after a minute. Or maybe it was two. "You two go on. I'll be fine on my own."

"You sure?" Lily took Carson's hand. Even the slight contact sent his heart racing. "I was just going to put a meatloaf in the oven."

"Sounds delicious." Cody patted his stomach and made appreciative noises. "How much time do you need?"

"Dinner will be ready in about an hour." Lily glanced at Carson with a look that indicated they wouldn't spend the whole time in the kitchen.

"I'll give you guys one hour," Cody said. "Then, I'm knocking on the door."

"One hour." Carson turned back toward Cody, as he led Lily back to her place.

"Sixty minutes," Cody reminded him.

"You realize we may never get rid of him." Carson turned to Lily. It was only fair to warn her now, before it was too late.

"I know." Lily gave an encouraging squeeze of his hand. "I'm getting a two for one deal."

"He doesn't step foot past the kitchen," Carson warned. He was not going to share Lily any more than he had to.

"We could let him use the bathroom." She had a teasing note to her voice, letting him know that she was taking his jealousy seriously. But not too seriously.

"He can use a tree."

"He's your brother." She leaned her head against his shoulder.

"He's going to be yours too." He put his arm around her.

"I guess I'll just have to live with that." Lily let out an exaggerated sigh.

"He's not going to live with us." He had to draw the line somewhere. Maybe he didn't need to live alone. But he certainly didn't need to live with Cody anymore. And the last six weeks had proven that Cody could handle living without him.

"He'll be fine."

"You think so?" He was so used to being the responsible one. The only responsible one.

"Yes. You don't have to worry about Cody." Lily did her best to assure him that everything would be all right. "He's a grown man. He can take care of himself. He's just never had to."

"Remind me not to make that mistake with our kids." Carson knew she'd keep him balanced. On the river, he knew to spread the load around, to keep from capsizing. He also knew that paddling only on one side, would send them around in circles. Teamwork was required to move forward. Lily helped him realize the same was true in life.

"I'm sure you'll guide them down the right path." Lily said. "I mean, we will. Together."

Yes. Together. He was still getting used to that feeling. Having someone he could rely on just as much as she relied on him.

Lily glanced at the river. "Thank you for saving me."

"No. Thank you." Carson wasn't sure if he could ever explain how close he'd felt to drowning before she'd come along. Not from the river, but from his responsibilities. From having to worry about Cody, and everyone else in his life. "You're the one who saved me."

Carson had worried that letting Lily into his life would only add to his burden. What he didn't know was that loving Lily actually made life easier. He had someone to share his responsibilities with. He had someone to share his life with.

And life was good.

Keep reading for an excerpt from

BETTER THAN PERFECT

Life beyond the game...

Johnny "The Monk" Scottsdale has won it all on the baseball diamond. He's even pitched a perfect game. Known for his legendary control both on and off the field, his pristine public image makes him the ideal person to work with young players in a preseason minicamp. Except the camp is run by the one woman he can't forget…the woman who made him a "monk."

Alice Harrison once traded her dreams so that Johnny Scottsdale could make it to the Majors—and then her dreams fell apart. Now here comes Johnny back into her life, just when she's ready to finally go after her dreams. This time she's not letting up. Even if she has to reveal what she kept secret for too long from her son and Johnny. She can't be sure how things will turn out, but she's not leaving until she swings for the fences…

A Lyrical book on sale now.

Learn more about Kristina at http://www.
kensingtonbooks.com/author.aspx/30540

Chapter 1

"Pitchers and catchers report to spring training in thirteen days, twenty-one hours and seventeen minutes," Hall of Fame broadcaster Kip Michaels announced, and the crowd went wild. "Kicking off today's Fan Fest, I'd like to introduce one of our newest players. Two-time Cy Young Award winner, perennial All-Star, and the last man to pitch a perfect game. Give a warm San Francisco welcome to Johnny 'The Monk' Scottsdale."

Thirty thousand people were expected at the ballpark today. A great crowd—for a baseball game. But instead of working the count, Johnny would be working the crowd. Answering questions. Signing autographs. Putting himself out there in a way he wasn't entirely comfortable with. He was as nervous as the day he'd made his professional debut fourteen years ago. Butterflies? Try every seagull on the West Coast taking roost in his stomach.

Focus. Breathe. Let it go.

"Thank you. I'm thrilled to be here." He'd much rather face the 1927 Yankees than sit in front of a camera and a microphone talking about his game instead of playing it. "I hope I can help the team bring home a World Series Championship."

He tried to relax his shoulders. Tried to hide his nerves. The Goliaths could be his last team. His last shot at a ring. His final chance to prove himself and leave a legacy that went beyond the diamond.

After fielding a few questions about what he could bring to the team, and deflecting some praise about his success so far, Johnny was released to another part of the park to sign autographs. Little Leaguers approached with wide eyes and big league dreams. Tiny tots with painted faces squirmed with excitement about getting cotton candy while their parents shoved them forward to collect an autograph. A shy boy with a broken arm asked him to sign his cast. The look on his face was more than worth the discomfort of being in the spotlight for something other than his on-field performance.

Johnny had signed the big contract. The team paid him a lot of money to pitch every five games. They also paid him to interact with the fans, to be an ambassador for the game he'd loved for so long. The game that had saved him from a completely different kind of life.

He shared a table with another new player, shortstop Bryce Baxter. They were set up near the home bullpen along the third base line. Several other stations were set up around the park, giving fans a chance to get up close and personal with the players. Some tried to get a little too personal.

"So you're the hot new pitcher." A busty brunette leaned over the autograph table, wearing what appeared to be a toddler-sized tank top. The team logo sparkled in rhinestones and she was obviously well aware of the attention she drew. "I'd be more than happy to show you around."

"No thanks. I'm pretty familiar with the city." He held his pen ready, although she didn't seem to have anything to autograph. Nothing he was willing to sign, anyway.

"I could take you places you've never been." She leaned over even more.

Johnny kept his head down, trying to avoid gazing at what she had to offer. He reached for a stock photo, scrawled his signature across the bottom, and slid the picture forward, hoping she'd take the hint and leave.

"You forgot your number." She pouted.

"Sorry. I don't give that out." Johnny wished he could retreat to the locker room. Get away from her and the crowd that seemed to be growing. He never understood why people would wait in line to make small talk and take his picture. He gripped the black marker, needing something to do with his hands. If he only had a baseball, he could roll it around in his palm. Feel the smoothness of the leather, the rough contrast of the raised stitches. Find comfort in the weight and the symmetry of the one thing he could always control.

His teammate inserted himself into the conversation. "Do you know who this is? The one and only Johnny 'The Monk' Scottsdale."

"The Monk?" She drew her gaze over Bryce, then glanced at Johnny before settling on Bryce once more.

"He's a god." He flashed a grin indicating he was more than willing to play her game. "Me? I'm a mere mortal." Bryce leaned toward her, clearly enjoying the interaction.

"You're new, too." She scooted over to his side of the table, dismissing Johnny's rejection as strike one. She must think she had a better chance of scoring with Bryce.

"I am. I think I left my heart somewhere in the city. Could you help me find it?" He slid one of his photos across the table to her.

"I can help you find whatever you're looking for." She took the pen from him and wrote something on the inside of his forearm. Her number, most likely.

Bryce grinned as if he enjoyed having a stranger tattoo him with a permanent marker.

"Bring your friend, too. If he's up for a challenge."

"I'll see what I can do, sweetheart." Bryce tipped his cap and winked at the woman.

Johnny exhaled, realizing he'd been holding his breath during the entire conversation.

"Thanks man, I owe you one." Johnny shook his head, as relieved as if Bryce had just snagged a line drive with two outs and the bases loaded.

"So it really isn't an act." Baxter eyed him carefully. "You really do walk the walk."

"What walk?"

"The celibacy thing. It's for real." A lot of guys thought he was full of it. That it was just for show. A way to get attention, and women. But once they realized he was genuine, most of the other players accepted him. Some even respected him. "You really don't mess around."

"No. I don't. I'm not perfect, but I try to stay out of trouble." Johnny removed his cap and ran his fingers through his hair. Since they were both new to the team, their booth wasn't as crowded as some of the others. They had a chance to catch their breath. He was able to finally sit back and enjoy the perfect weather. It was one of those glorious Northern California days when the sun came out to tease, dropping hints of spring and the fever that came with it.

"You looked like you were a little uncomfortable there." Bryce, on the other hand, seemed to relish the attention.

"I know it's part of the job, but it's not the part I'm good at."

"You let your game speak for itself. That's cool." Bryce reclined in his chair, looking as relaxed as if he was sitting in his own back yard. "Some of us have to use our charm to make up for lack of talent."

Johnny laughed. Baxter had plenty of talent. And more than enough charm to go around.

"She was pretty fine, though." Bryce continued to check her out as she walked away, collecting ballplayer's numbers like kids collected baseball cards. "Exactly what I need to get me in shape for spring training."

"Is that so?" Johnny managed to avoid the whole groupie scene. His entire career had been about control, both on and off the field. The Monk kept his cool. The Monk never got rattled. And The Monk maintained a spotless reputation. He had to, considering where he'd come from.

"There he is. Come on, Mom." A kid, about twelve or thirteen, rushed up to the booth, practically dragging his mother by the arm.

Johnny slipped on his best fan-friendly smile.

"We're, like, your number one fans." The boy was practically bursting at the seams. "Right, Mom?"

The boy's mother stepped forward, taking Johnny's breath away.

He'd had several reasons to come to San Francisco. Eleven million obvious ones, and several others that he'd done his best to articulate to the fans. There was only one reason he should have stayed away.

"Alice." Just saying her name sent a line drive straight to his heart. Even fourteen years later.

"Congratulations on your new contract. I know you're going to have a great year." She sounded like any other fan, wishing him well. She just marched right up to his table to ask for an autograph. A freaking autograph? Like he meant nothing to her.

A slight breeze blew her hair around her face. She tried to smile as she tucked a loose strand behind her ear. Blond, straight, silky—and if he remembered correctly—oh-so-soft. She wore modestly cut jeans and a soft blue sweater that on anyone else would have looked plain and proper. He didn't need to glance at her left hand to know she was off limits. Yet, she still moved him like no other woman ever could. Made him long for what he'd had. What he'd lost. What he'd tried for years to forget.

"Wait." The boy gaped at her. "You guys know each other? For real?"

"Yes. Johnny was…" She held Johnny's gaze just long enough for him to catch a flicker of regret. She turned to her son, who was about an inch or two taller than her. "He was your dad's college roommate."

"You knew my dad?" The boy seemed more impressed by that than the fact that people waited in line for his autograph.

"Yes. I knew him." Johnny swallowed the lump in his throat. "Before he married your mom."

"Cool." The kid smiled and nodded his head, like it was no big deal. "I mean, I know you played for the Wolf Pack when they went to Nevada, but I had no idea you guys were, like, friends."

Sure. Friends.

"Zach." She placed her hand on his shoulder, ready to steer him away. "I'm sure Mr. Scottsdale is a busy man. Let's leave him alone."

They'd once been as close as two people could be. But now he was Mr. Scottsdale.

The boy shrugged, dismissing her and looking up to Johnny with admiration. "It's totally awesome to meet you."

Johnny nodded, giving his most sincere smile, even though seeing Alice, and her kid, hit him like a 97-mile-an-hour fastball.

They started to walk away.

"Give my best to Mel." As if he hadn't already done that.

Alice turned around.

"Mel died. Eight years ago." A pained expression flashed across her face.

"I'm sorry. For your loss." Johnny said the words. He wanted more than anything to mean them, but he'd carried that resentment around for so long, it had become as much a part of him as his right arm.

"Thank you." Alice gave him a sad little smile. It was forced. Polite. The kind of smile she'd give a stranger. "It was good seeing you. Really good."

"Yeah. Sure." He could say the same, but he'd be lying. Seeing her again only reminded him of everything he'd sacrificed.

* * * *

The minute she'd seen Johnny on the stage, Alice's heart had swelled big enough to fill the stadium. There he'd been, larger than life. Damn. The man looked good. Better than on TV. Better than she remembered. He'd gained some muscle. A lot of muscle. Even without the jersey, there'd be no doubt he was an athlete. He moved with the kind of confidence and grace that came with being totally in tune with his body. Like he'd once been totally in tune with hers. She ached at the memory, but shook it off, uncomfortable having such thoughts with her son sitting next to her. Like Johnny had clearly been uncomfortable onstage, addressing the media and the crowds. He never did like to talk about his game. He'd simply let his talent speak for itself.

Just as she'd predicted, women lined up at his booth. They all wanted his autograph. Some of them wanted a little more. She hadn't been able to handle it back then. And now? What he did was his business. Especially since she'd been the one to walk out on him.

"Mom. Are you okay?" Zach was protective of her. And a little too observant.

"I'm fine, Zach." She shook her head to clear the fog of memories that rolled over her. With only the briefest look into his eyes, she couldn't forget the three years they'd spent together, nearly inseparable. Studying. Hanging out. Making love. "I'm surprised to see him, that's all."

"But you knew he'd be here." Zach had that tone, the unspoken *duh*. They'd been coming to Fan Fest every year since Mel's death. She'd known Johnny would be here. She just wasn't prepared for the impact of seeing him again. She'd thought she'd put those feelings behind her. Packed them away with her college sweatshirts and student ID card. "You were so excited when you heard it on the radio. Your favorite player finally becoming a Goliath. Why didn't you tell me you guys were, like, friends?"

"I didn't want you to think it's a big deal." She tried to place her hand on his shoulder, but he squirmed to avoid the contact. That was new. Not unexpected, given his age, but she missed her little boy. The first time they'd come to Fan Fest, he'd held her hand. Until they'd gotten to the miniature version of the ballpark. He'd joined the t-ball game like he was born to play.

"It is a big deal." Zach looked at her like she was hopelessly out of touch. Something he did a lot these days. "Mom, you actually know Johnny Scottsdale."

There it was. The star-struck admiration bordering on worship.

"I *knew* him, Zach." Alice tried to keep her tone neutral. She couldn't betray her emotions. A wave of regret washed over her. The question of what might have been. "But that was a long time ago."

"Wouldn't it be cool if he came to the foundation's minicamp?" Zach couldn't know why it would be such a bad idea.

She'd hoped to avoid him. Avoid digging up the past. And the question that had plagued her more and more as Zach grew. "I already have a pitcher lined up. Nathan Cooper. He's done it for years."

Alice had worked for the Mel Harrison Jr. Foundation since its inception, a little more than a year after her husband's death. The initial donations were privately funded, set up to provide grants to community schools and youth organizations. As the foundation had grown, they were able to provide services for greater numbers of children, but the more successful they'd become, the less contact she had with the kids.

Until a few years ago, when the team had approached her about setting up a minicamp for youth players. It evolved from a Saturday demonstration and meet-and-greet to a weeklong afterschool program where the ballplayers worked directly with the kids, helping them learn fundamentals of the game while boosting their confidence with the attention and mentorship of the pro athletes.

"Cooper's alright." Zach sounded disappointed, bordering on whiny. "But he's not Johnny Scottsdale."

"Zach, we made a commitment to Nathan Cooper."

"And Harrisons always keep their commitments." Zach parroted the family motto. She could tell by the tone of his voice he had to restrain himself from rolling his eyes.

"Yes, Zach, Harrisons keep their commitments." No matter what. She'd made a commitment to Mel, to the Harrison family. She'd hoped her feelings for Johnny would eventually fade. She'd made her choice. A desperate one at the time, but once she'd committed to Mel, she wouldn't look back. She still couldn't. "Cooper's a good player. A good guy. We can't just tell him we don't want him anymore."

"Well, maybe they could both do the pitching clinic," Zach suggested. "Since Cooper's a lefty, maybe it would be better to have a right-handed pitcher too."

"Johnny's a busy man. He doesn't need us bugging him." And she didn't need to be reminded of what she'd given up.

"Yeah, but he probably doesn't know very many people here yet." Zach sounded hopeful. Like they'd be doing Johnny a favor. "It would be good for him to get involved in the community."

"Zach. He doesn't need us." She'd made sure of it.

"But…" Zach couldn't let it go.

"I think it's time for some lunch." Lately, food seemed to be the best distraction.

"I could eat." Zach shrugged. "You want to split some garlic fries?"

"You know I do." The ballpark's signature fries had become a tradition. But if she ate a full order herself, she'd be sorry later.

"Can I get two hot dogs, then? Or maybe some nachos?"

"You're that hungry?" Wasn't it only yesterday that she begged him to eat? Playing airplane with the spoon or bribing him with a toy to take three more bites.

"Yeah. I guess meeting Johnny Scottsdale increased my appetite." He grinned at her. For a second there, he reminded her of someone she used to know.

"Oh, Zach…" She sighed, her emotions getting the better of her. Seeing Johnny for even a few minutes had her all mixed up.

It had been easier when Johnny was on the other side of the country. When he'd been nothing more than a box score. An image on TV. She'd followed his entire career. From his earliest days in the minor leagues, to his first start in Kansas City, to when he was traded to Tampa Bay. She'd watched him. Cheered for him. Wished him nothing but success.

"Oh please, Mom. Don't go there." She was embarrassing him. As she often did whenever she talked about how quickly he was growing up. Becoming a man. Neither of them was quite ready for it, but that didn't matter.

She put her arm around him but felt him struggling with the idea of pulling away. Reluctantly, she let him go, knowing it was only a matter of time before he wouldn't need her at all.

"Order whatever you want. Just don't complain about a stomach ache later."

"I won't." He ordered a hot dog, nachos and a root beer.

She stepped up behind him and ordered her hot dog, the garlic fries and a Diet Coke. She struck up a conversation with the lady behind the counter while they waited for their order.

"Geez, Mom. Why do you have to talk so much?" He'd waited until they were at the condiment station before complaining.

"I was only being friendly. There's nothing wrong with that." She unwrapped her hot dog and placed it under the mustard spout.

"Yeah, then why weren't you very friendly with Johnny Scottsdale?" He kept his head down, concentrating on his food. She'd learned to pay attention more when he seemed least interested in making conversation. "You actually knew him in college and you barely said a word to him."

She hit the pump on the mustard a little too hard and it splattered all over her sweater. She quickly grabbed a napkin to wipe up the stain.

"Is it... Is it because he reminds you of Dad? Does seeing him make you sad?"

"Oh, honey." She put her arm around him, pressing him against her. How could she possibly explain why seeing Johnny again was so painful?

"It seems kind of weird that they didn't keep in touch after college." Zach had no idea how weird it would have been if they had. The three of them had been the best of friends. How many times had they let Mel tag along on their dates? Or how many times had she made herself at home at their place? But Johnny had been at the heart of their little group. And when he'd moved on, she and Mel turned to each other.

"Johnny was trying to make it to the big leagues." She used the same story she'd told herself over the years. "He had to work very hard to get to where he is today. Mel had a job here in the city, and I was busy raising you. We just drifted apart, that's all."

"But, maybe you and Johnny can be friends again." He had a tiny hesitation in his voice. Telling her there was more to the story than he was willing to share.

She waited. Pushing him would never get him to open up.

"Maybe…" Zach took a long slurp of his soda. "Maybe he could tell me more about my dad."

* * * *

Well, that was a mistake. By bringing up his dad, he'd upset his mom. Zach could tell because she got really quiet. They sat in the stands to eat their lunch and watch the next round of interviews. She nibbled on her hot dog and absently picked at the garlic fries. He ended up eating most of them, which was fine. He loved garlic fries. But it was weird with her not talking. Normally she would chatter on and on about the upcoming season and especially all the new players. He'd expected her to be really excited about Johnny Scottsdale. She was probably an even bigger fan than he was.

She'd actually cried when he pitched his perfect game. Cried and hugged Zach like they'd been there. But she barely said a word to him when they met today. And they didn't even get an autograph.

Now, she was all quiet, and he wouldn't be surprised if she said she wanted to leave soon. He'd seen what he wanted to see. Johnny Scottsdale's first interview as one of the Goliaths, and then he'd gotten to meet him. Sort of.

Kip Michaels stepped onstage to introduce the next set of players. He was one of the best. He never had anything bad to say about an opponent, but he was a Goliath to the core. He also managed to throw out a few tips for young players during every game. He'd point out simple things, like keeping balanced in the batter's box or following through on a pitch. Plus, he'd been there. Way before Zach's time, but he'd pitched in the majors for ten years. So he knew what he was talking about.

"Thank you, San Francisco!" Nathan Cooper stepped up to the mic for his turn in the spotlight. "It's going to be a great season. I guarantee it."

Yeah, he was alright. Kind of a showoff, though. Like it was more about him than the team. Cooper played to the crowd, making them laugh and cheer and get pumped up for the season. Even if he was kind of obnoxious, he was a pretty good pitcher. Most of the time.

Zach glanced over at his mother. She was trying to rub the mustard stain out of her sweater. He wondered if that would be her excuse for leaving early. He wouldn't mind. Not really. He just wished he could have talked to Johnny Scottsdale more. He had a lot of questions. Mostly about baseball. Like what it was like to pitch a perfect game.

He had questions about his dad.

He barely even remembered him. Only a few fuzzy memories—mostly good—of a guy in a suit taking off his tie and getting down on the floor to play with the Thomas the Train set. He remembered watching movies and going to the park, but he didn't think he'd ever played catch with his dad.

He'd played catch with a few different major leaguers. As part of the minicamp. He never really felt like he was part of the program though. It was more like he tagged along, just because he could. Because his mom ran the show and his grandparents had started the whole charity thing after his dad died.

Some of the other kids had it real tough, though. Single parents who worked two jobs just to pay their rent. So they didn't have time to play catch with their kids. There were foster kids who never lived in one place long enough to be part of a team. Some of the kids had dads in the military, serving overseas in Afghanistan or places like that.

Zach felt kind of bad, taking up a spot for a kid who needed it more. At least he didn't have to worry about money. Or his mom didn't have to worry, anyways.

"Hey Mom?" He had an idea.

"Don't tell me you're still hungry." She smiled at him, but she was kind of distracted.

"No." Not really. But he would be after dinner. They'd probably have a big salad or vegetable stir-fry—something healthy to make up for all the junk food. "I was just thinking. Maybe I'm getting too old to be in the minicamp."

"You're not too old." She folded up her napkin and wrapped up the last of her unfinished hot dog. "There will be plenty of other kids your age."

"I guess." He wasn't as excited about it as he'd been the last few years.

"You don't have to do the minicamp." She tried to sound like it didn't matter to her, but he knew she'd be disappointed if he wasn't there. "I hope you're not quitting because I haven't asked Johnny Scottsdale to join us."

"That's not it." He grabbed the last garlic fry. Except maybe that was part of it. "I just don't know how much more I can learn from the same guys."

That kind of made him sound like a jerk. Like he thought he was some great baseball player already. That's not what he meant. He just didn't know how to say it without sounding like he was spoiled or something.

How many kids got to work with real Major League baseball players every year? Not many. For most of them it was a once-in-a-lifetime kind of thing.

"If you don't want to come, that's okay. You won't hurt my feelings." She said that, but she didn't like when he didn't want to do stuff with her. It was hard for him to tell her he'd rather be with his friends. She always worked so hard at finding fun things to do together. Maybe it was because he didn't have his dad around anymore and she felt like she had to make it up to him. Or maybe it was because she didn't have his dad around and she was lonely.

"I'll come," Zach said. But he didn't really want to.

* * * *

Johnny plopped down in front of his locker to change out of his jersey and into his street clothes. He was wiped out, but not in a good way like after a game. His muscles were sore from tension, not exertion. He was still reeling after his encounter with Alice. For years he'd pretended they were both dead to him. Come to find out, Mel had died. And even though they hadn't spoken in years, it still came as a big blow. The man had once been Johnny's best friend. Almost a brother. And now he was gone. Was it an accident? A long and painful battle with disease? Whatever the cause, Alice was left to raise their son alone.

Alice was a mother. Not a big surprise. She'd always loved kids. She was going to be a teacher. Until she'd married Mel and didn't have to work. Mel was rich. Came from money and probably couldn't help but make even more money once he graduated and went to work for his father, helping make other rich people richer.

It bothered him more than he wanted to admit. Her having a kid. Not that Johnny had ever really wanted to be a father. But maybe a part of him would have wanted to be the one to give her that gift.

He was wrestling with that thought when his manager, Juan Javier, approached him.

"Just the man I need to see." Javier had been a catcher during his playing days. A pretty good one too, until his knees gave out. But he was still in good shape. Still had a commanding presence.

"Sure, what do you need?" Johnny didn't know the man well enough to determine whether he should address him by his first name, last name or just call him "Skip." His reputation around the league was that of a player's manager. Well respected and well liked, with a thorough knowledge of the game and an uncanny ability to get the most out of his players. Johnny looked forward to working with him.

"I need a hero." Javier parked himself next to Johnny. "Got word this morning that Nathan Cooper didn't pass a drug test. He's out fifty games, unless he appeals."

Did that mean Johnny would be moved to the bullpen? Cooper was a relief pitcher, a left-handed specialist. Johnny was a right-handed starter. At least he had been his entire career.

"Don't worry, you're still a starter." Javier clapped him on the back. "This is a PR nightmare. At least it didn't leak out this morning. That would have put a dark cloud on the Fan Fest."

"So what can I do?"

"Your reputation is spotless. It's one of the reasons the team was so interested in signing you." They didn't call him The Monk for nothing. His composure on the mound was only part of the story. "We had a few years where...well, you catch the news. The fans are sick of this stuff. Sick of the cheaters. We need someone like you. Someone the kids can look up to."

"I try to be one of the good guys." Johnny shrugged. It's all he'd ever wanted to be. He wanted his name to be associated with honor, integrity and respect.

"Russ Crawford, from the front office, had Cooper lined up for this charity event." His manager placed a sturdy hand on Johnny's shoulder. "We don't want a guy suspended for drugs representing us to the community."

"No. We don't." Johnny never understood what would drive a guy to take such a risk. Or why there were still guys who felt they could get away with it. He balled his fists, thinking about how much harder the rest of them had to work at proving they were clean.

"We need someone to take his place. I thought you'd be perfect." He gave Johnny a friendly pat on the back.

"I was perfect once in my life." Twenty-seven batters had faced him. Every one of them had walked back to the dugout shaking their heads. None of them had reached first base. No hits, no walks, no errors.

"You and only about twenty-three other guys." Javier gave him a smile of admiration. Of respect. Not only for Johnny, but for all the players who'd come before him. "But you're not just perfect on the field."

That was his reputation. No wild parties, drugs or women. When he went out with his teammates, he stuck with one beer. Just to be one of the guys. Then he would return quietly to his room. Alone. He politely refused advances and room keys from his female fans.

"What kind of charity thing are we looking at?" *Let's get to the point.* What really mattered. As long as it wasn't a speaking engagement. He could pitch in front of a sold-out stadium. Or an empty one where the few fans in attendance tried to make up for the lack of numbers with an abundance of noise. But talking to a room full of people? No thanks. He'd much rather run the bleachers, drag the field, or even cut the grass by hand, one blade at a time.

"It's a minicamp for youth players," Javier explained. "They come to the ballpark after school and we take them through a few drills, demo mechanics and basically share your knowledge of the game."

"That sounds like something I could do." Johnny was just beginning to think about what he might do after his career was over. Coaching was something to consider; it would keep him in the game. But he wasn't sure if he'd be any good at it. He didn't know if he could explain things in a way others would understand. He could show them, though. He could demonstrate what worked for him.

"So you'll do the pitching clinic." It wasn't a question. The new guy on the team had to prove himself, no matter his reputation, and picking up a teammate was a good way to do just that.

Johnny nodded. Why not? Anything to keep his mind off Alice and Mel. And their kid.

"Tell me about the kids." Johnny didn't have a lot of experience with kids. Like, none. Even when he'd been a kid, he didn't really know how to relate to them. He was the quiet boy in school and in the dugout. "How old are they?"

"I think anywhere from about nine to twelve or thirteen."

"Old enough to tie their own shoes, then." In other words, about Zach's age.

"Yet still young enough that they don't think they know everything," Javier added with a slight smile. "About baseball, at least."

"So these kids should be coachable." When he'd been that age, he'd soaked up every tip and tidbit of information about the game. He'd been eager to learn and apply the knowledge to his rapidly growing skills.

Could he be the kind of mentor he'd had back then? Could he pass down his knowledge of the game to the next generation? He hoped so.

"They're good kids. Some of them may have caught a bad break. Single parent homes, families fallen on hard times. Some of these boys might be homeless or in foster care." Javier was starting to make Johnny a little nervous. He'd been one of those kids. He'd known hard times.

Lived with a single mother who'd worked too much. Without a father or a man to look up to.

Until his coach had stepped up.

"I guess you've got your man." Johnny hoped he could be the kind of man these kids needed. "Just give me the time and place."

"I knew I could count on you. The camp starts Monday. Here's your contact at the Harrison Foundation." The manager handed him a slick business card. Johnny's heart seized as he read the name.

Alice Harrison, Director

"She's a great gal. Professional. Knowledgeable." Javier seemed not to notice all the air had been sucked out of the room. "You'll love her."

Oh yeah. Johnny had loved her. He'd once loved her even more than he loved the game.

Meet the Author

Kristina Mathews doesn't remember a time when she didn't have a book in her hand. Or in her head. Kristina lives in Northern California with her husband of twenty years, two sons and a black lab. She is a veteran road tripper, amateur renovator, and sports fanatic. She hopes to one day travel all 3,073 miles of Highway 50 from Sacramento, CA, to Ocean City, MD, replace her carpet with hardwood floors, and throw out the first pitch for the San Francisco Giants. Visit her on the web at kristinamathews.com.

www.ingramcontent.com/pod-product-compliance
Lightning Source LLC
Chambersburg PA
CBHW050737250626
47155CB00005B/1805